The Madman

&

His Mistress

History in the Making

Roswitha McIntosh

Cover painting by Mimi Stuart

ISBN 0-7414-3971-9

Published by:

INFINITY
PUBLISHING.COM

1094 New DeHaven Street, Suite 100
West Conshohocken, PA 19428-2713
Info@buybooksontheweb.com
www.buybooksontheweb.com
Toll-free (877) BUY BOOK
Local Phone (610) 941-9999
Fax (610) 941-9959

Printed in the United States of America

Printed on Recycled Paper

Published June 2007

Also written by Roswitha (Ros) McIntosh

Live, Laugh & Learn
An Autobiography
*
Texts on
Risk Management

Acknowledgment

My warmest thanks go to David Warren, who read each chapter, some of them twice, and rid them of Germanisms. I owe gratitude to Erin Oberli, who gave valuable last minute advice, and to my former husband, Charles McIntosh, who has written all his life and whose encouragement was heartening. I also like to thank Sol Stein, whose book, *Stein on Writing*, taught me to be sparing with words and lavish with suspense.

My deepest gratitude goes to my children, Mimi Stuart and Alison Poulsen, for their love and support, for the splendid book cover that Mimi painted and for their wise words of counsel.

This book is a tribute to my parents, Edith and Edgar Leuthold, passed away many years ago, whose example of integrity, courage and wisdom provided the substance of this book.

Table of Contents

I. Prelude

II.
39 Reasons Not to Rush into War

Foreword

The wisdom of our rulers or the lack of it has varied widely in the course of history. Heads of state shape the lives of their people, often for generations to come. And yet, people have chosen and applauded rulers devoid of wisdom, who have brought them to the brink of disaster.

Of all the unwise rulers, few have exerted a stronger hold on their people than Hitler and Stalin. These dictators ruled with an iron hand, controlling every aspect of their subjects' lives, exerting power even over their thinking.

Though written as fiction, the events of this book are true. They are the stories of three college friends (one of whom was my father) and their families. It shows life in Germany as it was during the tumultuous first half of the last century. I was born when Hitler came to power. Nine years of his reign are deeply engraved in my memory—years that raised many questions. Is life perpetual struggle? Does good prevail over evil? Can we choose future leaders more wisely?

History does give us answers.

Roswitha Leuthold McIntosh
Alameda, California
May 2007

I. Prelude

The Buried Past

Truth is stranger than fiction —Mark Twain

D r. Sigurd Siegel, Vienna's prominent psychologist, was turning the pages of his patient's file. It was a puzzling case—the patient was as sound as anyone, yet something had to be done, and soon.

Elly, his young nurse, stood in the door trying to get his attention, her face flushed with agitation. Chords of a Vienna waltz floated through the open window.

"Your patient won't be coming," she said. "He was ... ," she pushed back an innocuous curl. "I called his boarding house," she started again. "Mr. Renholt was murdered last night."

Dr. Siegel's hand froze in mid-air. The late afternoon sun caught it and flitted merrily over his neatly penned notes. The grandfather clock in the hall ticked more audibly, more audaciously. Like an irksome intruder, it spoke of the passage of time, of the brevity of life.

"Why?" she whispered. Renholt, a harmless, good-natured chap murdered? It made no sense. His greatest joy was to come twenty minutes early to the doctor's office and often talk another patient out of a coin.

It was a strange case. A friend had sent Renholt because of their mutual aversion toward the National Socialists. Vienna was swarming with them, more every day. Many wore the uniform with the swastika and promoted the annexation of Austria to the German Reich. Renholt was terrified of them.

"They are after me, Doc," he kept telling the doctor. He even changed his name. His real name was Reinhold Hanisch.[1]

In Dr. Siegel's opinion, Hanisch was not paranoid. But why would the National Socialists be after a penniless, happy-go-lucky tramp? Hanisch had told him why: During the cold winter back in 1910, Hanisch had befriended Adolf Hitler. Night after night, the two men had stood in line at Vienna's Meidlinger Asylum for the Homeless[2] waiting for a bed. In the mornings they had to vacate the place. When they did not get in again at night, they slept on a park bench or under the bridge.

Twenty-eight years later, Hitler, Vienna's street rat, had become the big boss in neighboring Germany, getting ready to march into Austria. Yet no one seemed to know about Hitler's shady past. In Germany, Hitler paraded as the unknown savior, cloaked in mystery, sent by God. Hanisch was certain that the big boss wanted to keep it that way; that is why Hitler was after him; he wanted to silence him.

Back in 1910, Hanisch had shared his bread with young Hitler, a pale and friendless chap with blistered feet, sitting for hours staring into space, building castles in the air. Hanisch, a long-time tramp and well versed in the tricks of a hobo's life, was fishing for more reliable quarters than the Asylum and probed young Hitler about his trade.

"I'm a painter," Hitler told him.

"There must be plenty of jobs for painters," Hanisch replied in hopeful anticipation.

"Not one of those," Hitler bristled with contempt. "I'm an Academician and an Artist."

---

[1] Hitler searched four years to track down Hanisch. *"Hitler, eine Biographie"* by Joachim Fest, p. 83

[2] Ibid. p. 41

4

"Then make use of your art!" Encouragingly, Hanisch patted the young man's arm. But the arm swiftly withdrew. Nonetheless, Hanisch got postcards of Viennese landmarks and paper and paints, and Hitler painstakingly copied them. Enterprising Hanisch sold them to tourist stores, and with the proceeds they were able to move to a cheap dorm on Meldemann Street.

Dr. Siegel knew the Meldemann dormitory.

The Hanisch/Hitler partnership lasted seven months; then greed got the better of the young artist. He had copied the Vienna House of Parliament, "a Hellenistic marvel on Austrian soil," Hitler called it and proudly declared, "It's worth fifty kronen, not a penny less." When Hanisch delivered the customary ten, Hitler flew into a rage and persuaded a fellow roommate, a young policeman, to throw Hanisch into jail. Hanisch never saw Hitler again.

"Why?" Elly repeated. "Why would anyone want to murder Mr. Renholt?"

Dr. Siegel's hand slid over his forehead. "Who knows, Elly," he replied with a slight tremor in his voice and gathered the victim's file. "Get your coat, Elly. I'll drive you home."

Elly shook her head. "I'll go to the concert in the park," she said. "I need music to clear my head."

"The Friday afternoon concert!" the Doctor became aware again of the lively strains of a waltz. He smiled kindly at his young nurse. "Of course, Elly. Go and enjoy yourself! Just remember, it is better not to talk about murder victims. Less harm comes to the ignorant."

Troubled, the doctor drove to the Vienna Woods, his eyes nervously scanning the rear mirror—he, too, was privy to the knowledge for which Hanisch had been murdered. He settled on a secluded bench to rewrite the victim's file. His temples throbbed. He took a deep breath to calm his nerves—never

5

before had he altered a patient's records or changed a dead man's past. Yet he was certain that those National Socialists would be looking for this file to see what Hanisch had told him. No, he was not willing to be murdered, too.

The task completed, he tore his prior notes into a thousand shreds and drowned them in a public latrine. Then he went home, pondering Hanisch's story and his own recollections of the Meldemann dorm:

The year was 1914. Sigurd Siegel was a young student at the University of Vienna then. For the last three weeks, though, he had roamed the countryside blinded by jealousy, with a bottle of wine as his only companion. It was cold that evening when he found himself in the Vienna Woods where it had happened.

Sigurd did not want to be in the Vienna Woods! Every tree reminded him of his Sylvia. His hopes and dreams were buried there. He hastened downtown and turned into the first dorm on Meldemann Street. He needed a bed for the night.

Sigurd was a newcomer to the dorm, a stuffy place, but he did not notice. A gaunt man in a caftan disrupted his thought—a humorless chap, holding forth on politics, shouting, and gesturing with his fists. He seemed to be at home there. Sigurd chose a bunk farthest away from the chap. Even then he could not tune out the man's ranting. There was something irritating about him—his anger, his intensity. Leaning against his bunk, Sigurd tugged on his youthful chin.

"A fanatic," he postulated. "A merciless fanatic."

Sigurd, being a student of psychology, could tell the signs. He glanced at the others in the dorm. They, too, seemed to be mesmerized by the speaker's harangues. He turned away, disturbed by the speaker's cold, hypnotic eyes.

A bearded male was lighting a cigarette and Sigurd strolled over to him. "Got a light?" he asked. "Ran out of matches." Arching his brow, he pointed his head toward the speaker.

The bearded male took in the newcomer with curiosity—a hale and hearty youngster in a place like this? He shrugged his shoulders and took his time to answer, "Maybe a madman. Maybe a politician out of work. Can't choose your roommates in a flophouse."

A flophouse! Had he sunk that low? All because of a girl? He thought of the lusty banter among his fraternity brothers and longed for his roommate Edgar and his counsel.

The speaker's ranting caught Sigurd's attention again; he was attacking minorities now, fueled, it seemed, by a deep-seated rage. Sigurd recoiled from those angry outbursts. Yet he too was caught in the clutches of passion. He did not like what he saw.

Slowly, he strode back to his bunk. His slender fingers reached under the pillow to pull out his bottle. "This is not the answer," he decided on his way to the sink, and poured the cheap wine down the drain. The gurgling of the liquid synchronized well with the speaker's drone.

The orator was raving against the Slavs and the Serbs now.

"He's got fierce determination," Sigurd continued his analysis. "I would not want to be on his black list." Being fair-minded, he turned to analyze his own actions. "I've been a jealous fool, forsaking my studies," he realized. He suddenly felt a great sense of relief—in the morning, he would return to the university. And maybe have a talk with Sylvia.

"Quiet!" someone shouted from below.

Annoyed, the orator adjusted his long sleeves and carefully closed the top button of his black caftan. For weeks he had combed Vienna's hand-me-down shops for something dramatic

7

to wear, something that would set off his gray complexion and go well with his dark hair and eyes and his black mustache. He found the old caftan at St. Paul's, and had worn it ever since, three years now. His only garment.

He wanted people to remember him when he spoke. He exulted in his political views. Despite his young years, he had collected a vast list of *enemies* who were the target of his verbal slaughter—among them the Serbs, the Jews, the Slavs, the rich, the poor, and the educated.

For six long years he had roamed the streets of Vienna, listening to its coffeehouse orators and street corner politicians. The city was a hotbed of anti-Semitism and ethnic rivalries, and eagerly he drank in the abusive talk. Words of scorn and contempt suited his mood. They expressed precisely what he felt. They soothed his tortured soul.

"Quiet! I say," came from the door. A heavy-set woman, the owner of the flophouse, stood in its opening.

"Must you shout like this? It's time you did some honest work! A young man like you, hanging around, living off charity!"

The young man disliked opposition and confrontation. He turned and stole out the backdoor.

"He is a coward to boot!" Sigurd spit out his cigarette and ground it into the floor. "The man would use deceit and cunning to get his way."

That man was Adolf Hitler.

It was close to suppertime; the charity kitchens were about to open. Hitler stood in line for food, listened to more political talk, and practiced his own version on other vagrants.

His own words were music to his ears.

But work? That was another matter.

He had never worked, and never intended to. Work was for others, not for him.

Sigurd eagerly welcomed the light of dawn. He was glad to return to the university and his studies. During the night, his thoughts had gyrated around Sylvia, but from a different angle. He wanted to see her. Would she be willing?

He mulled over their last encounter, a moment vividly engraved in his memory. She had stared at him, and then abruptly left the parlor without saying a single word!

If only he could remember what led up to it, but the facts were hazy in his memory. He decided to write her a letter. With paper, pen and envelope, he headed for the Vienna Woods. He settled on the bench where he last saw her, twenty-two days earlier—Sylvia, radiant in the company of another man! Turmoil overcame him and he fled to another bench facing in the opposite direction. He wanted to think calmly, not blinded by passion. He recalled the flophouse orator, shouting and shaking his fists; it had deeply repulsed him. He took out paper and pen, and began:

My beloved Sylvia,

Should he call her *his beloved* after what he had seen? He had intended to marry her, but ... Nonsense, he did have to address her somehow. Besides, he had no other sheet of paper.

My beloved Sylvia,

I am sitting in the Vienna Woods where we used to stroll and dream of ever-lasting love, where we got engaged, where I saw you three weeks earlier arm in arm with that other man, and all my dreams of happiness came crashing down.

What happened then? He had barred it from his thoughts, but he needed to remember. He tried to recreate the scene. Sitting on a bench, he had noticed her from a distance—Sylvia arm in arm with another man. Blinded by jealousy, he had hastened downtown to drown his wrath.

He went from tavern to tavern that night, drinking and looking for the young man who had accompanied her. That man, he was handsome, annoyingly handsome! Probably ten years older than Sylvia. Probably well established, not just a student as he was. Reluctantly, he had to admit to a flood of jealousy.

I have never loved anyone but you, Sylvia. And when I saw the arm of another man linked to yours, my world collapsed. I spent all night in nearby taverns. In the morning, I came straight to your door. A big mistake, I realize now. I was not sober, not kempt, not rational.

He remembered it vaguely through the haze of the unaccustomed alcohol and his crushing disillusionment. She opened the door happy to see him. She led him into the parlor while he poured forth his anger and suspicions. She just stared at him, without a word.

I may have accused you of infidelity. I do not remember. But I do remember your look of shock and disbelief. I never gave you a chance to explain, did I?

Could she possibly have an explanation? How could she! The other man was obviously not a casual acquaintance. And that was the worst part of it. At a glance, Sigurd detected affection and intimacy between the two—they were obviously not talking about the weather or about books. They were sharing confidences. Sigurd jumped to his feet. Furiously, he paced up and down the lane. Ten minutes later he continued his epistle.

For the last three weeks I've agonized, roaming the countryside, but I have found no answer. Today, I will be returning to the university and my studies. Will you allow me to apologize in person and talk with you?

Your ever faithful Sigurd

The last paragraph took him great effort to write, but he did it. Swiftly he folded the letter, tucked it into the envelope, and licked the glue. Had he judged her too hastily three weeks earlier? With vigor he spit out the taste of glue and marched off to the post office.

A few days later, on June 28, 1914, newspaper headlines electrified the world: "Archduke Francis Ferdinand, Heir to the Habsburg Throne, Assassinated!"

Politicians rejoiced. They saw their opportunity to declare war. Hitler rejoiced with them. It had been a tough six years, eking out a living from charity and surviving in what he called the jungle of a corrupt city. He had enough of the filth and loneliness that went with it. Tomorrow he would enlist in the German Army. He had dodged the draft six years earlier. Now the army offered salvation. He needed a change. He was ready and eager to work off his hatred in glorious, hands-on battle.

Marriage for Dowry
Where there's marriage without love,
There will be love without marriage —B. Franklin

Eighteen years had passed.

Festive guests crowded Leipzig's famous Thomas Church where Johann Sebastian Bach used to play the organ. Among the guests were Sigurd and his wife Sylvia. His college roommate Edgar had invited him to the wedding of his sister-in-law. The year was 1932.

To the measured pace of the Wedding March, Nobel, Edgar's father-in-law, was walking his radiant daughter Viola down the aisle. Yet his heart was heavy with apprehension. Why had he given his consent to the marriage? Why?

He had not given it willingly. Granted, Arno was tall, good-looking, and always ready with an amusing tale, but as Nobel saw it, Arno was a ladies' man—he owned nothing, knew nothing and talked too much. Worst of all, he had never done an honest day's of work. Did he love Viola? Unlikely. Arno loved himself and his comforts. He did not desire Viola; he desired her family's wealth.

The words of an old Argentinean soothsayer crossed Nobel's mind. He had not thought of them in thirty years. "Beware of wealth," the old gypsy had told him. "Someone will covet it and stop at nothing to get it." Nobel, a young man then with no assets to his name, had laughed at her words, but seeing her ragged clothes and bony hands, had given her a coin.

Nobel's "no" to the union did not deter the young suitor. "I'll get support," Arno laughed, and refocused his courting efforts on Mina, Nobel's wife. He regaled her with amusing gossip, brought her chocolates and flowers, and flattered her unstintingly; and gently Mina began nudging her husband in the right direction.

Nobel, well aware of his daughter's expensive tastes and her insatiable delight in things, tried to explain the realities of life. But he found that wives and daughters are deaf to words they do not want to hear. Twelve months later he succumbed to the pressure and accepted the man into the family.

Arno, the groom, was waiting near the altar. He looked splendid in the fine attire Mina had chosen for him. But what was hidden beneath it?

"My parents were political refugees; they died when I was an infant," he sighed to Mina one day when she asked about his family. "My dear aunt, my only relative who brought me up, has also passed away."

A sad tale; all fiction.

His parents had come to Germany to find work. And both were alive. When their only child disappeared, his father took his sorrow to the corner bar, and his mother to a dark corner of the church. For years they had prayed for a child. When Arno finally arrived, they smothered him with attention and pandered to his every wish. In their eyes, Arno was the center of the universe. And Arno intended to keep it that way.

At fourteen, Arno dropped out of school and cultivated girlfriends. Two years later, one of the young girls got pregnant, and Arno, who had promised her eternal love and a grand wedding, quietly slipped out of town. He decided to hide his lowly birth and pretend to be an orphan. It would evoke sympathy, he figured, while his good looks would open doors for him. His doting parents had proved it to him. And so had his girlfriends. He knew what he wanted from life—wealth without having to work for it, and power beyond his humble station. In a rigid, class-structured society like Germany, this was a good-sized challenge.

His strategy worked. For the next ten years he lived a life of idle pleasure.

Now also his future looked secure.

He stood near the altar exultantly, about to be married into one of Leipzig's respected and wealthy families. Nobel searched Arno's eyes for warmth and love; after all, this was the man's wedding day. But they gave him little reassurance.

Those eyes! Nobel broke into a cold sweat. Nobel's eyes were a serene gray that evoked trust in total strangers. Arno's eyes were blue but hard like steel. Eyes held a great fascination for Nobel. When he grew up on his parents' farm, he kept a journal about the eyes of their animals. Were they aggressive eyes? Devious? Good-natured? Nervous? Playful? Scared? His impressions were seldom wrong. As a businessman, he had

13

continued this practice and paid great attention to a person's eyes and gaze.

Would he buy a car from Arno?

No, not from Arno.

Yet here he was, about to give his daughter in marriage to this man. He took another look at the groom. He had seen cold eyes like his before, but could not remember where. He would have to take that man into his business. The thought weighed heavily on him.

Beware of wealth! Someone will covet it. There it was again, the gypsy's warning. His business and investments had flourished. He was a wealthy man.

He had given much thought to Arno's future and agreed with Mina that they would send Arno to his branch in London for a year, and then a year to his office in Paris.

"Good," was Mina's reaction. "It will improve Viola's French and broaden Arno's education."

"I hope he will learn the business," Nobel interjected quietly. He did not believe in miracles, but he would spare no effort to turn Arno into an upright member of society. Time alone would tell.

"I shall miss him," Mina concluded. Her words still puzzled him. It was one of her charms that she had her own and definite ideas.

In any event, Arno could not take Viola's assets and run. Nobel and his lawyers had seen to that.

The reception was in full swing. In need of a moment's respite, Nobel retreated to his library. Wrapped in troubling thoughts, he did not hear the door open.

A voice apologized, bringing Nobel back to the present.

"Don't leave, Edgar. Come on in," he called, delighted to see his other son-in-law. He liked Edgar, a man of indisputable integrity.

"A new member in the family," Nobel advanced, hoping for the younger man's opinion.

Edgar nodded slowly. He loathed the groom. Arno reminded him of a slimy worm. No, a deceitful snake. Yet sensing his father-in-law's pain, he chose kinder words. "I've never seen Viola happier," he said. "Time will tell."

"Well spoken, Edgar, like a diplomat," Nobel smiled. Obviously, they agreed in their low opinion of their in-law.

"I wish I could play a game of chess with you, Edgar, but duty calls. I must return to my guests."

"I'll stay here if you don't mind." Edgar excused himself.

He, too, needed a reprieve from Arno, who was oozing charm from every pore. He shuddered at the thought of running into Arno at clubs and social events, and at family gatherings. Yet for Edith, his joy and pillar of strength and the mother of their three children, he would do anything.

Election — 1932
Political ploys are legally enacted games-playing —B. Fuller

The wedding guests departed and so did the young couple. Peace returned to the residence. Nobel was smoking his pipe, while reading the late news.

Paul von Hindenburg, supported by anti-Hitler forces, had won the election. It was good news. Yet Hindenburg was eighty-five and his advisors had feared civil unrest if Hindenburg failed. He needed the support of the National Socialists, Germany's strongest party. So before the elections, Hindenburg had made a deal with the party: in exchange for their support he promised to appoint their man Hitler as chancellor.[3]

Nobel studied the new chancellor's photograph. He had heard Hitler speak, and had judged him a crude, cold and calculating demagogue. And yet, this Hitler had recognized the wave of patriotism that swept the nation after the devastating Treaty of Versailles. His inflammatory speeches promised the people what they wanted to hear, and like a tsunami they carried him to the top.

Ruefully, Nobel thought of the fine democratic constitution that the German Cabinet drew up after Word War I. It contained the best features from the governing documents of England, France, Switzerland and the United States. The monarchy had been abolished and Communism stopped. The new constitution seemed to "guarantee an almost flawless democracy.[4]"

Then in June of 1919, a year after the armistice, the country was confronted with the Versailles Peace Treaty. Germany was stripped of its colonies. Large chunks of its territories were awarded to neighboring countries, its population dispossessed and driven out. Horrendous reparations had to be paid—five billion marks in gold as a first payment. Ships, lumber, cattle and coal had to be delivered. And the country was forced to disarm. For a nation that revered its corps of officers and honored the bearing of arms, this was harsh punishment.

The immediate response was anti-Treaty violence. Passionate demonstrations and riots swept the country and lasted for years. The German cabinet could no longer cope and fell into chaos. The German judiciary became a center for counterrevo-

---

[3] Germany's Chancellor, Heinrich Brüning, was forced to retire. He emigrated to the United States and became a professor at Harvard.

[4] "The Rise and Fall of the Third Reich" by William L. Shirer, p. 89

lution, beset by the worst corruption it had ever seen, and perverted justice for reactionary political ends.[5]

The German currency began to slide. By 1921, its value dropped to 75 marks to the dollar; by 1923, it stood at 18,000 to 1; by November, people had to use a wheelbarrow filled with 4,000,000 marks to buy one loaf of bread. The German currency had become worthless; the savings and hard-earned money of the population were wiped out.

Despair united the people against their government that had signed the treaty. They felt betrayed and destroyed, and yearned for nationalism and someone who would save them from starvation and ruin. Hitler's timing for his patriotic tirades against the allies and the government was perfect. He could not fail.

Nobel took another look at the Chancellor's photo when it suddenly struck him—those cold and calculating eyes. He turned to Mina.

"Have you noticed Hitler's eyes, Mina? Don't they resemble Arno's?"

"No, dear," she replied matter-of-factly. "Hitler's eyes are brown, Arno's are blue."

"True, but when you look at the expression of their eyes, there's a significant resemblance."

"Whatever their expression, I'm glad he married Viola. Both our younger daughters have children by now. It's high time our oldest found a husband, too."

Nobel looked doubtful.

"He's such a dear, " she added warmly. "He has great charm."

---

[5] Ibid. p. 92

17

Nobel reached for his pipe. He did not value men with charming chatter and idle hands; those were the devil's tools. He valued men for their integrity, their industry and their learning. Uneasily he puffed on his pipe. As the fifth of ten children he had left the family farm at an early age since farms passed undivided to the oldest son. He worked his way around the globe—as cabin boy on a steamer, as cook's helper in the Amazon jungle, as an explorer's assistant on the African continent. Eventually, in the city of New York, he found an employer he liked, and worked for him with great diligence. After four years, Mr. Mautner the furrier, made Nobel a partner, and later, when he wanted to retire, sold the business to him.

Nobel returned home, set up his headquarters in Leipzig, Germany's capital of furs, and married Mina, who had waited for him.

"We've been married for twenty-four years," he reflected contentedly, while his eyes came to rest on a photo of Mina and their three daughters. He turned to her, smiling; she was sitting at the little rococo table writing invitations for their next dinner. A few years earlier, Nobel had been named Honorary Consul General for Persia, and Mina took great pride in being one of Leipzig's prominent hostesses.

"Mina," he said affectionately, "among my four pretty women you are the most beautiful."

"Thank you my dear," she smiled graciously. "Tell me, shall we invite Otterbach? I hear he's become an ardent admirer of Hitler."

"Preferably not. He's opinionated and anti-Semitic. Many of the people I work with are Jewish."

"We won't then. I dislike political diatribes."

Nobel picked up the paper again. The new chancellor was an unknown quantity, an uneducated nobody who had never done an honest day of work, and for a moment, Nobel was reminded of Arno again. Inciting the masses with inflammatory speeches did not fit with Nobel's concept of honest work. Nobel reached for his pipe. Why did Hitler, an Austrian citizen, come to Germany and volunteer in its army?

A knock at the door interrupted his thoughts. It was the butler.

"Dr. Selig has arrived. He is waiting in the study, sir."

"Ah, my chess partner. Thank you, Barns. Bring us a beer."

"Glad to see you, Doc," Nobel greeted his chess partner warmly. "The election results are most disturbing."

Doc sank into the leather chair. "Devastating! If people had read Hitler's *Mein Kampf*, they'd realize that this man is a madman, a dangerous madman." Doc was the only one among Nobel's friends who had read the book.

"No one wants to struggle through long-winded, half-baked theories."

"True. It is laborious reading," Doc agreed. "But people don't know what they are in for. Hitler has bizarre ideas. Take racial purity, for example, and I quote: *a people must preserve the purity of its bloodline or it will weaken and perish.*[6] What will this lead to?"

"It's pathetic nonsense."

"You know my wife is Jewish, Nobel, and I'm half-Jewish. We are seriously thinking of emigrating."

"It won't come to that. Hindenburg plans to reinstate the monarchy. Hitler won't last long. He's uneducated, not even German. I still can't understand why he enlisted in our army?"

---

[6] "The mixture of blood and the resultant drop in the racial level are the sole cause that old cultures have died out." *Mein Kampf*, p. 17

"An opportunity to escape from a life of frustration and rejection. He exchanged extreme poverty and morbid loneliness for the excitement of a common goal and the glory of collective action. It gave him an outlet for his deep-seated hatreds. He hates everything his Austrian father stood for." Doc knew; he had worked at the hospital in Braunau where Hitler was born.

"You knew him as a child, didn't you? What was he like?"

"He was smart in a limited sort of way, but cantankerous and lazy. He was a ringleader at school and demanded absolute subservience from his playmates. Yet he fiercely resented the slightest admonition from his elders. He'd strike a pretentious pose for his class photo, but he failed in his studies. Three times he did not get promoted."

"Didn't he drop out of school?"

"He did. He never studied. Studying was work. And work was for others, not for him. Besides, he was exceedingly arrogant. At the Realschule in Linz, he boarded with five of his classmates. While they used the informal *you*, he addressed them with the formal *thou* —at age fourteen! He never mingled with them. What he wrote about his life and family is mostly fiction."

"Why would he resort to fiction?"

"To hide his background. He wants to be superman, the g Godsent savior. Did you ever find anything in the press about his personal life, or see a photo of him before the elections?"

"Not that I recall."

"He likes to shroud himself in mystery—appear aloof, grand and mysterious!"

"He certainly is aloof. I wish he had stayed in Vienna!"

"A pity indeed," Doc clutched his beer and took a large swallow.

20

Nobel, too, reached for the restorative brew. "His campaign slogans certainly appealed to the hungry masses," Nobel mused, setting up the chessboard. *"I will restore order...create jobs... combat the Communist threat...unite Germany...and re-establish our national pride,* all issues that are irresistible to a defeated nation and millions of unemployed and destitute. But talk is cheap. Let's see his actions."

Doc looked at his friend in dismay, "Tell me, why do people who cannot manage their own affairs insist on managing everyone else's?"

The Black Sheep

A man should treat his brothers lovingly and with justice, according to the deserts of each. But the deserts of every brother are not the same —A. Huxley

It was overcast. After a two-year absence, Viola and Arno returned to Leipzig, and with them their baby son. The young parents looked splendid in their latest Parisian outfits. The simple, well-tailored black suited Viola well—she enjoyed good food, and it tended to show.

Nobel introduced Arno to his staff and showed him his office. "Your place will be here in the anteroom to my office," he explained. "You'll be my special assistant." He intended to keep a close eye on his son-in-law.

Mina invited the family to a festive dinner to welcome the young couple home. In return, Arno took family and friends to dine at Auerbach's Keller, one of Leipzig's fashionable, old restaurants, well known from Goethe's *Faust*.

Arno escorted Mina to her seat.

"This man Hitler," he exclaimed, "What a hero, what an inspiration! Admirable, how he's risen."

"You seem to like him, don't you?" Mina replied amicably.

"A capital man. Mark my words, he will rule the world," he added in high spirits. "Did you see last night's torchlight parade?"

Mina shook her head.

"A thousand young people marching with torches through the city. On the lawn of the sports arena they formed a perfect swastika. A dozen bands played. Thousands of people cheered. It was spectacular."

"Did he speak?"

"What a speech! Dynamite. He swept everyone off their feet; the crowd went wild. Hundreds joined his Party. So did I. I've applied to become a member of Hitler's elite, the SS[7]. This man will go places."

After dinner over coffee, Arno sidled up to Edgar, his brother-in-law.

"A most embarrassing situation, Edgar. I forgot to bring my wallet," he began, looking suitably downcast. "You wouldn't mind paying; I'll need ...," he paused and showed Edgar the bill for the extravagant dinner. He had judged Edgar well. Without a word, Edgar pulled out his wallet and handed Arno what he needed. Inwardly, Arno chuckled with delight, calculating how soon he could use this ploy again. Edgar's upper-class upbringing was a painful thorn in his side.

Nobel was an early riser. He traded furs worldwide, and daily over his cup of coffee skimmed the London and New York Times, El Figaro and the local press. By the time the family awoke, he had left for work.

---

[7] SS is the commonly used word for Hitler's *Schutzstaffel* or bodyguard that he created in the mid-1920s.

That evening, he and Mina attended the opening of the opera season—a splendid performance of Giuseppe Verdi's *Il Trovatore*. During intermission, while enjoying a glass of champagne with their friends, they saw Hitler approaching. Hitler liked operas, especially Wagner's, and attended them often. He looked no longer the part of the beer garden demagogue; he was well dressed and aimed his charm at the ladies.

"A fine performance," Hitler pronounced, while Nobel shook the outstretched hand and introduced his friends.

Nobel and Hitler had not met before. Political posturing, Nobel figured—Hitler is seeking acceptance in the class that least applauds him. He searched the man's eyes; they were blood-shot that evening and in spite of the smile, his eyes remained cold and calculating.

"I shall walk to the office, Alexi," Nobel called next morning to his Ukrainian chauffer, and set off through the Rosenthal, Leipzig's park known for its roses. He was humming Verdi's haunting *Miserére*, and was still humming when he opened his mail.

In the outer office, Arno was looking through a men's clothing catalog. He had a weakness for expensive clothes and always managed to wear the best. The boss's humming reminded him that Mina had sent him tickets for that evening's performance. He was looking forward to being seen at the opera. He and Viola made a good-looking couple.

"I've got a fine position and a bright future in a prosperous company," Arno gloated to himself. "One day, it shall all be mine."

A sudden thump interrupted his reverie; the humming stopped. Arno jumped up and within seconds stood in Nobel's office. His father-in-law's head had slumped on top of his mail.

The letter opener had fallen from his hand. He seemed to be unconscious, or was he dead?

Arno's head reeled. Was this his opportunity? Noiselessly, he closed the door and touched the man's shoulder whispering his name, but Nobel did not respond.

The shadow of a grin crept over Arno's face. "The safe," he thought, as he gingerly reached into the unconscious man's pocket. A knock at his door made his hand jerk. He withdrew it and flew back to his anteroom to slide into his chair.

"Come in," he called, his heart racing.

It was Helga, Nobel's secretary. She had been with the firm for many years. "SS Führer Pohl is here to see you."

Not now, Arno agonized, while his mind hunted for an appropriate excuse. Too late. Pohl's person appeared in the doorframe. Arno jumped up and snapped to attention with a crisp "Heil Hitler!" and added quick-wittedly, "I'm honored to see you." He moved his chair in Pohl's direction. "Would you like to take a seat?"

"No thanks." Pohl's voice was hard but not unfriendly. "You've applied to become a member of the SS. It will require a background check and a detailed medical/physical report. Only persons with unblemished Aryan characteristics and ancestry will be accepted." He looked approvingly at Arno, who was tall, good-looking, fair-skinned, blue-eyed and blond. Exactly the type Hitler wanted.

"Where do I obtain the forms? I shall do my best to answer all questions," Arno replied.

"I brought them with me."

Pohl located the questionnaire in his briefcase and handed it to Arno. Political questions and answers flew back and forth; no lack of enthusiasm on Arno's part. An eternity seemed to have elapsed when Pohl finally left.

Arno felt drained, but pleased. "This is my day," he thought and took a deep breath to collect himself. "The safe," he exalted. "The safe!" Cautiously, he knocked at the boss's door. No answer. Quietly, he slid open the door. Nothing had changed. Eagerly, he fingered inside his father-in-law's pocket to locate the key. To Arno's chagrin, Nobel had never taken him to the safe. Arno certainly had tried. The safe, he figured, had to contain loads of funds. It was customary to pay everything in cash: salaries, services, even major purchases, such as cars and real estate. There it was. Gently he extracted the ring with the keys.

"I'll need a container to carry the loot," he thought, and rushed back to his desk to get his briefcase. While emptying its contents into a drawer, there was another knock at his door. Should he ignore it? He decided against it. He slid into his chair, got hold of a pen and the catalog and called, "Come in."

It was Helga again. "I've typed the letter for Mr. Nobel. May I take it to him?"

"Thank you, Helga," Arno beamed his most endearing smile. "You're the best of secretaries. Let me take it to him. I need to talk with him."

He locked his eyes into hers while gently taking the letter from her hand. She nodded and withdrew, while Arno heaved a sigh of relief. He reached for the keys and his briefcase and hastened to the safe. Eight keys were on the ring, but it did not take him long to find the right one. When the safe opened, he gazed at its contents in ecstasy. Bank notes were neatly rolled and marked. Papers were stacked in boxes clearly labeled.

Eagerly he reached in to clean out the cash. With great reluctance he returned a few notes. It would look better, he felt. He gathered bonds and other valuables, then locked the safe and returned the keys to the owner's pocket. He looked at his unconscious father-in-law with a touch of satisfied self-righteousness, "I've married your daughter. It'll stay in the family," he said and placed his briefcase near the backdoor. He took a deep breath to remove the grin from his face. Then, with an expression of deep concern, he opened the door to the outer office and called to Helga.

"Herr Nobel needs his doctor. Please call him right away, Helga. I will drive to the house and fetch Frau Nobel." He picked up his bulging briefcase and left through the backdoor.

An hour and ten minutes later Helga was still trying to reach Arno at the Nobel residence. The doctor and the ambulance had come and gone, taking the patient to the hospital. She wanted to tell him so, but Arno had still not arrived. She nervously watched the clock; it was only a short drive to the house. Luckily it had been the butler, not Frau Nobel, who had answered the phone, and Helga had been able to leave an urgent message for Arno to call her.

At last, Helga's telephone rang.

"What's up, Helga?" Arno's voice came over the wire.

"Take Mrs. Nobel directly to the hospital," she said. "Mr. Nobel is . . . " Her voice broke off, choking, and the line went dead.

The funeral was held a week later. Several hundred people came to bid Nobel farewell. Heinz, the doorman, was wiping a tear from his eyes, thinking of his little boy whose life Nobel had saved. The boy had come down with scarlet fever when he'd been out of work, unable to afford medical help. Nobel heard about it and sent him his own doctor. Heinz would miss the kind gentleman.

Many Jewish fur traders had come. They used to go to Nobel with their squabbles and arguments. They trusted Nobel, who was a patient listener and came up with solutions they could live with.

Three weeks later, Mina announced the new head of the company: She chose Arno, her favorite son-in-law. When the near-empty safe cast suspicions on the man, Mina refused to discuss the matter.

"We see what we wish to see," Edgar explained to Edith. "And we close our ears to what we don't want to hear." And they held their tongues.

In the meantime, Arno stood elatedly in front of his mirror, practicing the look of a grief-stricken relative.

Madness of the Masses
Evil will triumph if good men do nothing —Edmund Burke

Nobel had been buried less than a month, when news of Hindenburg's death[8] rocked the country—a year and a half after being reelected to office.

Shock and grief shook the nation, mixed with the inevitable question, what now? To the thunderous applause of many and the stunned disbelief of others, Chancellor Adolf Hitler was named Hindenburg's uncontested successor. Not only that, the President's Office was merged with that of the Chancellor's. Hitler was Head of State now as well as Supreme Commander of the Armed Forces.

He had reached his first goal: he was absolute ruler of Germany.

Edgar and Sigurd went to Berlin to attend Hindenburg's funeral. In reverential silence, the coffin of the former Field Marshal was carried on a World-War-One gun carriage, accom-

---

[8] August 2, 1934

panied by torchbearers clad in black. Not a word was spoken, not a command given.

In his Last Will, Hindenburg had decreed that after his death the monarchy—the House of Hohenzollern—was to be reinstated. Hitler knew Hindenburg's wishes. Yet Hitler did not intend to share his power with anyone. During the weeks of Hindenburg's illness, Hitler and his henchmen had ruthlessly cleared Hitler's path to succession. Hitler traveled to charm people of influence, while Himmler, Göbbels and Göring saw to it that all opposition was permanently silenced.

Röhm,[9] the man who had maneuvered Hitler into power and for a decade had provided indispensable army protection for Hitler and his Party, was outraged. Not so much at their ruthless methods, but that Hitler deviated from the Party platform. Hitler was courting the rich and influential, and was getting too powerful. Röhm was a person to be reckoned with; he controlled an army of two and a half million well-trained SA men, whom some people referred to as thugs.

In June, Röhm's strongmen forced their way into the Krupp Works. They disrupted the assembly line and promised the men a second workers' revolution. Mr. Krupp, however, Europe's largest manufacturer of weaponry, wanted war and favored Hitler. He was tired of making peacetime products as stipulated by the Versailles Treaty and warned Hitler of Röhm's opposition. And Hitler decided to strike.

During the Night of the Long Knives, some five hundred SA[10] men were murdered, among them Röhm. That Sunday,

---

[9] Without Röhm's protection, Hitler's methods of intimidation, incitement and violence would not have been tolerated. Röhm also provided funds for the Party's purchase of a newspaper, *Voelkischer Beobachter.*

[10] SA stands for Sturm Abteilung (Storm Troopers), a strong-arm squad of the German Workers Party. It was formed in 1920 from among

July 1, 1934, while the killers were still hunting down the opposition, Hitler held an impromptu tea party for the cabinet in the garden of his Chancellery to assure the nation that all was well.

"Hindenburg was no match for Hitler's cunning," Sigurd murmured. "It was a tough year for the aging President."

"A contest he lost on all fronts."

"Look at the way Hitler orchestrated his brown-shirts to create terror in the streets."

"So it was Hitler who was behind the rioting!"

"Of course it was. Terror justified his seizing more power to police us."

"Have you noticed how quiet Hitler is keeping his victories? His new laws are barely mentioned in the press."

"He's afraid to alarm his enemies—he's got many. He plans to consolidate his power first. Do you realize that Hitler achieved equal power with Hindenburg in just two months?[11] In fact, he has been running the country ever since, and hardly anyone noticed."

"We simply have no idea of what is going on. I used to get information from Sam, but he was fired from his government job. And so were Arthur and Simon. All good men."

"They are Jewish. Hitler banned all non-Aryans from government jobs."[12]

"It does not make sense! Some of our brightest people are Jewish. Is he enforcing the law?"

---

the ex-service men and ex-Freikorps organizations, which Röhm absorbed into the German Workers Party to swell its ranks.

[11] On March 23, 1933, Hitler forced Hindenburg and the German Reichstag into approving Gleichschaltung, the Enabling Act, which gave Hitler equal power.

[12] The Civil Service Act marked the beginning of Jewish isolation and impoverishment.

"He seems to be."

"Sam is still looking for a job. I wrote him a character reference; but it hasn't helped. People are afraid to employ him."

"He would be smart to emigrate."

"It's tough to emigrate when you don't know the language."

"I feel like emigrating myself. Remember the recent book burnings! All those great Jewish authors, Freud, Einstein, Brecht, Mann, Remarque, Hesse, Kafka. Monstrous, to burn my favorite books!"

The funeral was over. Edgar and Sigurd moved away from the crowd. Even so, they continued talking in whispers. The wrath and passion of the flophouse orator of eighteen years ago still stuck in Sigurd's mind. He had learned of Hitler's meteoric rise to power only eighteen months earlier, when on the front pages of the newspapers he recognized the madman of the Meldemann dorm. That small mustache in the gaunt face and those cold and calculating eyes were a dead give-away. Yet nowhere did Sigurd find a word about Hitler's unsavory past. Did Hitler silence all voices, like Hanisch? Shortly after Hanisch's murder, the Secret police came to Sigurd's office to request Hanisch's file. That is to say, they asked for the Renholt file.

"Hitler has shut down all my clubs," Edgar interrupted Sigurd's worrisome thoughts. "It's an infringement on our liberty."

"He's closed down *all* organizations, even the Freemasons and Rotarians."

"It's an outrage."

"He's afraid of opposition to spread," Sigurd explained. "It certainly caused a loud outcry of anguish."

"...which Göbbels swiftly squashed. Do you recall him crowing like a mother hen? *Join Hitler's labor party. It's the best and only party to belong to.*" Edgar mocked, *"It has cleaner bathrooms, beautiful aesthetics. .... . If you don't join, we'll bite off your head."*

"Göbbels would have gladly enrolled everyone in Hitler's labor party. I have never seen such effort to get people signed up for the DAV[13].

"It certainly is versatile with a branch for everyone—all creatively abbreviated," Edgar laughed. "My manager belongs to the SA, his wife to the NS-Frauenschaft, his daughter to the BDM, his boy to the HJ[14], and their toddler to AA-Männer."

"Not a moment left for the family!" Sigurd, the psychologist, objected.

"That is the idea. As the humorist says, the family can meet once a year in Nürnberg—at the Annual Day of the Party."

"How does Sylvia feel about Hitler's new anti-abortion and pro-birth laws and his motherhood medals?"

"You mean bearing one child a year? No! Three children are enough for us."

"The government's pressure is enormous. In time, we'll be seeing many mothers with eight children, proudly wearing Hitler's Gold Medal of Motherhood."

"Do you suppose Hitler is planning to have a family?"

"No. He presumes to be Superman; it demands celibacy," Sigurd mocked. "Besides, I'd rather he does not multiply!"

"Tell me, why does he want all those children? Fill the ranks of his Hitler Youth? Fight future wars?"

"I would not bet on peace, Edgar."

---

[13] The DAV (Deutscher Arbeiter Verein) was the only party permitted. By government mandate, it absorbed all unions and many other organizations. Later, it was renamed the National Socialist Party.

[14] Hitler Youth (J=Jugend). They wore brown shirts, were trained in combat and street fighting, and after 1926 focused on sports and national pride. They proved a valuable force when Hitler seized power. Membership became mandatory and rose to several million.

31

"Sigurd! Where do you get your information? You know more than the papers print."

"I have my secret source," Sigurd grinned with a touch of embarrassment. "Do you remember Sylvia's cousin?"

"The one who caused you fits of jealousy, and your fraternity brothers gray hair worrying what became of you?"

"I was gone for only three weeks," Sigurd protested.

"You can sow a lot of wild oats in three weeks," Edgar laughed. He patted his friend on his shoulder. "Glad you came back to your studies, Sigurd, and made up with Sylvia. Tell me about her cousin, the handsome Romeo."

"In strictest confidence, he is my source. He is working in the government. Don't mention it to anyone."

"Don't worry, I know Hitler's cardinal rule—keep the people ignorant and subservient."

"And the women pregnant."

"Did you know that he has forced even the Catholic Church—mind you, the all-powerful Catholic Church—to surrender its political rights to him?[15] *All* rights, except control over its parochial schools."

"Who would have anticipated it? What a superb democratic constitution we had."

"Shocking, that one single man was able to destroy and abolish it! And settled us with Compulsory Sterilization Laws instead." Edgar kicked a rock. "Laws to sterilize the less fit. It won't be long, and we shan't need psychologists anymore."

He looked searchingly at his friend. As of January 1934, all mentally and physically handicapped, manic-depressives, alcoholics and criminals had to be sterilized. Who would be judging these cases? Their severity? Their permanence?

---

[15] The Concordat with Rome, July 8th 1933.

Sigurd nodded. "I am thinking of changing my profession. I can't sit in judgment of people's sanity. Do you realize that I am required to report all mentally ill patients to the government?" His fist was clenched, his knuckles white. "I can't do that. I must find a way out, Edgar. Sylvia agrees with me."

For several minutes, they walked in anguished silence. Then Sigurd resumed.

"Let me quote Hitler: 'The weak must be chiseled away. I want young men and women who can suffer pain. A young German must be as swift as a greyhound, as tough as leather, and as hard as Krupp steel.'"

"As hard as Krupp steel?"

"It may be a sinister hint of what is to come, Edgar. The Krupps have armed Europe for three centuries and a half. Europe's finest weapons have come from their factories. The Krupps are Europe's wealthiest and most influential family. I hear that old man Krupp financed Hitler's election."

"Gustav Krupp would certainly favor war. What a letdown for him to produce teakettles instead of guns. Do you remember Krupp's giant guns that shelled Paris and Verdun in 1918 at an unheard-of range?"

"And his first anti-aircraft guns that shot down observation balloons during the Franco-Prussian war?"

"They have made the best weapons for generations. People at the London Fair were agog when Gustav Krupp unveiled his 2400-pound piece of perfectly cast iron, perfect for making larger guns."

"I've often wondered whether they named Gusstahl (cast iron) after Gustav or after the verb *giessen* (poured iron)?"

"Probably the verb. Nonetheless, the Krupps rank with royalty. Do you remember our Emperor, how he doted on the Krupp heir, Beth? He called her his Queen Beth."

"And arranged her marriage to the perfect queen consort. She made an admirable Krupp president, though. It makes you wonder about the impact of the environment on our genes."

"You are the psychologist, Sigurd. Fourteen generations of Krupps. What do you conclude?"

"It certainly has affected their genes. Look at Gustav Krupp; he is Europe's richest man. And yet he spends his life inside his steel mills. Twenty-four hours a day he is surrounded by horrendous noise and smoke. He adores his wife, and yet he built a house for her right in the middle of his steel plant. The poor woman is practically asphyxiated by the fumes and deafened by those steel hammers. The wine glasses on her table keep shattering from the constant vibration.

"The truth is, he cannot function outside his mills. Did you know that every morning he sits in his observation tower to monitor his employees—he's got over 60,000 in his Essen plant—to make sure no one is late?"

"It surprises me that the Krupp Works survived the Versailles Treaty. Do you remember the consternation when in 1919 all weapons and much of the machinery were destroyed or taken away and the company closed down?"

"Followed by a huge uproar among the workers! The government had to let Krupp continue operations to keep his people employed. Nothing but peacetime products, of course. The city has been swarming with people of the Peace Commission ever since to make sure no weapons are made."

"And journalists from around the globe keep coming to tour his Steel Works."

"Did you read last Friday's Christian Science Monitor? They "loved" Krupp's vast "arsenal of peacetime products," hundreds of them—from kitchen utensils to locomotives, while old man Krupp would sell his soul to build tanks again! The amusing thing is, the journalists come equipped with large cameras, but I've never seen a printed picture. Have you?"

"No, and for a good reason. After each tour, sly man Krupp serves splendid refreshments to the journalists. Well, you can't fill your plate lugging a bulky camera, so Krupp provides a secure room where they can leave them. By the time they've eaten, radiation beams have overexposed all films." [16]

"I hear old man Krupp didn't just fool the journalists. He's fooled the commission, too. His engineers have been working secretly in Berlin designing better weapons. Weaponry runs in the Krupp blood."

"I recently read their annual report. Their peacetime production ran at a heavy loss. Krupp calls it his 'camouflage with a purpose, ... the need to safeguard our irreplaceable experience for the military potential of our nation and to keep the employees and shops in readiness for later armament orders, if or when the occasion should arise.'" [17]

"Speaking of camouflage, just before the Röhm purge Hitler paid a visit to Gustav Krupp. The purpose seemed obvious, to discuss armament. To *camouflage* the obvious, a few days before the visit Hitler appointed Gördeler, an archenemy of militarism, as his price commissioner. Göbbels made sure that all journalists knew about it and would write about Hitler's obvious intentions of peace."

"Didn't Gördeler resign?"

"Yes, shortly afterwards, after he had served Hitler's purpose."

"But our national budget does not show a penny for military spending."

---

[16] *"The Arms of Krupp,"* by William Manchester, p. 334
[17] Ibid. p. 335

"Let's call it creative accounting. Since the Röhm purge, re-armament is receiving top priority. Hitler's allocation for the military is five times larger than for public works, but it's carefully concealed. Krupp and other industrialists are paid in IOU's that are honored by dummy banks and corporations, and not a penny shows up in the budget."

"Probably a brainchild of Schacht's, Hitler's financial man."

"Exactly. A brilliant man. My cousin works for him. Did you know that in 1921, just two years after the Versailles Treaty, old man Krupp was manufacturing weapons again?"

"Not possible!"

"He exchanged patents for shares in the Swedish firm Aktielbolaget Bofors, and bought enough voting rights to control production. By year's end, they were producing Krupp weapons under the Swedish firm's name."[18]

"No wonder Krupp is a stout SS man today."

In October 1934, Krupp publicly lauded Hitler's withdrawal from the European Disarmament Conference and the League of Nations, while Hitler declared Krupp the country's Leading Industrialist. The armed forces were handed a blank check to rearm. Steel production soared, and munitions makers were granted first call on all raw materials from overseas.

A year later, in the fall of 1935, Edgar and Sigurd resumed their conversation about Krupp. Sigurd had just returned from Essen.

"You would not recognize the city. It's a forest of smoke stacks. Hundreds of new factories have been added, especially since last spring when Hitler declared Military Sovereignty and universal subscription."

---

[18] Ibid. p. 335

"I remember that day. Memorial Day, 1935; six months after Hindenburg's death. Tempestuous fanfare! Not like commemorating the dead, more like celebrating a victory."

"Hitler defied Versailles."

Nöller, Edgar's fraternity brother, invited Edgar on a fishing trip. Nöller was still unmarried and always ready to join Edgar and Edith on as many trips as Edgar would let him, which was often—Nöller's jovial presence was always welcome. During their student days, the two men had skied and climbed mountains together and shared their views over Munich beer. Nöller and Sigurd were Edgar's last remaining friends with whom he still felt safe to exchange political confidences. With the speed of lightning Hitler had turned the nation into a police state.

"Remember Hitler's beer garden rally?" Nöller asked. During the twenties, when rumors reached the university that a mustached young man was bandying political buzzwords at beer-garden gatherings, a few students went to look him over.

"You didn't take any of Hitler's free beer, did you?" Edgar replied. Just outside the beer garden, a dozen of Hitler's cronies, soon to be known as the *brown-shirts,* were handing out free beer to attract a crowd, while Hitler held forth attacking Communists and Jews, promising bread, work and glory.

"I hope I did. I hope I took two bottles of his free beer," Nöller grinned, but he didn't recall. "It certainly attracted a crowd ... "

"Willing to drink and repeat the nonsense those *brown-shirts* shouted."

"Remember Hitler's ludicrous words?" Nöller asked.

"Why don't we have work?"

"Because of the Jews," his cronies and the crowd yelled.

"Why don't we have food?"

"Because of the Jews," they shouted back.

"Why did the crops fail? ..." Edgar shook his head. "Ridiculous. But the crowd loved it. They got free beer."

"You quoted Nietzsche when we left: 'Madness is the exception in the individual; it is the rule in a group.' That day we saw both, a madman and a mindless, mad crowd."

"My dear Edgar, let's forget politics today! We are headed for my favorite fishing creek." Nöller lovingly patted his steering wheel. "Ah, the succulent trout my little creek harbors! You've never seen finer. Anna will cook them for us."

But Edgar could not shake his frustration. "We have no liberties left! Look at his latest insult, his *Youth Laws*. Parents no longer have authority over their children. I quote: 'Children's obedience, devotion and loyalty belong solely to Hitler and the Party.'"

"I'll bet you a beer, Hitler has already issued directives that children must report every word that is spoken in the home. So watch your language and remember, it's *for the good of the fatherland.*" Nöller gestured pompously in Hitler-like fashion.

"Be glad, you don't have children, Nöller. I wish Hindenburg had reinstated the monarchy during his lifetime."

"Yes. Better an educated monarch than an unscrupulous egomaniac."

"When the educated silently acquiesce," Edgar quoted sadly, "they relinquish their power to the vocal multitude."

"You're not realistic, Edgar. Hitler eliminates all opposition. Utter one word against Hitler, and you end up in the KZ[19]."

A smile flitted across Nöller's face. "Did Sigurd tell you the latest joke about Dachau?"

---

[19] The standard name for concentration camp.

Edgar shook his head, "I hope your car isn't bugged."

"Hans ran into a friend who was recently released from Dachau."

"I didn't know anyone ever got out," Edgar interjected.

"Not anyone I know, but here's the story: *What was it like in Dachau, Hans wanted to know.*

Just fine, said his friend. Fine breakfast, fine lunch, fine re-training, then a fine supper and a fine movie afterwards."

"Doesn't sound like Dachau," Edgar interrupted again.

"Well, Hans didn't believe him either and elbowed his friend: *Hey, that's not what the other guy told me.*

Yep, replied his friend. That's why the other guy is back in Dachau."

"No more politics, Edgar. Let's enjoy nature while we can. It's our last chance before you're off to Berlin to compete in *Hitler's* Olympics." They had entered Nöller's sacred grove of trees near his fishing creek.

Olympic Gold

In matters of principle stand like a rock.

—Thomas Jefferson

Hitler in person was hosting the 1936 Olympic Games. One hundred and fifty new buildings stood in readiness, one of them a vast Olympic stadium. Hitler wanted to impress upon the world that he was Ruler of the *Master Race*.

The city hummed with activity. Foreign reporters were lavishly provided with microphones and radio vans so they could broadcast to every corner of the world. Huge screens, a novelty then, were placed throughout the city. Hitler wanted everyone to view the German victories.

For special effect and a historic first, Hitler ordered a torch to be lit at the ancient stadium of Olympia and had it carried to his stadium in Berlin. And for ultimate splendor, his foreign guests were beguiled on an island of the Wannsee where an *Italian Night* was staged. Over a thousand guests reveled in luxuriant gardens, and were transfixed by the magic of an Arabian night.

Exhilarated, Edgar rode in from his last run before the Games. His horse had performed splendidly. Dismounting his Trekener, he was about to enter the stables when two SS officials stepped out and blocked his way. He had dodged them the day before. He could not elude them this time.

Clinching his fist, he ignored their officious "Heil Hitler!" and turned to his horse. Sensing her master's tension, she whinnied and shook her mane.

"Are you planning to ride in the Olympics, sir?" one of the SS men demanded. The Games were to open in the morning.

Leuthold nodded assent, but thought it better to speak, "Yes, I do." He had registered for dressage and jumping.

"Then we must ask you to sign this paper." They handed him a pen. "Simply a formality."

He glanced at the form, "Membership in the Nazi Party?" [20]

"Yes sir," they confirmed crisply. "Only members of the Nazi Party have permission to participate in the Games."

Leuthold returned the pen and pocketed the document. "Let me think about it."

Before they let him pass, they made sure he understood. "All Germans participating in the Games must be members of the Nationalist Socialist Party."

Leuthold walked away swiftly to conceal his indignation. The two uniformed men glanced at each other—this Leuthold

---

[20] The word *Nazi* was not used until after the war. The word in usage was *Nationalsozialisten*.

needed watching. The older one pulled a black notebook from his pocket and made an entry.

In the dim light of the stable Leuthold realized the bitter truth. He stroked the noble head of his horse. She had won him many trophies over the last three years. In frustration, he tightened his grip on the saddle. He had to be a Nazi to ride in the Games! He loved the sport and wanted to ride; he had trained diligently. Family and friends had come to Berlin to watch him. But join the Nazi Party? He had strong political convictions, but expediency was not one of them.

Hitler nursed great expectations of the Games. He wanted his protégé, Lutz Long, to prove to the world that the *Aryan Race* was indeed superior. To Hitler's intense disappointment, it did not happen. African-American Jesse Owens was the unrivaled victor of the Games. He broke eleven Olympic records and won four Gold. And he prevailed over Hitler's Lutz Long.

Hitler was beside himself. He refused to shake Owens' hand, and refused to present him with his medals. Fortunately, Lutz Long knew better. The great athlete embraced Jesse Owens and congratulated him, while onlookers smiled in relief.

Leuthold and his wife Edith watched from the bleachers, studying Hitler's anger-distorted face. What ambitions lurked behind those cold and calculating eyes? Leuthold distrusted this man and deeply disliked him. He had torn up the papers for membership, and did not ride in the Games.

The Last Ride

Tyranny is always better organized than freedom —C. Peguy

Five months had passed. Leuthold's voice trembled with urgency as he requested, "Professor Dr. Goldstein, please."

41

"No longer here, sir," was the crisp reply of the hospital's admissions clerk.

"Then Professor Simons."

"No longer here, sir."

"And Dr. Roth?" Leuthold's anxiety mounted. These men were the hospital's most experienced doctors. He knew them well. Being attached to the Fifth Mounted Regiment, he was no stranger to Hohenluechen, Germany's top-ranking hospital for sports injuries.

"No longer here, sir," the attendant repeated.

"Who is the new head of the Orthopedics Division?" Leuthold inquired impatiently. "I wish to see him." Edith, his beloved wife, was being brought here in an ambulance.

An orderly accompanied him to see the new chief.

A clean-shaven, blond youngster, barely thirty-five, occupied the chair of the venerable Professor and greeted him with a brisk "Heil Hitler!"

Goldstein, I need you, Leuthold agonized. He had known the Professor well. His long, delicate hands had inspired confidence in his most injured patients, and so had his keen and kind, dark eyes.

"Who is your best orthopedic specialist, Doctor?" Leuthold came straight to the point. "My wife's leg has been severely crushed."

"We have many good doctors. All new, all Aryan, sir. Some are members of the Schutzstaffel." His pride was evident as he pronounced the last word.

Leuthold cringed. "Any of the old guard left?" he cautiously inquired.

"None. Instructions from Berlin," the young chief replied. "All Jewish doctors have been replaced."

Edgar tried to steady his nerves; he needed a good doctor. He took a deep breath and tried another approach. "If you were in my shoes, Doctor, whom would you choose?"

On that fine October morning in 1936, Edith and her friends had ridden out on horseback. She had married young, perhaps to escape the maternal taboo against exercise. Edith loved sports. For her, life was movement and music. Yet at the time sports were considered highly unsuitable for a lady. In her mother's opinion, a lady's value lay in her skill of running a large household, her graciousness in entertaining guests, and her bountiful support of the arts and charities. After her marriage to Edgar, Edith learned to ride horses, ski the mountains, and chase after tennis balls. Life, for her, had just begun. And Edgar, an eager sportsman himself, encouraged her.

On a recent trip to London he had found a tiny, beautiful compass for her. Edith carried it with her on all excursions. Galloping across the open plain or trotting under the serene trees of the forest, Edith discovered infinite bliss.

On that October morning, however, Edgar had actually tried to dissuade Edith from riding out. He was at a loss for words, though. How does a man explain an uneasy feeling deep within his gut? Even for an intuitive woman it would be a difficult case to plead. And Edith, young and full of joy, had ridden out. She galloped ahead of the group when suddenly, riding around a bend, she and her horse were confronted by a group of children kneeling in the bridle path, rolling marbles. Her horse shied and jammed her leg into a tree.

After a long day at the hospital, Leuthold returned home, tired and dismayed. Maxi, the family's shepherd dog, met him at the door. Sensing his master's despair, his intelligent eyes conveyed his concern: "Where is my mistress? Why your worried face?"

"The children are in bed, sir," the housekeeper reported. "Where may we serve you supper?"

"None. Thanks, Maria," Leuthold replied and sought refuge in his study, accompanied by his four-legged friend.

Would Edith ever ride again? With Goldstein at the operating table he had no doubt that she would. But without a knowledgeable, experienced surgeon? He shuddered. What had become of them? In the twenties and early thirties, most doctors at reputable German hospitals were Jewish. Why had Hitler given orders to have them replaced? As if the mythical word *Aryan* could substitute for years of experience. The headlines of one of Hitler's speeches flashed through Leuthold's mind: "You are a superior people, a superior race." Apparently, a *superior* people did not need doctors.

Nobel's chess partner, Doc, had predicted that this would happen: "If Hitler ever gets into power," he said, "he'll take vengeance on all Jewish doctors." True to his conviction, when Hitler was named Hindenburg's successor, the doctor pulled up his roots and left the country, much to Edgar's regret. Leuthold recalled their discussions when playing chess.

"Why would he take vengeance on Jewish doctors?" Nobel had asked.

"Hitler's mother," Doc explained, "the poor woman, lost three of her children. Hitler blamed the Jewish doctor for it. Also for his mother's death."

Slowly, Leuthold surfaced from his recollections. His shoulders slumped under the weight of helplessness. He looked at his bruised hand where his car keys had dug into his palm when he heard about Goldstein and Simons' dismissal and could not voice his opinion.

Hitler tolerated no dissent and abolished free speech. Leuthold had a wife now and three children; he could not sacrifice them on the altar of his political convictions. Expressing even the slightest disapproval of the government would have dire consequences, and everyone knew it. A humorist formulated it thus: "Lieber Gott, mach mich stumm, dass ich nicht nach Dachau kumm!" ("Dear Gott, make me dumb, that to Dachau I won't come.") It was the fervent mantra of anyone who wanted to survive.

People with misgivings about Hitler were in a minority that kept diminishing as dissenters disappeared.

The majority idolized Hitler and applauded what he did. Three years earlier, they had been unemployed and starving— 33% of the population. Rioting had been rampant. Angry mobs attacked every car that ventured into certain neighborhoods, turned them over and set them ablaze. By 1936, the streets were safe. People had jobs again. They were building highways and factories, or marched in Hitler's new army.

Nonetheless, Leuthold remained troubled. What had become of personal liberty and freedom of speech? Earlier that day at the hospital, if he had voiced his disapproval, his wife would have been refused admission. And he? He would have been carted off to the KZ as others before him.

He anchored his elbows on his desk and buried his head in his hands. His eyes came to rest on the magazine in front of him, but for a long time he saw nothing but a worrisome future. When his eyes focused, he was looking at Germany's prestigious riding journal. Ironically, just a few days before the accident the magazine had portrayed on its cover the radiant face of his wife, mounted on her Trekener, holding her latest trophy. The headlines read: *A New Star is Born.*

Eleven months passed. Edith was still in the hospital, struggling daily with therapy and exercise, suffering excruciating pain. She could not walk, not even stand. Edgar wanted her transferred to a well-known clinic in Switzerland, but the Nazi doctors refused to give their consent. At long last, Edgar found a way to circumvent the government's interference and took her there himself.

It was early September, a clear and crisp autumn day. Contentedly, he squeezed Edith's hand. At last, he had her by his side again. He felt new hope. Those last eleven months had dragged like an eternity. Slowly, shifting from third to second to first gear, they climbed the Swiss Alps to reach the Brenner Pass that would take them into Switzerland. The sun-bathed beauty of Europe's highest mountain peaks was melting away the pain they both had suffered.

They talked about the day they met, nine years ago, at a costume dance given by Edith's mother. Mina, with three daughters nearing marriageable age, gloried in entertaining the sons and daughters of her friends. They congregated in the large hall with its festive chandeliers and fine parquet floor and danced the Charleston and the Jitterbug. To ensure plenty of dance partners for the young ladies, she sent invitations to the officers of the Fifth Regiment at Grimma, of which Edgar was a member then.

Edith at seventeen was guileless, full of fun and surrounded by beaus; marriage was not on her mind. To her, life was a daily adventure to be explored. She wanted to bicycle, play the piano, ice skate, and dance.

She had recently returned from *Le Rosé*, her Swiss boarding school, and found life at home trying. Her elder sister, Viola, envied her free spirit and many suitors, while her mother frowned upon her fondness of sports and the out-of-doors. Marriage would mean liberation and a chance to ride, ski, and play tennis. She knew that Edgar cherished these sports.

When Edgar asked Nobel for Edith's hand in marriage, her father, a wise and just man, queried his daughter first.

"Do you love Edgar? Do you want to marry him?"

"I don't know," Edith answered truthfully. Her thoughts were more focused on escaping the confines of the parental home rather than on love and marriage.

Edgar was ten years her senior, tall, dashing and popular with the ladies. He was one of the first to drive a car in the city of Leipzig, a Bugatti that could easily outrun the police.

"Edith is still young," Nobel explained to Edgar, while setting up the chessboard; he enjoyed a match with the young man. "You have a degree in law, don't you? Didn't you work in the Public Defender's Office?

"Yes, briefly. Defending criminals does not appeal to me."

"Do you plan to practice law?"

"I don't think so," Edgar looked slightly embarrassed. "Too much twisting of words, too little consideration for the truth."

Nobel puffed on his pipe. "Before we set a wedding date, Edgar, let me suggest that you obtain your PhD. Even if you never practice law, the title of *doctor* is a worthwhile asset. Germans have a passion for titles. It may prove useful one day."

Edgar had dated extensively, but had never been in love until he met Edith. He was determined to gain her hand no matter what dragons had to be slain. That very same week he met with his old professor, enrolled at the university again, and embarked on his doctoral dissertation.

47

Edgar held Edith's hand as they entered the Swiss Clinic. He was as worried as Edith was.

The prognosis of the Swiss doctors was not good. The young Nazi doctors had set her femur, tibia and fibula, but they had overlooked four fractures in her foot. Months of exercising had caused irreparable wear and tear to the broken bones. The Swiss doctors would try to make repairs; but the damage was done.

Blood Money

Nothing is so permanent as a temporary government program
—Milton Friedman

Maria, Edith's faithful housekeeper, dropped her sewing and hurried to the front door. That hard, impatient knock boded no good. Two SS men confronted her.

"We wish to see Dr. Leuthold."

"Let me see if he is in," Maria replied timidly.

"No need. We know he is in, and he **will** see us. Is he in his study?"

"I don't know. I'll go and see." Maria, torn between fear and duty, anxiously turned. But one of the men grabbed her arm.

"We'll see for ourselves. Go back to your kitchen."

Leuthold was working at his desk when the two men entered and noisily clicked their heels, an unpleasant reminder of his encounter with SS officials at the Olympic Games.

Shortly after his marriage, Leuthold had resigned from the Fifth Regiment and taken over his father's company that was deeply in debt. His father had died, probably of despair. His oldest daughter Kåte had married a dashing young hussar of the cavalry, who had a passion for gambling and a knack for losing.

48

Quietly, his father-in-law kept paying his gambling debts to protect his daughter from scandal and hardship. But it did not cure the young man's addiction—he kept at it, and scandal was imminent. The old gentleman got a loan from his bank and secured it with the young man's livestock and farm.

Yet when the bank called the loan, there were no assets to be sold. The young man had obtained prior loans on everything he owned, and the old man was stuck with huge debts. At least, he had fulfilled the promise he had made to his young wife who died when Edgar was born—he had given their four children the best possible upbringing and education.

At his father's sudden death, Leuthold took on the challenge of resurrecting the company to pay off the debt. To his surprise, he found the business to his liking. He was used to breeding racehorses. Now he was dealing with seeds of every description, corn, wheat, flax, alfalfa, ... they also could be cultivated and improved. In densely settled Europe, where farmland is at a premium, the cultivation of seeds to achieve larger and better yield was of vital importance.

His business flourished. He traveled throughout Europe, especially in Eastern Europe where farmland is abundant, and persuaded farmers to cultivate seed for him. In his warehouses, machines sorted, dried and cleaned the incoming seed to prepare it for the next round of cultivation.

"You are making a worthwhile contribution to the economy," Edith commented on one of their trips. "You are improving the quality and quantity of the food supply."

Edgar agreed. He loved his work.

"The best part is that you accompany me on most trips," he replied and squeezed her hand.

When the two SS men entered his home office that day, he was poring over his map to plan the next trip to his growing clientele—another trip without Edith. She was still hospitalized. The clicking of their heels jerked him from his thoughts.

"It is time you joined the Party," the taller of his SS visitors came straight to the point. "It is expected of every good citizen."

Leuthold knew it was not only expected, membership was mandatory. Hess' favorite slogan could be seen and heard everywhere:

Hitler is the Party. The Party is Hitler. Hitler is Germany.

"Let me think about it," Leuthold replied, trying to remain noncommittal. It was the same excuse he had used at the Olympics. But this time he did not get away with it.

"You do understand that people who do not join the Party are suspect of subversive activities?" one of the men queried. He paused to let the words sink in. "Nonetheless, we will offer you a chance to show your goodwill toward the government by signing this check." He took a pre-written check from his black notebook and placed it on the desk. Leuthold hesitated, but the SS man anticipated his reluctance and clarified the situation.

"The check will be signed now, or we shall have to accompany you to headquarters to explain yourself."

Slowly, Leuthold reached for his pen. He knew the meaning of *explaining oneself at headquarters*; it meant being sent to an unknown destination like Dachau. He glanced at the amount and gulped. It was not cheap to stay out of the Party!

At long last, Edith was home again—after more surgery, more therapy, more patience. But in time, Edith walked again. The injured leg remained shorter and her foot stiff. Pain became her constant companion and to walk without limping a continuous challenge.

50

The children had not seen their mother for a year, nothing but their father's worried face and the servants' ominous whispers—it had been a year of traumatic anxiety. Now, at long last, the house radiated warmth and joy again. It was as if life had finally resumed.

Before long, Edith was thinking of sports again. She felt sports were a pivotal part of a family's life and was thrilled when Edgar suggested they build a ski cabin. They found an ideal spot on the slopes of the Keilberg, the highest peak of the Erzgebirge. The mountain range was known for severe winters and much snow, yet close to the city—ideal for weekend skiing.

Construction progressed well, but not for long. The contractor called, requesting their Party membership number to get pipes for water and gas, and cables for electricity and telephone.

"I don't belong." Leuthold replied. "Don't you?"

"Of course I do. If I didn't, I couldn't get a license, not even a job!" he protested. "Nowadays, many materials are classified and available only to Party members."

"So what is the problem?"

"I've tried everything," the contractor explained. "They say the house is for you; therefore, you have to belong to the Party."

The year was 1937. Was Hitler planning for war, or was he on a rampage to chastise non-Nazi citizens?

Whatever the reason, Edgar did not cave in. If the house had to be built without gas, running water, electricity and telephone connection, so be it. If the government denied him a permit to build an access road, the family would carry what they needed on their backs. The cabin was two miles from the main road and five miles from the nearest grocery store in the valley. Rather a pack mule than a Nazi. It would call for Spartan living. Edith, with her unflappable good humor, had a sign mounted

51

over the entry of the cabin that announced: *Gelobt sei was hart macht.* (Praise be given to what makes us tough!)

The cabin had fine carved woodwork, but candles provided the only light. It had five bedrooms upstairs, but only one working toilet on the lower level with a manual flushing system—a bucket of water. Wood was the only source of energy, both for cooking and heating, requiring loads of wood that had to be hauled, sawed, chopped, and stacked.

"For an occasional weekend it will do nicely," Edgar reasoned. "Hitler's days are bound to be numbered." Hitler, in the meantime, was proclaiming his Thousand-year Reich.

Boxing—Playoff or Political Payoff
The 1938 Joe Louis/Max Schmeling Match

"Peter," Rosi called to her brother, "Uncle Nöller is here."

They were Nöller's devoted fans. Nöller radiated a contagious love for life, and was always ready for fun and adventure.

It was June 22, 1938, the day of the highly anticipated boxing match between Germany's Max Schmeling and America's Joe Louis. Schmeling was the world's most recent heavyweight champion and beloved by his people as a quiet, kind and very private person. Joe Louis was America's hero and the world champion, admired by the nation at large. The fight was to take place in New York's Yankee Stadium, to be broadcasted live.

Everyone clustered around the radio, even the children thanks to Nöller's intervention. Since all stations were government controlled and saturated with propaganda, the children were normally not allowed to listen to the radio. If they wanted music, their father felt, they could play the piano or crank the record player.

"Hitler is expecting another Schmeling victory," Nöller grinned. "The match has been prodigiously publicized."

"Yes, everywhere," Edith nodded. "Remember how ecstatically Hitler celebrated Schmeling's victory against Louis two years ago? He personally wined and dined Schmeling after his victory. What was the crazy title of the film that Hitler had made?"

"*Schmeling's Victory: A German Victory*," Nöller cited amusedly, "he ordered it to be shown in every theater."

Edgar frowned and increased the volume of the music to drown out the conversation. He looked reproachfully at Edith and Nöller. No one could safely voice such thoughts.

He turned to Nöller, "You were in New York for the match, weren't you?"

Nöller beamed. "Indeed I was. What a fight! Yankee Stadium was half empty. Still, some 46,000 spectators attended. Usually it is packed for a Joe Louis fight."

"Why half empty?" Rosi timidly interjected.

"Ah, a good question." Nöller smiled at the little girl. "You see, the fans expected Louis, the unquestioned world champ, to win the fight in five minutes flat. And that, they figured, did not justify the purchase of an expensive ticket, did it?"

She nodded. "Did it last five minutes?"

"It lasted much longer." Nöller punched the palm of his hand in delight. "Schmeling is an intelligent and very thorough fellow; he came well prepared. For weeks he had watched and studied films of Louis' techniques and had discovered a flaw. Let me demonstrate. Who wants to volunteer?"

He looked at the two boys. Seven- and four-year old Peter and Paul gazed at the well-built man towering over them in visible alarm. Before they could react, Rosi had swung up both arms and shouted: "I do."

53

Nöller looked at the tiny girl in front of him and shook his head. "It's against my code as a gentleman to hit a lady," he said gravely, trying to look big and tough, "but we will give it a try."

She smiled and stretched to gain another inch, knowing full well that Nöller would never hurt her. He would not hurt a fly.

"Here's what we'll do," he explained. "We use our arms to protect our faces at all times. Like this. Then we punch each other. You hit first. Punch me with your left fist as HARD as you can. Now punch!"

Rosi punched as hard as she could, but Nöller had nimbly stepped aside and before she knew it, he had pinched her right cheek.

"You weren't protecting your face," he exclaimed triumphantly. "And this is exactly what Louis did. After each jab, Louis dropped his arm and exposed his head. Schmeling decided to exploit this flaw by hitting back with short, straight rights, like this. He spent weeks perfecting his punch."

"What happened during the match," the boys asked eagerly.

"What a fight! Everyone watched in shocked amazement as Schmeling, round after round, kept throwing straight rights at Louis' face. Finally, in round twelve, poor, battered Joe Louis had enough."

Edgar groaned, "And today is the rematch."

"I wouldn't want to be in Schmeling's shoes," Nöller replied, looking troubled. "The tide of American sentiment is strongly running against him. He's considered Hitler's patsy, though quite unjustly so." Edgar had turned up the music again, and Nöller spoke more softly. "Schmeling's dining with Hitler after his victory, and Hitler's title of the film gave the boxer a bad name overseas. In addition, Hitler used Schmeling to assure Mr. Brundage, the head of the American Olympic Committee, that Hitler would welcome the American team at the Olympic

Games in Berlin and treat it well. You were at the Games, Edgar; you know what happened." He was whispering discreetly, and Edgar adjusted the volume again.

The radio was playing one of Hitler's favorite operas, Richard Wagner's *Die Meistersinger*. Wagner was the only person Hitler admired; he identified with Wagner and considered him his soul mate. "Wagner creates a hysterical excitement in me," Hitler would say. And indeed, the two men had much in common. Both were fiercely anti-Semitic; both had unknown grandfathers, both failed in school, both evaded military service when drafted, and both were vegetarians. Wagner was convinced that only a strict vegetarian diet could save humanity.

The Overture to the Meistersinger ended, and the German announcer set the stage for the big event, recounting the highlights of the Schmeling/Louis victory two years earlier.

"Tonight," he continued, "every seat in New York's giant Yankee Stadium is sold out."

Nöller leaned toward Edgar and whispered, "My friends in New York tell me that Louis has vowed to get even with Schmeling; he has not forgotten those painful straight rights. It will be quite a fight."

Loud jubilation for Louis could be heard, mingled with insults and booing for his German opponent. At last, the big match began. Rosi settled on a cushion next to her mother's chair, the boys sat on the sofa with Nöller. The radio announcer's words came hard and fast now, but not for long. Suddenly, an animal-like howl pierced the air, followed by a hard thump. Rosi covered her ears and dug her head into her mother's lap.

"Dreadful static," Nöller exclaimed, rubbing his ears while winking at Edith. "Probably one of those giant turtles dragging itself over the underwater radio cables."

Edgar was about to turn down the radio, but the broadcast had ceased. After a long silence, the announcer returned. He apologized for technical difficulties that interrupted the broadcast of the boxing match. A medley of marching songs would be played instead. Edith rose to accompany the children to their bedrooms where they could ponder in leisure the strangeness of the event.

At breakfast, resourceful Nöller was ready to share the latest news. He had contacted his friends in New York.

"The match did not go well for Schmeling," he said. "Max is a methodical and slow starter, but yesterday he never got started at all. After a couple of rapid punches, Louis landed a knockout in Schmeling's kidney—so powerful that it broke two vertebrae." He paused, while everyone cringed.

"And then?"

"That was the end of the fight or what Hitler's announcer called 'technical difficulties'. One single round! Probably the shortest fight in boxing history."

"Expensive tickets," the boys declared.

"True," Nöller laughed, "but a great victory for Joe Louis. All America is celebrating."

"Poor Schmeling[21], he'll be coming home on a stretcher. No flowers and invitations from Berlin anymore."

---

[21] Hitler never forgave Schmeling for losing the Joe Louis fight. Schmeling remained a friend of Joe Louis. Later, when Louis was down-and-out, Schmeling sent him money and quietly paid for his funeral. In 1989, Henry Lewin invited Schmeling to Las Vegas to thank him for saving his and his brother's life. During the Kristallnacht, Schmeling had hidden the boys in his hotel room and later helped them escape to America—a feat Schmeling never revealed to anyone. Schmeling died in 2005 at age 99, honored by thousands.

Grandeur in Stone

My monuments shall last for centuries and shall be admired by generations to come. —Hitler

November, 1938. Five years had passed since Arno took over the Nobel fur company and Hitler became leader of the German people. Arno moved into a palatial residence and stopped paying dividends to family stockholders. Hitler designed and built his Obersalzberg residence, the Berghof.

Hitler drew the plans himself. Not even Speer, his architect, was allowed to see them. Hitler's greatest pride, however, was the site of the Berghof. It faced the famous Unterberg, where according to legend the Emperor Charlemagne slept. Hitler designed a large picture window with a semi-circle of sofas and chairs, where his guests could view the mountain while listening to the legend that he never tired of telling. Emperor Charlemagne, so the story went, would rise again and restore the glory of the German Empire.

Was it a legend?

Not to Hitler. He and many of the local residents looked upon it as fact. They were certain that Emperor Charlemagne had indeed risen and was ruling now from the Berghof. Wherever Hitler went, people showered him with jubilation and adoration. They saw in him a man of the people, yet aloof like a god. He restored their hope and self-esteem. He set new goals for them and gave them tasks to be done. They were willing to follow him wherever he chose to take them.

While Hitler remained simple in his personal habits, he was extravagant in his plans for the future. He and Speer designed magnificent neoclassical monuments, grander than anything built before. The structure for the Zeppelin Field in Nuremberg measured thirteen hundred feet, its height eighty feet and was modeled after the Pergamum altar, but immensely larger.

Nuremberg's Great Stadium was the largest ever built, with a seating capacity of 400,000. It was completed in record time and Hitler assigned Speer, its architect, to stage in it the 6th Congress of the Nazi Party. Every seat was filled. Thousands of spectators lined the streets. Over a thousand well-rehearsed Party members carried torches and formed a symbolic swastika in the center of the stadium. Around its perimeter, Speer placed one hundred thirty anti-aircraft searchlights reaching 20,000' feet into the sky. The effect was phenomenal, like a surrealistic cathedral of light. The British Ambassador Henderson called it "solemn and beautiful ... like a cathedral of ice."

Hitler allowed no budgetary limitations for his construction. Only the biggest and best in design and materials were good enough. Albert Speer, a brilliant, capable young architect, was ideal for the position and became Hitler's closest associate. Berlin was to be the seat of Hitler's future empire, to be adorned with magnificent avenues. Hitler himself designed the Arch of Triumph, five times larger than its counterpart in Paris. Even Speer had to admit that Hitler had drawn it in perfect architectural perspective.

"The splendor of my construction," Hitler told Speer, "must reflect my own greatness and the spirit of my time. My monuments shall last for centuries, and shall be marveled at by generations to come."

Hitler showed no such sentiment for the ancient churches that graced Germany's landscape. He wanted no other gods beside him. *He* was their god. And churches fell on hard times. For nineteen centuries, the church had been the country's wealthiest and most powerful influence. It could forgive all sins, and, with approriate donations, guaranteed entry into heaven.

Even after the Thirty-Year religious War, when the northern half of Germany became Protestant, and the southern half stayed Catholic, the church remained all-powerful.

The people loved their churches. Hitler was a Catholic, but no longer attended services. Yet he kept telling his people that God personally had chosen him to be their leader.

"The essence of religion is propaganda," he told Göbbels, who needed no prodding. "Whatever we want the people to believe, we must repeat over and over again, and do so loudly until it becomes faith," So far, he had done well in this respect, and the people obeyed.

Maria's favorite church was not far from the Leuthold residence, a church with lofty spires. Her friend Anna attended it, too. Edith was blessed with a free spirit that preferred to look for the grace of God in nature. She had a tacit understanding with Maria: if Maria took the children to church, she could choose the place of worship.

On a balmy Sunday in 1938, Maria and the children had barely taken their seats, when vicious voices thundered through the sacred place.

"Juden, raus mit Euch!" (Jews get out!)

Fear darted like sparks from head to head. With great presence of mind, the minister motioned to the organist to play the first hymn, while he, with great dignity and seemingly oblivious of the ugly outbursts, climbed the stairs to the lectern. Before the organ's last sound had died away, he began his sermon as if nothing had happened. And miraculously, peace returned.

Rosi, holding on to Maria's hand, surreptitiously searched for the cause of the turmoil, but remained baffled. Here and there among the worshippers sat a dozen Hitler Youths in uniform. She knew it was they who had shouted the nasty words. But why? And at whom? And what did they mean?

After the service, Maria rushed off with her young charges to meet Anna and share her alarm.

"Did you see old Marion wearing the Star of David?" she asked.

"The poor woman was in tears."

"The Brauns and Neumans were wearing it, too. I've never seen them wearing the yellow star."

"Nor have I," Anna replied in a hushed voice, barely audible to the children. "It beats me. They've been members of the church for years. Why did they boo them?"

"Those youngsters must have been put up to it. I've never seen them in our church before, have you?"

"Those kids in uniform? No respect, those boys!"

"But pretending they own the world."

"Did you notice old Max? He got even with them for their insults."

"Max? Who's in charge of the collection plates? He did?" Maria's voice rose a pitch in pleased anticipation.

"He sure did. He stationed his collection boys right by those loud-mouthed kids so they couldn't escape without a donation."

"What a sense of humor he has," Maria laughed impishly.

"They patiently held the collection plates right in front of those boys until they coughed up some coins."

"That serves them right," Maria laughed with delight; but she looked puzzled: "Tell me, Anna, why are they wearing the Star of David now? The law was passed a long time ago."

"I guess nobody knew they were Jewish. I didn't know. Did you?"

"'Course not. They've belonged to the church for years. They're like one of us."

"But how were they found out? And how come those youngsters knew. You work for the church; you must know something."

"Well, the church does keep very complete records, better than the government does. They record every birth, christening, conversion, wedding, death and many other details."

Maria's eyes popped wide open, "Do you mean that the church squealed ... "

"Naw, not our pastor. The records are kept at church headquarters. The Vatican is said to have the most complete records in the world."

Rosi skipped over to Anna's side to hear her better. Why do they have to whisper like willows in the wind, she thought impatiently.

"You know what bureaucrats are like," Anna continued. "They don't care. They don't know Marion or the Brauns as we do. For them they are just numbers. Those bureaucrats think only of their own advantage. Mind you, this isn't right!"

Maria shook her head vigorously, "Politics, even in church!"

"But that's how it is; people like us will never know the truth," Anna declared resignedly.

Rosi wrinkled her forehead: Why can't they find out? Don't adults know?

When they arrived home, Rosi summoned her courage to ask her mother. Questions were not welcome during the Hitler years, especially questions of a political nature. Edith sadly patted her daughter's head.

"We don't know who denounced them," she said softly. "Politics is a very secretive matter, something we can no longer talk about." And so it remained a mystery until after the war.[22] Even the discussion of philosophical thoughts that did not express precisely the National Socialist point of view were considered anti-government and therefore dangerous. As a consequence, conversation had largely died.

The children did not go to church again. They said grace before meals and a prayer at bedtime.

"God," Edith taught them, "does not confine himself to churches; he lives in people's hearts. He is all around us, in the sky and the clouds, the trees and the wind, and in song and dance."

---

[22] After the war, ample evidence was found that Maria's supposition had been correct. The Church, primarily the Vatican, provided the Nazis with names and addresses of persons converted from the Jewish to the Christian faith. See Sam Harris' *End of Faith*.

39 Reasons Not to Rush into War

The Gathering Storm
Man survives solely by means of the most brutal struggle —Hitler

Distraught, Edgar watched from his balcony as the sun disappeared behind an ominous weather front. Was it an omen of Germany's political future? Politics was on everyone's mind, but to discuss it, even in the privacy of one's home, was out of the question. Informers were listening everywhere. He turned to Edith, his pillar of joy and strength. She was sitting across the table from him, smiling, her eyes focused on the children in the garden below.

"Faster," her five-year old son Paul was shouting, "faster!" He was sitting next to his sister, Rosi, clutching the side rail of their new rickshaw that Nöller had brought.

Peter, their older brother, was pulling them, galloping in wild exuberance up the gravel walk, across the lawn, around the rhododendron bush; and over they went! Maxi barked, wagging his tail. They scrambled to their feet ready to continue the wild ride. But Maria, their young housekeeper, intervened. Time to come in.

Ten minutes later, they joined their parents on the balcony for strawberries and cream. They were still beaming from their adventures with the new rickshaw.

"Did you ride by the Forbidden City? Did you bow low to the Chinese elders?" Their mother bowed in Chinese fashion and they mimicked her, aiming their noses for the whipped cream on their strawberries.

Maria reappeared at the door. "Telephone from Berlin, sir."

Their father's smile vanished as he followed Maria into the house. When he returned, he was in uniform, wearing a long, military coat with a saber at his side. He looked handsome, but deeply somber. Maxi eyed him gravely. Did he perceive his master's premonition of the darkness that would soon engulf them? Edgar patted the children goodbye and Edith, pale and wordless, left with him to accompany him to the station. In the distance thunder began to rumble and large raindrops drove the children inside. Why goodbye, they wondered; they were five, seven, and nine. The curtain on their carefree world had fallen.

Hitler had consolidated his power and was ruling with an iron fist. Germany had become a police state. Boldly, Hitler marched into Austria, his native land.

"I am carrying out the will of God," he told the perplexed people of Vienna in his victory address. "I am convinced that it was the will of God to send me, a boy from Austria, into the Reich, to let him grow up and to raise him to be the leader of the nation so that he would lead back his homeland into the Reich."[23]

Next he annexed the Sudetenland, and Europe grew alarmed. The British Prime Minister, Mr. Chamberlain, flew to Munich to meet with the German potentate. But Hitler, with hypnotic charm, disarmed the British Prime Minister's concern. On his return to London, Mr. Chamberlain proclaimed, "There will be peace in our time." Mr. Chamberlain heard what he wanted to hear. He had not read *Mein Kampf.*

Hitler had no patience for peace. While the world sighed in relief, Hitler readied his troops. On September 1, 1939, German tanks and infantry swept into Poland. Victory was won with the

---

[23] Hitler's speech given in Vienna after the Anschluss, April 9, 1938

speed of lightning, known as the *Blitzkrieg*. England and France no longer hesitated; they declared war on Germany.

Leuthold had managed to stay out of the Nazi Party, but the military was a different matter. The Officers' Corps considered obedience a matter of honor and duty. Its refusal meant cowardice and disloyalty, punishable by death. Nor did men drafted into the military have any options; they followed orders or they were shot. Leuthold, attached to the Cavalry, was sent to the western front. France fell as quickly as Poland did.

While he was gone, Edith received government orders, too. She had to hand over the keys to her husband's Mercedes and release their beloved horses to be shipped to the front. The government's orders promised, "Compensation to be determined after the glorious victory of the fatherland."

The Haunting Past

The greatest tyrannies are perpetrated in the name of the noblest causes —Thomas Paine

Who was this man who was so ardently hailed, feared and hated?

Ancestry: Hitler's ancestry is still a mystery and a cause for speculation because records were altered or destroyed.

Adolf Hitler's father, Alois, was the illegitimate son of sixteen-year old Maria Anna Schickelgruber. The father of the child was not recorded. Five years later, his mother, Maria Anna, married John Georg Hiedler[24] who was too poor to support her son. Consequently, her son was sent off to live with John's brother, Johann Hiedler, who had no sons of his own.

---

[24] The name was spelled also Hitler and Huetler. Few people could read and write then; therefore the varied spellings.

By 1876, Alois Schickelgruber had become a minor customs official, a finer job than any of his destitute relatives ever held, and his proud foster father prodded Alois to change his name from Schickelgruber to Hiedler. To expedite the change, Johann and three of his friends posed as witnesses and persuaded the local priest to enter his brother as the father of Alois. The kind priest liked the idea. After all, a child had to have a father. He made the entry in the church records, but forgot to sign and date it. Alois liked the idea too; it held promises of an inheritance. By then, Alois had a young wife and two former wives and several children to support. So, Alois Schickelgruber became Alois Hiedler or Hitler—twelve years before Adolf Hitler was born. During Adolf Hitler's reign, John Georg Hitler (or Hiedler) was named as Hitler's legitimate father—and thus beyond the reach of doubters.

Amusingly, after the Führer's death, someone pointed out that in 1876, when Johann claimed fatherhood for his brother, his brother had been dead for nineteen years. His mother, too, had long been buried. The true identity of Hitler's paternal grandfather, it seems, lies safely buried with the child's mother, Maria Anna Schickelgruber.

Rumors have it that Hitler's unknown grandfather had Jewish blood. Was Hitler aware of it? All we know is that during his reign his family's birth and baptismal records were changed and the town of his ancestors was thoroughly obliterated by being turned into an artillery practice ground. Irrelevant as these rumors may be, they are based on the fact that Maria Anna gave birth to Alois while living with and working for a Jewish family named Frankenberger, who had an eighteen-year old son. Maria Anna was sixteen.

Childhood. Twice divorced, Alois took in his sixteen-year old niece, Klara Poelzl, to keep house for him. When she got pregnant, he married his twenty-year younger niece, who continued to call him *Uncle*. Their first three children died; on 4/20/1889, in the small Austrian town of Braunau she gave birth to her fourth, Adolf Hitler. His 52-year older father, Alois, was short-tempered and stern, and often beat the child, but Klara adored and spoiled the little boy. She was a weak woman and Adolf learned to manipulate her with great skill.

Adolf did poorly in school, but he did not lack talent. In the words of his teacher, Dr. Eduard Huelmer: "Hitler lacked self-discipline. He was notoriously cantankerous, willful, arrogant and bad-tempered. He was lazy and reacted with ill-concealed hostility to advice or reproof; at the same time he demanded of his fellow pupils unqualified subservience."[25]

It was the same unqualified subservience Hitler demanded from every German, including his girlfriends, his generals and his closest associates for as long as he lived.

Early Ambitions. The priesthood was his earliest ambition. When he was seven, the family moved to Linz, seat of the Benedictine Monastery, where Adolf became a choirboy. Prominently displayed on the monastery wall was a swastika, part of the Benedictine coat of arms. The power of mystery and faith deeply impressed the young boy, and he later adopted many of its techniques to captivate his own followers.

When eleven, he showed an aptitude for drawing and his father enrolled him in technical drawing classes. Drawing and sports constituted his only passing grades. When sixteen, after his father's death, Hitler failed yet another grade and dropped out of school. He stayed home with his mother and enjoyed a life of leisure. Klara's pension as a widow enabled her to sup-

---

[25] Edward Huelmer testified at Hitler's trial in Munich. Quoted in *Hitler's Youth*, by Franz Jetzinger, pp.68 - 69

port the young man. He slept until noon, dressed with care and sporadically painted. Sometimes, in the middle of a meal he'd jump up to design another monument.

He visited Vienna and was overwhelmed by its beauty, its parks and its opera. In spite of his mother's poor health—she was dying of cancer—he decided to stay in Vienna. He applied at Vienna's prestigious Academy of Art, but to his bitter disappointment he was rejected.

Hitler's Vienna Years, 1908 to 1914: When Klara died, Hitler returned to Linz to attend her funeral and pocket his legacy. His financial support gone now, he claimed to be a student, which entitled him to an orphan's pension. Blissfully, he returned to Vienna and continued his life of leisure. He slept late, dressed with care, swung a student's dainty walking cane and strolled through the park. He read in the library, and frequented the opera. "I saw Wagner's Tristan & Isolde 30-40 times during that year," he later boasted.

He had a penchant for sitting hours at a time, staring before him and roaming the world of fantasy. Mentally, he built opera houses and monuments, grander than ever built before. He dreamt of being remembered by future generations for the magnificence of his monuments. When he was drafted into the service, he applied at the Academy of Art for a second time, and for a second time he was rejected. They suggested that he apply at the School of Architecture, but the lack of a high school diploma barred him from admission. He did not consider getting his degree.

Hitler could not handle the second rejection. Intense resentment against the academy gnawed on him until he died. At every opportunity, he would voice bitter and biting remarks about teachers and universities, the educated and the privileged. When he got word of his rejection, he flew into a violent temper, and then, without a word, disappeared from his apartment into the anonymous underworld of Vienna. Was it to escape the compulsory draft or to hide his shame and fury? No one knows. His roommate Kubizek, and his half-sister Angelika searched for him in vain. No one heard from him for years. His orphan's pension for students had ended. He was penniless. He slept in hallways, parks and flophouses, stood in line at charity kitchens, and for four years scraped out an existence among the poorest of Vienna's poor.

World War I, 1914 to 1918: To escape the misery, Hitler enlisted in the German army. He rose to lance corporal and was awarded the Iron Cross Second and First Class that he wore until he died. When WWI ended, Communist-inspired insurrections shook Germany, the Kaiser abdicated and the Socialists gained control of the government. Anarchy ruled the cities.

Political Orator: Hitler returned to Munich and testified for the army against a Communist takeover bid. Pleased with his testimony, the army offered him a job to dissuade returning soldiers from joining the Communist party. He was sent to get oratory training, and to spy on certain political groups, in particular, the new **German Workers Party**.

At one of the Party meetings, Hitler became so incensed about a speaker that he exploded into one of his violent tirades. Impressed, the founder of the Party made Hitler their Committee Member #7. A year later, in 1920, Hitler changed the Party's name to the National Socialist German Workers Party, later known as **Nazis**.

In Prison: In 1923, at a Munich beer hall rally, Hitler proclaimed a revolution and led two thousand armed *brown-shirts* to take over the Bavarian government. When police fired the first shot, Hitler was the first to flee. Two days later the police caught up with him, and arrested him. At the trial, Hitler brazenly promoted himself and his ideas. He was given a five-year sentence. While in prison, Party member Rudolf Hess joined him to write down Hitler's version of his early life and his future vision of Germany, which later, after extensive editing, became *Mein Kampf*.

After serving only nine months, Hitler was released. He knew what he wanted—not a job, not work; he wanted political power. He would seek it not by force, but patiently, through the backing of his Party. He returned to the NSDAP and became its spokesman. Untiringly, he campaigned and advertised for new members and spoke to scores of audiences, promising a Thousand-year Republic that would rule the world.

Geli Raubal: Early in 1928, Hitler rented a small house in Obersalzberg and asked his half-sister Angelica and her 17-year old daughter Geli to keep house for him, and 39-year old Hitler fell in love with his pretty niece. Their romance lasted four years, the most blissful years for Hitler. Politics moved on the back burner. He rarely left his Obersalzberg house, except in Geli's company. Blithely, they went for long drives in the country, strolled along the promenade, and visited the Munich Opera. In her company, Hitler was a changed and happy man. The first volume of *Mein Kampf* was published then, and even though it sold poorly, he embarked on a second volume.

Hitler stayed away from all NSDAP meetings, which Party members deeply resented. Membership dropped off alarmingly. The Party's Committee looked upon Geli as its major foe. She stood between Hitler and his historic mission. Most of all, they were enraged about the large amounts of Party funds Hitler was squandering for their personal pleasure.

Hitler and Geli lived together for four stormy years. Hitler, or *Uncle Alf* as she called him, dominated Geli's every move. He forbade her to smoke and go out with others. He painted nudes

70

of her that still exist. Yet in spite of his possessive love for her, Hitler refused to marry her. He was determined to remain single—he envisioned himself as a mythological figure of greatness, unattached and unmoved by human emotions, and consequently, Geli was to remain single, too.

Geli enjoyed the attentions of her illustrious uncle, the eloquent leader of the Nazi Party. She was furious, when Hitler took seventeen-year old Eva Braun for a ride in his Mercedes. Yet Geli was not in love with Hitler. She was in love with Hitler's chauffeur Emil, whom Hitler promptly fired when he found out. She wrote passionate love letters to Emil, but Hitler would not hear of her marrying him, let alone go out with him. She met him only in secret rendezvous.

On September 19, 1931, Hitler had a speaking engagement in Hamburg, and Geli decided to spend a few days in Vienna. Yet Hitler forbade her to go. According to the neighbors, they had a stormy row. While getting into his car, Hitler reportedly shouted, "For the last time, NO!"

Several hours later, she was found dead in their apartment. According to the newspaper, *Die Münchner Post* and the police report, her nose was broken, her body severely bruised, and a bullet from Hitler's revolver sent through her heart. On her writing table the police found the letter that Geli had just written to her friend in Vienna announcing her visit.

The news of Geli's death reached Hitler on his way to Hamburg, and he returned to Munich at once, a broken man. Hitler's political opposition had already spread word about his niece's death. It claimed that the SS was tired of Hitler wasting his time with Geli. They got rid of her so he could focus on his historic mission. Hitler categorically denied it. He insisted that her death was clearly a suicide. Thanks to Röhm's influence with the media, his version of her death was published. The reason for her suicide? Depression, because she realized that she lacked sufficient talent to become a Wagnerian soprano.

Hitler swore vengeance to his political opponents. As soon as he regained his composure, he hurried off to Hamburg to give his address, the most impassioned he ever gave. He continued his rabble-rousing tour for many months, driven by fury and an obsession to succeed. He poured his entire emotional ardor into his speeches. Verbally and emotionally he embraced the crowd—in his own words: "The crowd is my mistress."

Chancellor: Within one year, the Nazi Party became Germany's strongest party. In 1932, Hindenburg ran for reelection, and needed their support. In exchange, he promised to appoint their man Hitler as chancellor. The rest is history.

The Mood of the People
Never believe anything the government says —George Carlin

On Furlough: It was spring, 1940. Edgar was home on a brief furlough. The mood of the people was not as optimistic anymore; they had plenty of work, but they were still at war—contrary to what Hitler had promised them. Little did they know that much worst was yet to come.

Edith invited Nöller for lunch. The two men stood at the veranda door, undecided. Glorious sunshine caressed the first daffodils, tempting them to walk in the garden. Yet they wanted to discuss politics, and to do so they needed privacy. They retreated to Edith's domain. She had promised to play the piano to drown out their conversation.

"What became of our friend in Shanghai? Did he get out?" Edgar was eager to know.

"He did. I talked to him a month ago. Would you believe that the children of European residents in Shanghai are studying German in preparation of the future? I would have thought they'd learn Japanese. Obviously, they expect Hitler to be victorious."

"I am not averse to victory and peace, but Hitler may create hell on earth! Do the people find Hitler still irresistible?"

"He's got them in his clutches more than ever. But it is fear that motivates them now. Just to complain these days is against the law, sufficient reason to get you locked up or sent to the front."

"Is the pressure still on to join the Party?" Edgar whispered.

"You had better believe it. Not to be a National Socialist gets you automatically blacklisted."

"What a government—a strong man and his spies!"

"You said it," Nöller got up to pace the floor. "Spying on your neighbors has become a national pastime. Do you realize that those stool pigeons are getting paid for denouncing their friends and neighbors!"

"Sounds like you got denounced, too; did you?"

"Who hasn't," Nöller growled. "Sometimes I am tempted to join the Party just to stop these annoying interrogations. Next Monday I shall be off to pilot school."

"Flying missions?"

"No, to be an instructor. But I guess when we run out of boys to train, we'll be sent to drop bombs. War is insane! They sent my friend Max Schmeling, the heavyweight champ, on that suicide mission to Crete."[26]

---

[26] Schmeling eventually recovered. He remained blacklisted for expressing sympathy toward the USA, as reported by the Gestapo.

"The paratrooper mission? Did anyone survive it?"

"He was severely wounded and will be spending many months in the hospital."

"What was his crime?"

"Hitler never forgave him for losing the boxing match against Joe Louis. To boot, he's still not joined the Party."

"Good old Max. I like a man of principle."

"Standing up for your principles, my dear Edgar, is suicidal these days."

Both men sank into silence. The beguiling strains of Schuman's *Träumerei* Edith was playing did not soothe their qualms.

"Tell me, how did you get off at Gestapo headquarters?" Edgar resumed.

Nöller laughed. "I made a lucky guess. I fired one of my employees for stealing eggs and lying about it. I figured he wanted to get even. I told the Gestapo men that dishonesty should not be tolerated among German citizens, and they could not very well disagree with that."

"So they drafted you to train pilots?"

"My orders arrived two weeks later," he nodded. "Headquarters is not my favorite place to go. I'd rather climb the Matterhorn with you in a snowstorm. Remember that day, and the howling blizzard? Suddenly no visibility! It moved in like lightning and without warning."

"Just like Hitler."

An hour later, Nöller took leave, but not without stopping by the children's room. They were lying on the floor with Maxi, playing the word guessing game that Nöller had found for them in his attic. It dated back to Nöller's own childhood days.

Later that evening, Edgar's friend, Dr. Werner von N., stopped by. He, too, was a close friend of Edgar's since college days. Werner had recently dined with Hitler at the Berghof, and

Edgar was eager to hear about the visit. After dinner, the two men retreated to Edgar's study to talk while the gramophone player concealed their words. Werner was a conservative and a man of broad learning. When barnstormers began to captivate the imagination of the Western world, Werner took up the study of aerodynamics and began building airplanes.

"The Führer is brilliant and persuasive, Edgar. He has a captivating way about him. His vision for Germany is extraordinary."

"You cannot be serious, Werner! I clearly recall your prior opinion of the man."

"True, Edgar, but he is a different person now. When I saw him at the Berghof, he looked commanding, not at all like the street barker of the early twenties. At dinner, he was smooth and charming to the ladies and talked with firm determination about his goals. I tell you, the man is hypnotic in getting his wishes across. Impossible to say *No* or disagree."

"Did he ask you to build planes for the war?"

"He did. I saw him privately before dinner. He had requested that I bring sketches of the planes I am building. He studied them attentively and came up with rather ingenious suggestions. He wants me to design them more simply and efficiently so they can be built quickly and in great quantities. I can't wait to talk to my engineers. The man is compelling."

"Werner, the man is a demagogue, a dictator! He is the ruin of every independently thinking man and woman. Don't you remember his speech in Kulmbach in 1928? He spoke like a savage, not a civilized human being. Do you remember his words? You were as shocked as I was. I still remember some of it verbatim:

"It is not by the principles of humanity that man lives or is able to preserve himself above the level of the animal world, but solely by means of the most brutal struggle!"[27]

"The rhetoric of a young man," Werner shrugged. "But consider what he has done. He has restored Germany's dignity. People have work again. Don't you remember that a third of our population and their families were starving? Look at our extraordinary victory over Poland and France. He wants airplanes to be affordable for the common man. Think of it! A plane in every backyard!"

"You are thinking of airplanes and are overlooking the political implications of his policies. Werner, you come from an old, aristocratic Austrian family. How does your family feel about the man? Are they glad that he brought Austria home to the Reich?"

"I cannot speak for my family," Werner replied icily. "I do not discuss politics with them; I don't have time to visit them."

"They were not pro-Hitler when I last visited you," Edgar answered reproachfully, wondering if this rift in their political outlook would mark the end of their long friendship. His head was throbbing. It cost him great effort to remain civil.

In spite of their political differences, Werner harbored a deep liking for Edgar and realized that he needed to explain his thinking.

"When I was studying aerodynamics in Berlin, Edgar, two of my friends persuaded me to accompany them to hear Hitler speak. I was skeptical, but went. The hall was packed. Hitler invited the professors to sit with him on the platform, which lent a definite air of authority and endorsement to the meeting.

---

[27] Hitler's speech at Kulmbach, 2/5/1928; *Hitler's Words,* by G. W. Prange, p. 8.

76

Hitler himself appeared in a plain blue suit. No one introduced him."

"No one ever does. He dislikes sharing the limelight. The audience is to focus on him alone," Edgar added.

"He does like to make a theatrical entrance." Werner grinned and nodded. "He looked modest and rather shy at first; totally different from what you and I saw in the beer garden of Munich. He spoke about history, quite dull at first. But slowly, the enthusiastic crowd carried him forward while he warmed to his topic. Total silence at first, then the first hypnotic gasps, then full abandon. It was hard to tell who mesmerized whom, Hitler the crowd, or the passionate crowd Hitler. They became like one, ecstatic, more and more uninhibited, until they reached a climax. Hitler, I'm told, calls this adoring crowd *my only mistress*. Probably his substitute for women."

Edgar could not argue with his friend's account. He knew it was true.

"I've heard him on other occasions. He usually arrives late, letting his audience wait so it can work itself into a feverish frenzy before he makes his appearance. In Hamburg, an audience of 10,000 waited seven hours for his appearance! He arrived at three in the morning. Yet people did not leave. They patiently waited. The waiting establishes a sort of brotherhood among them. It creates a common bond to their leader."

"I've heard similar reports from other people. He likes to generate a common creed," Edgar replied, troubled. "I remember one of my professors in Berlin saying that the people of today want an uneducated, simple man who can carry forward one simple idea. Maybe it's true. But where will it lead us? History shows that countries prosper only during times of wise and learned leadership. Hitler has neither wisdom nor learning. His prowess is willpower and unbending determination."

"Edgar, you can't imagine the enthusiasm of the crowd!"

"I have seen the enthusiastic crowds. Unfortunately, the crowd is seldom right in assessing political leadership. Do you remember wise Phoecion,[28] who ruled Athens for many years? When he was applauded by too many people, he asked himself, *What have I done amiss?*"

"And when his wisdom did not suit the people, they condemned him to take poison."

Edgar nodded sadly. "One of their wisest rulers. Forced to take poison like Socrates."

He was glad that Werner took his leave before harsh words were spoken. Distraught, he went in search of Edith to share his dismay.

"I may have lost another friend," he protested. "Werner is going to work for Hitler."

"Building airplanes for the war?"

"More planes to prolong the war," Edgar objected, and Edith soothingly interjected, "You know that airplanes are Werner's passion. He is like a child with a toy when it comes to flight. Besides, does he have a choice but to follow Hitler's orders?"

"He is doing it willingly. He is quite taken by Hitler."

Edith thought for a long moment, "Do you recall that the same thing happened to Porsche, Krupp and other industrialists? Hitler must have something captivating and irresistible." Teasingly, she added, "Maybe you would feel the same way, if he were to suggest some brilliant plan to improve agricultural seeds."

---

[28] Phoecion the Good (402 to 318 B.C.), one of the wisest and most virtuous Greek rulers and generals. He was condemned to die by poison like Socrates, when he proposed peace instead of war, which the people wanted.

"Not in a million years," Edgar burst out, and Edith quickly went to his side to assuage him.

After a few moments, Edith approached the topic again. "I am very fond of Werner's wife; you know Martha is my best friend. I would hate to lose her." She looked at her husband searchingly, "Do you think Martha and I can continue to be friends? We never talk politics." Seeing Edgar's grim face, and knowing his unalterable views, she feared a *No* and quickly forestalled it. "It has been a long day, Edgar, and a difficult one. Let me get us a snack from the kitchen. I am hungry."

But even the snack did not appease Edgar.

"Hitler is a fanatic. He is dangerous. Money-grubbing capitalists are harmless in comparison. They are only after money. Hitler is after power and control."

"But who would believe his crazy ideas? After all, we are all human, Aryans and Jews alike; we all have runny noses at times and need a hug." Edith's faith in humanity was unshakable. And so was her sense of humor.

"Hitler believes in his theories and acts accordingly. He is superstitious to boot, and steeped in Germanic mysticism."

"His mysticism may be just a ploy to prove his strange assumptions," Edith suggested.

"It is possible. He picked up those ideas from Guido von List and Jorg Lanz, when he lived in Vienna."

"The romantic mystics of thirty years ago?"

"Exactly. Hitler's ideas are not new. The creation of a superman and an Aryan race has been advocated ever since the turn of the century. Hitler is following in their footsteps."

Edgar paused for breath, also to rewind the record player to drown out their conversation. Edith sat down; she knew there was more to come. She had heard about these mystics at school.

"Wasn't Lanz the run-away monk, who founded the Aryan-Heroic Order of blue-eyed, blond-haired men?" she asked.

"Right. Lanz preached class warfare, the extermination and sterilization of mixed races, and the birth and creation of a New Man. Lanz held his meetings under a huge flag with a black swastika."

"Like Hitler's?"

Edgar nodded, "Lanz's followers bought him a handsome castle near Vienna. That is where he held his Aryan pageants and beauty contests."

"Of blond and blue-eyed maidens?"

"And blond and blue-eyed men," Edgar could not help grinning. "Hitler went to visit him there to get his pamphlets; he was an ardent collector of Lanz's publications. Apparently, Lanz deeply impressed him. Since the Anschluss, however, Lanz has been ordered never to write or publish again."

"Understandable. Hitler is using Lanz's ideas as his own. Weren't there several other proponents of a master race?"

"Schönerer. Hitler greatly admired Schönerer, a bitter and arrogant demagogue, who promoted extreme fear of Jews and minorities among Vienna's society. Fear became the basis of his anti-Semitic movement."

"Sounds like Hitler."

"Hitler's favorite was Lueger, the Mayor of Vienna."

"Lueger?"

"Lueger was Hitler's absolute idol. In *Mein Kampf* he refers to Lueger "as the shrewdest and most powerful mayor of all times." Actually, both men have much in common. They are both self-made men, inventive, clever and eloquent, and both used existing institutions to achieve their goals."

"I remember that the Austrian Emperor refused to accept Lueger as mayor because he came from the lower classes."

"He did, three times. But Lueger got around the Emperor. He was mayor for fifteen years and accomplished much, but he was strongly anti-Semitic; Hitler joined his Anti-Semitic Alliance while he lived in Vienna. Oddly enough, you cannot mention this today or you would be locked up."

"Did Lueger promote sterilization and racial purity, too?"

"Not only that, he ardently advocated breeding a superman. A crazy idea!" Edgar exclaimed. "You can't breed people. Look at the pharaohs of Egypt; they married their own daughters; their sons married their sisters; and eventually, their offspring became demented."

"Like our beautiful Dame. What a gorgeous greyhound she was." Edith cried out.

Edgar nodded. "Like our Dame—a pure-bred dog with less brain than a pair of shoelaces. There are limitations even to breeding animals."

Edith sighed. Her mother had brought them a beautiful greyhound when their first child was born, but Dame did not live long; she ran in front of a coming train.

"We simply cannot breed people. Think of it, Edith, what would we do with the people who are **not** desirable?"

"You draw a dark scenario, Edgar. Odd, that this same Hitler preaches hard work, honesty, toughness, loyalty, and *Kraft durch Freude.*[29] He disdains money and capitalists, and the people love him for it."

"He wants a lot more than money. He wants absolute power—power over everyone."

"Like puppets on his string," Edith wrinkled her nose disapprovingly and playfully pulled on the lace cloth on the little table; it obligingly slid to the floor.

---

[29] Strength through Joy, Hitler's vacation program for workers.

Edgar nodded. He had not noticed the slipping lace. "And yet, this same Hitler is haunted by fear and feelings of inferiority. His life is nothing but pretense. Do you know that he used to kiss the hands of his secretaries, assuming it to be worldly?"

Edith burst out laughing.

Edgar rewound the record player. "We are no longer free to think or speak. Why does Werner not see it?"

"Maybe our views are filtered by our interests," Edith tried again; she did not want to lose her best friend. "Werner sees in Hitler a man who shares his love of flying and of developing a better plane."

"Hitler is a demagogue. Or—as he would phrase it— sent by God to rule us."

"I wonder what is it like to be a messiah?" Edith mockingly stroked her upper lip pretending a Hitlerian mustache. "A lot of responsibility."

Edgar stifled a small smile. "No responsibility at all; not if you assume to be God. I am sure Hitler considers himself above law and conscience. He wouldn't dream of questioning his actions."

"Edgar, I think you are an incorrigible royalist. You see in Hitler the demagogue who blocked the restoration of the monarchy." She smiled and added: "Let us drink a toast to your illustrious uncle[30] and the House of Hohenzollern." This said she hurried off to fetch glasses and a bottle of wine.

Politics! A merciless divider, Edgar thought. Yet Edith's mentioning of his uncle did evoke pleasant memories. An amusing anecdote was told about the old strategist. When Kaiser Wilhelm II appointed Leuthold to be his commander-in-chief, it caused quite a stir. Leuthold was a commoner. The po-

---

[30] Commander-in-chief of Emperor Wilhelm II

sition had always gone to a member of the aristocracy, and the Kaiser was reproached about this unseemly appointment.

"I like Leuthold," the Emperor contentedly replied, "he is a man of action and integrity, not of words."

The Emperor had judged his new appointee well; Leuthold was not a man of words. On the occasion of the Kaiser's birthday, it was customary for the commander-in-chief to deliver a two-hour dinner speech, and bets as to the length of Leuthold's address reached an all-time high.

The brevity of Leuthold's speech surpassed all expectations. At the appointed hour, in the festive hall of the palace, Leuthold rose, wine glass in hand, to deliver his speech:

"The first drop of wine," he said, "and the last drop of blood for our Emperor!"

He toasted Wilhelm II and sat down. One brief sentence without a verb! It caused quite a stir and can still be read in the history books of the time.

Later that night, Edgar turned to Edith with a smile, "I hope you and Martha will remain friends for many years to come."

Betrayal

When the rights of one are denied, the rights of all are in jeopardy —Jo Ann Roach

Two days later, Edgar received a letter from Frankfurt—a summons to Gestapo headquarters. He looked like a man on his way to the gallows, sick and pale. His only consolation was that Edith insisted on accompanying him.

Official summons never revealed the reason for investigation, which added to the nerve-racking suspense and made preparation impossible. The Gestapo inquisitors began by questioning Leuthold about his forebears. Leuthold knew his ancestral history well and, to Edith's relief, he cooperated. She dreaded Edgar's frank disdain of the Nazi regime and his lack of political correctness. It was her daily worry that Edgar might implicate himself. In spite of his answers, though, the inquisitors were not satisfied. Leuthold even drew the family tree for them, but they looked grimmer still. Edith watched the proceedings with growing curiosity.

"You seem to be looking for a particular name," she finally interrupted.

"Yes," the Gestapo man fired at Leuthold: "We have been informed that you have a relative named Riess."

"Riess?" Leuthold's face was blank.

"You mean Mathilde Riess?" Edith chimed in.

"Do you know her?" they turned on her.

"She's my great-aunt; she died before I was born." The Gestapo man looked at her, taken aback. Mathilde Riess was presumed to be Jewish. They had expected Leuthold to be a descendant. Leuthold had brown eyes and black hair. They would have been glad to send him away. But Edith? She was blond, fair and blue-eyed—her paternal as well as maternal ancestors had come from Sweden. By Hitler's standards, Edith looked Aryan.

Thwarted and annoyed, the inquisitors left the room. Edgar and Edith were locked up and left alone in the chamber of interrogation. Would Edith be incarcerated? What would happen to the children? Sent away, too?

Edith slowly repeated what she had said before. "I remember my grandmother mentioning her name. I wish I knew more about her." She knew the inquisitors would be listening to their every word.

84

For an hour they sat in absolute silence. Then another hour. A third hour passed. It was torture for Edgar who by nature was impatient and impetuous. Tense, barely breathing, they waited. Their fate hung on a thread. Time seemed to stand still.

At long last, a young secretary entered. "Heil Hitler!" she saluted. "You may leave now." She turned smartly on her heels, saluted again and left.

Edgar's clammy hand reached for Edith's. She still was his. Grateful and yet haunted by this menacing place, he rapidly guided her through its endless corridors. He wanted to sprint down the hall, away from this anti-chamber of hell. But he did not dare to. Edith, his fountain of strength, was still by his side, and this was all that mattered. She always found a way of keeping the family alive and together, and had an uncanny knack for focusing on the bright side of life.

When safely in their car, Edgar breathed a sigh of relief. During the interrogation, however, he had made a frightening discovery. It took possession of him now with full force.

"We were lucky they did not keep us," Edith ventured, trying to break his unexpected tension.

Edgar did not respond. His hands were nervously gripping the steering wheel.

"Something is worrying you, Edgar." Edith gently touched his arm. "You can share your burden with me. You will feel better when you do."

Edgar took a deep breath. He knew she was right. His concern weighed like a sack of cement on his mind. "Let us pull over and go for a walk," he suggested. He had an unpleasant feeling that his car might be bugged.

"How about the woods over there?"

"No. Too many trees." He did not want to be overheard by anyone.

"Then let's walk along the pasture."

"Good," Edgar agreed. "Not even the SS can hide behind the dandelions."

They had barely walked a dozen paces, when Edgar plunged into the reason for his trepidation.

"Who knows about your Jewish great-aunt Mathilde Riess?"

"No one except the immediate family. It puzzled me, too, that the SS knew about her."

"Someone has tipped them off. Did you notice the papers the investigator kept looking at?"

"No, except that he kept shuffling them."

"One of the papers had Arno's signature."

"Arno's signature?" Edith stared in disbelief. "How can you tell? His signature is illegible."

"That's just it; it is large, ornate and ostentatious. There is no other quite like it."

"But why would he ... ?" Edith could not say the dreaded word. She had turned pale. A deadly enemy within the family? How could Viola denounce her own sister? Or was it Arno's doing to denounce his brother-in-law? It endangered their very existence.

"A few months ago," Edgar confessed, "the annual reports of the Nobel fur company were due. You are one of the heirs and should have received a report, also the annual dividend. But ever since Arno took over the firm, he has not paid a dime or sent a single report. So I wrote him a brief note requesting it; a copy went to your mother. I did the same last year. It didn't do any good, of course. Arno does not respond to this sort of thing."

Edith was quiet for a long time. She knew her husband's honest, orderly mind. He was a person of absolute integrity and expected the same of others.

"Perhaps," she began haltingly, "we should forget about the company and let Arno have it. He desperately wants it. Arno is cold and calculating, too formidable to have as an enemy. I would rather live in peace and harmony than have to deal with him."

"It is your rightful share, and there is plenty for everyone," Edgar protested.

"Are you sure it was Arno's signature?" Edith queried again. Betrayal within the family? It was too horrible to contemplate.

"I wish I had the smallest doubt, but I do not." More pensively he added, "Have you ever looked at his signature?"

"No. It certainly has a grandiose flair."

"Exactly. Just as his personality—pretentious. It is also illegible—he is hiding his true character. I have a hand-written note from him. It's most illuminating. If you like, I shall explain some of his basic characteristics. Ego and greed are by far his strongest traits."

"I thought you studied law. What do you know about graphology?"

"Not much," Edgar laughed. "Graphology is a field that requires many years of study. I only took a basic course. It is a fascinating eye opener, though."

"Does handwriting really reveal a person's character?"

"Absolutely. That is why employers require a handwritten résumé for all management positions. Look at your handwriting. It shows you are open, honest, kind, modest, and very understanding."

"Is that why you married me?"

"No, Liebling, mostly for your looks." Edgar teased her. He felt a huge relief now that Edith knew the situation and carried part of the burden.

The Informer

The greater the power, the more dangerous the abuse

— Edmund Burke

Maria lowered her voice to a whisper, "Who is our Blockwart, Gnädige Frau?"

Hitler had given the people work. Now he demanded his payback. They had to march for him, spy for him and help him maintain a totalitarian police state. People to him were nothing but numbers. Their purpose was to fight for his glory and make him ruler of the world.

"I don't know, Maria." Edith replied softly, and with a furtive smile added, "I wish I knew." Each and every city block had a "Blockwart" or informer. Their identity was often unknown.

"Anna said it could be a neighbor or one's best friend," Maria whispered with deep concern.

"I hope not, but it could be."

"In my home town," Maria continued, "the Blockwart is well known. She's an older woman and goes around snooping and visiting people in their homes. She asks them a lot of questions. People don't like her; they are afraid of her. Sometimes, the people she has visited disappear."

Edith patted her arm, and whispered back, "Cheer up, Maria, we cannot change the world. You are right, though, we do have to watch what we say. It seems the less we say, the better it is."

But Maria was not in a mood for cheerfulness. She had another worrisome issue on her mind. "Frau Gerhard says she has to be ever so careful when her two little boys are home. Their

Hitler Youth leader keeps urging the boys to spy on their parents and denounce them. Their own parents!"

Edith's cheerfulness was dwindling, too. Aren't we all living in constant fear, she thought, every moment aware that it may be our last? But she did not dare put it into words.

The new law of *Sippenhaftung*[31] was especially frightening. Each member of a family was held responsible for the political actions of all other members. If her Edgar were to desert the cavalry or not salute properly, all members of his family would suffer the consequences. It could take many forms—no food rations for minor offenses, jail or firing squad for major ones.

Thanks to the informer, the government knew everything—who visited whom, what was said, what you owned and owed. Fear paralyzed the very faculty to think.

During that first cold winter of the war, a Nazi official appeared at the Leuthold's door. One solitary SS-man, not the customary group of two or three. He clicked his heels, lifted his arm in salute, and announced, "I have come to inspect the closets in this house."

"Come in," Maria answered, timidly. "I will fetch the lady of the house."

Edith greeted him, calm and composed. "Which closets would you like to see?" She would have preferred to ask for a search warrant, but that would have been a serious affront. Civilians had no rights against the government.

"Yours, Ma'am," the SS man replied. If nothing else, her question and his answer had pinpointed his investigation.

"Certainly. Anything in particular you would like to see?"

---

[31] Clan liability

"Yes," he said, taken aback by her unruffled amiability. He was used to people trembling with fear when he appeared at their door. "It has come to our attention that you own fur coats," he said. "You will agree that our soldiers at the front need them more than you do."

Shaken, Edith took him to the wardrobe that held her treasured furs, given to her by Edgar and her beloved father, the furrier. If only they were not hanging all in one place, she winced inwardly, deeply regretting her orderly arrangement.

The SS man collected her coats and left, his eyes gleaming. He clicked his heels and his voice sounded an octave higher as he brightly saluted her. Edith sank into the nearest chair and gazed at the empty wardrobe. Even if her coats had gone to the front, it would have been little comfort. As it was, she knew they were not intended for the men. They would be warming the wives or girlfriends of some Nazi officials.

That evening, Arno sat in his usual bar having a beer with his friend, Hans, the SS man.

"Eh, thanks for the tip, Arno. It was a great haul!" Hans beamed. "Never saw so many furs in one closet!"

"Glad to hear it," Arno smiled. "Why should the rich and privileged have it all."

A devilish delight played around his mouth; it was the perfect punishment for Edgar's impertinence. Arno had given Rosi a little fur jacket on her birthday. And Edgar, with an innocent grin, had turned to him and asked, "Will I get billed for it?" Right in front of Mina. Arno could have strangled him. Certainly he would bill Edgar; he always did. But Edgar did not have to squeal about it in front of Mina.

Tyranny at School

Authoritarians do not surrender power voluntarily

—Victor Davis Hanson

Tears were rolling down the pale cheeks of eight-year old Rosi. She lay on her bed, eyeing the boots on the floor— beautiful riding boots made of soft leather, hand-crafted for the small feet of her mother long before the war. They fitted Rosi to perfection. What joy she felt that morning when her mother brought them for her to wear. What heavenly comfort for her feet! Her own shoes were too small and had caused painful blisters, and new shoes could only be bought with a government permit. Hers was not due for another five months. Nothing but military boots were being manufactured—boots for the soldiers at the front.

Rosi reached longingly for one of the boots and gently stroked the delicate leather. New tears welled up in her eyes and she dropped the boot back to the floor. She could never wear the boots again; the memory of that morning was too painful.

When she had entered the classroom, stout Liza immediately noticed her boots. She followed Rosi to her desk. Then, with her hands on her hips, she sneered for everyone to hear:

"Good God, here comes Miss dainty horsewoman, riding to school on her pony." Her scornful laughter still echoed in Rosi's head. Liza was the class bully and lost no time summoning everyone to Rosi's desk. They stared and laughed, pulled her hair, kicked her boots, and made mean remarks. Rosi dug her face deeper into her pillow to block out the memory, but she did not succeed.

When the teacher entered the classroom, Liza coyly raised her hand.

"Yes, Liza. What is it?"

"Excuse our standing here, Fräulein Neunübel, but Rosi wanted us to admire her brand new, dainty riding boots." Liza demurely pointed, and with a nasty stare at Rosi returned to her seat.

The teacher's stern face darkened, "Rosi, where did you get those boots?" she demanded.

Rosi, choking with tears, swallowed hard and obediently opened her mouth to answer. But the teacher was quicker and brought down the verdict.

"You shall stay after school and write two hundred times how and where you got those boots!"

It took Rosi nearly three hours to finish her punitive assignment and was allowed to go home. She was deeply hurt and puzzled. Why did the teacher punish her? Why did she glare at her boots with such contempt? Longingly she thought of her former school. What friendly environment; how pleasant its teachers and her classmates! But Hitler had closed all private schools. He did not approve of privilege and education.

Hitler wanted all schools to reflect the government's attitude of absolute and ruthless authority. Children were to be indoctrinated and disciplined at an early age. They were to obey and follow him, no one but him. They were to be his future soldiers and child-bearers.

School was Rosi's worst nightmare. A stern old spinster and a sergeant who had been wounded at the front were her teachers. Strict disciplinarians both. The younger teachers had been sent to the front, and if female, to work in hospitals or war-related industries. School for her was nothing but pain and suffering.

Maxi was the only one who shared her misery. Hanging his tail, he dolefully listened as Rosi lamented. "All day long, they stuff our heads with boring facts. Grammar drills, word drills, more grammar drills. For history we memorize dates, battles, names and places."

She once overheard her parents remark that her history book lacked color and drama, and contained no lessons to be learned. She wasn't sure what it meant, but her parents were undoubtedly right.

Her classroom teacher was Fräulein Neunübel, a singularly fitting name, meaning nine evils. A frigid scowl firmly engraved her gray-green face. Had she ever smiled, ever? Certainly none of her students dared to laugh or smile in class. Through thick, horn-rimmed glasses she glared at the girls, who sat in silent fear. One could have heard a pin drop.

Her lessons began by summoning each child to her desk for inspection of the homework. She'd study it somberly, while the student braced for the worst. It was next to impossible to please her. "Stretch out your hand!" she would finally command, and reach for her ruler. Then, mercilessly, she would whip the outstretched hand.

After school, the students had to collect for the war effort—bones on Mondays, rags on Tuesdays, scrap iron and glass on Thursdays, paper on Fridays.

It was not a happy time. The very air was saturated with anguish, grief and woe. And they were hungry, cold and miserable much of the time.

If at least they could have complained or talked about their misery, they could have unburdened their hearts. But Hitler had outlawed complaints and discontent. Everyone was to do his part and like it! "It is for the good of the fatherland," Hitler kept telling his people.

When Rosi and Peter talked about their misery, which was seldom, they whispered like conspirators. One never knew which inquisitive informers might be listening.

It was Monday—a long time before Sunday came again, their only day off from school. The children were lying on the floor in the playroom, studying.

"Much homework, Peter?" Rosi asked her brother sympathetically; he looked downcast and depressed.

"Can't say," he mumbled unhappily. "My stomach rumbled all day with hunger pangs. I didn't hear what the teacher said."

Paul nodded; his mind was conjuring up visions of butter and bread. "And it was miserably cold," he added. "My fingers were too stiff to hold my pen."

"Mine, too," Rosi murmured. "It's so awkward to knit with gloves on." Throughout the war, the girls knitted socks for soldiers at the front. Classrooms were no longer heated; every bit of fuel was needed in factories and at the front.

WAR! WAR! WAR!

All of life was focused on the war. During the long, cold winter months, when outside temperatures dropped below freezing, children sat in their classrooms wearing coats, scarves and wool mittens.

"Did you march again during your math class?" Paul piped up. "I wish we could, too."

Rosi's math teacher had been a career sergeant. When he lost his left arm and leg at the front, the army planted him as teacher on a class of little girls. It was not a happy fit. It never dawned on the sergeant that the girls were not green recruits.

"You'd hate it! We march like broomsticks around a dragon spitting fire at us," Rosi laughed, visualizing the fire-spitting sergeant.

On very cold days, he took the girls to the gym and had them march. "We have to salute every time we pass him. If we don't do it properly, he yells until the walls shake. Well, maybe not the walls, but my knees do," she corrected herself. They were taught to be meticulously truthful.

During the first ten minutes of each class, he would test their multiplication skills.

"8 times 9," he would bark, or "7 times 13."

They had to stand for the exercise. If you were first with the answer, you were allowed to sit down. It could have been fun, but his yelling was utterly unnerving. Rosi could not have told him her name.

Civilian greetings, such as good morning or *Gruess Gott*, were no longer permitted. A crisp *Heil Hitler* had to be used for all occasions. Some children even heil-Hitlered their parents.

A tiny scratching noise could be heard at the children's door and Maxi showed his friendly face. The children's room was his favorite place. They'd lounge together on the big sofa or on the lion skin on the floor. He was their only trusted friend sharing their joys and sorrows.

At the sight of Maxi, Paul jumped from the sofa and tried to click his heels—not successfully—he was in socks. He swung his arm into the air and barked at Maxi, "Heil Hitler!"

Startled, Maxi stopped in his tracks. No one had ever saluted him that formally. When the children exploded into muffled laughter, he wagged his tail, visibly relieved. And Rosi wrapped her arm around Maxi and whispered, "Don't ever leave us, Maxi. Not ever." These were uncertain times.

The children's father had his own version of the government-mandated salute. Leuthold added a little "t" after the "heil" which changed the *Hail Hitler* into *Cure Hitler!* Since secretaries were in short supply, he often had occasion to type a letter himself. When he did, he never left out that little "t."

As was to be expected, one of these letters got into the wrong hands and he was summoned by the Gestapo. Knowing her husband's aversion to the SS and his unwillingness to simulate political correctness, Edith managed to go on his behalf.

Here is what happened.

"Who types your husband's business correspondence?" Edith was questioned at headquarters.

"Different people," she replied. "Why do you ask?"

A letter with the offensive "Cure Hitler!" was produced. Edgar had refrained from sharing this bit of humor with her, but she could vividly picture his satisfied grin every time he added that meaningful "t." She studied the letter gravely and at great length. Then she whispered: "A very bad typo. I'm afraid I typed this letter."

The Gestapo man was aghast at her guileless admission of so serious a crime. Even lesser offenses were punished with incarceration.

"You see," she explained pleadingly, "My husband's secretaries are working at hospitals or factories, and the men are at the front. He is very short-handed. Whenever I can, I help out. The trouble is, I've never typed before the war. It takes me much time and effort. It was late at night when I typed this letter, with a sick and restless child on my lap. I'm truly sorry."

The official was a young man. Edith was blond, blue-eyed and young. He probably shrugged his shoulders and thought, "Oh well, a blonde," and let her go, but not without stern exhortations that she must improve her typing skills.

Edith had never typed. But from then on, ever so often, she could be seen tapping away gingerly at a typing machine. Perhaps atoning for her tale.

The Joys of Summer

Summertime, when the living is easy —Ira Gershwin

Edith opened the windows to let in the warm breeze. Flowers were in bloom, birds were singing—it seemed like peacetime. Down below in the neighbor's garden Otto, the new gardener, was cutting the hedge. A good-looking young chap, Edith thought. He certainly had made a deep impression on Maria. Edith went in search of the young girl and found her near the dining room window, gazing at the young man. Maria did not hear her coming, and Edith quietly backed out, went down the hall and called Maria.

"Here I am," came Maria's joyous voice as she hurried out to the hall.

"Maria, have you noticed what a lovely summer day it is? Too beautiful to be inside. I have letters to write. But why don't you go in the garden and enjoy it for the both of us. Perhaps you can find some flowers for the table or some herbs for dinner. Go and enjoy."

"Thank you, Ma'am; I'd love to," came the eager reply, and off she went blushing happily, while Edith returned to her desk, smiling. She was writing a letter to her children—she knew they would want to hear about Maxi. They were at the Nobel's lakeside home on summer vacation, a glorious reprieve from air raids and school.

At the lake, it drizzled mercilessly for the first three days, but it did not dampen the children's joy. They climbed the tall wild cherry tree loaded with tiny, tasty cherries and merrily aimed the pits at the climbers below, wishing they could aim them at their teachers. They watched the raindrops make a thousand little ripples on the lake, and welcomed the gentle sound after the harsh commands of their Hitler Youth leaders.

They ran with abandon on the large meadows, glad to be far away from their collection routes for the war effort. And when no one was watching, they took off into the strawberry and gooseberry patches to eat their fill.

Grandmother Mina whole-heartedly approved of the children playing outdoors. Of course, when Paul returned to the house covered with mud, a few well-chosen words were to be expected.

"But why do you have clean sand down by the water and dirty mud up here in the garden?" Paul countered. While scrubbing him, Mina explained.

"Some sixty years ago, there was nothing but rock and stone here. When they needed stones to build the War Memorial to commemorate Europe's victory over Napoleon, they excavated it right here."

"And they filled the hole with water?"

"Better than that. They dynamited 30' into the ground and struck water, which created the lake."

"With the sandy beach?"

"No sandy beach. Your grandfather bought the land, built the house, and ordered sand for the beach and many truckloads of fertile soil for the garden. Nothing will grow without good soil."

"I shall become a farmer," Paul beamed, thinking of the huge strawberry patch he would plant to assuage his constantly empty stomach.

Mina loved her garden. Rain or shine, that is where she spent the early hours of her day, and no one but the gardener was allowed to disturb her. The children were instructed to sleep late, and they gladly obliged, romping about their bedrooms with muffled cries of laughter. Around ten, they were rewarded with breakfast in bed: bowls of hot oatmeal topped with fresh fruit.

By mid-morning, the kitchen hummed with activity. Pots steamed with fruit, jams, and vegetables, while sulfur fumes swirled and sterilized the jars. Each summer, Mina canned two to three hundred jars of produce from her garden to prepare for the long winter.

The White Ship

The secret of happiness is freedom, and the secret of freedom is courage —Thucydides

During the summer of 1940 an air of secrecy pervaded grandmother's house. Some of the children's clothing disappeared. "Other people need them more than you do," they were told. There were furtive goings-on in the guesthouse. Strangers came to confer with Mina and disappeared again. Mina was widowed then and was deeply involved with *The White Ship* that was to save people of Jewish faith from Hitler's persecution.

Nobel had known many Jews. When Hitler embarked on his road to power, he singled them out for his verbal attacks; he expounded his Aryan theories in *Mein Kampf*; and when he became chancellor, he barred non-Aryans from government employment. Yet when he achieved *absolute* power, he no longer mentioned the Jews—they quietly disappeared, as did Hitler's political opponents.

So Mina joined underground forces to sponsor *The White Ship*. They raised funds, helped and hid the persecuted, and procured a ship with captain and crew. In 1940, all was set. The

Jewish families, many of whom had spent the last weeks or months in hiding, were safely brought aboard. With some 900 people aboard, *The White Ship* lifted anchor.

They successfully escaped from Hitler's persecution. Yet they lacked a destination. Their German sponsors were unable to communicate with the outside world, and port after port turned *The White Ship* away. American ports, too, denied them entry. Immigration quotas were exhausted.

Eventually, one door did open—thanks to the US Jewish Relief Fund that succeeded in negotiating a deal with Trujillo, the dictator of the Dominican Republic. He was to amend his country's constitution to guarantee civil rights and freedom to people of Jewish faith to practice their religion; and they would purchase large parcels of land from him on which the refugees could settle.[32] El Generalissimo Trujillo did as he promised, and each person received eighty acres, ten cows and a horse. And before long, their barren land flourished.

Trujillo's laudable action was triggered by surprising motives. Many months earlier, he ordered 25,000 Haitians killed, and the foreign press took him harshly to task. By performing this humanitarian act, Trujillo intended to restore his image.

In regard to the Haitians, however, Trujillo felt that his action was justified. For years, he and the Haitian government had a standing agreement that during the cane-cutting season 25,000 to 100,000 Haitians would enter the Dominican Republic to cut sugar cane. As soon as the cane was cut, the Haitians were to return to Haiti. In 1937, however, the Haitian dictator refused the Haitian workers to return to their home country,

---

[32] Near Santa Domingo and in Sosua near Puerto Plata in the north of the country. They produce most of the country's meat and dairy products today.

claiming that Haiti had too much poverty and too little work. They were to stay in the Dominican Republic.

Trujillo did not like to be foiled. If Haiti did not want them, he did not want them either, and ordered them killed. The plea of the Jewish Relief Fund on behalf of the refugees aboard *The White Ship* offered a welcome opportunity.[33]

Like Father, Like Son
Force always attracts men of low morality —Albert Einstein

"Arno!" Mina called delightedly as she hugged her handsome son-in-law, "My dear Arno, I thought you were somewhere governing the Baltic States."

"I was, and still am. I had to come home on a secret mission. But I wanted to see you first. Have to leave again in the morning." Beaming broadly, he dug into his pocket to produce a small bag of coffee. Mina dearly loved coffee, but coffee could no longer be bought. Stores sold a roasted-rye substitute, which resembled coffee only in color.

"Latvian coffee!" Mina exclaimed, studying the bag. "Don't tell me Latvian stores still have coffee on their shelves?"

"Of course not," Arno laughed. "But I have my ways and the uniform helps," he grinned slyly.

"You mean your SS-uniform? Let me look at you." She backed off a step, her joy sagging.

"It got me that fine post in the Baltic," he beamed. "Otherwise I'd be fighting in the trenches."

---

[33] The settlements flourished, in spite of the poverty that still exists in the country. Many refugees intermarried with the native people, and a climate of harmony and wellbeing prevails.

"How is Viola, and how is little Wolfie?" Mina changed the topic. With Arno, she preferred to steer clear of controversial subjects.

"Viola and Wolfie will be coming here by train. I would have loved to chauffer the family, but I can't when on an SS mission. Got to be circumspect."

"Come in, dear, and we'll find something to eat and drink for you," she said and took another look at his waistline. Obviously, he had not gone hungry.

"Tell me about Latvia and what you are doing with yourself?" she asked.

"Grave responsibilities. Got to keep those Latvians in line, make sure they don't hoard food or wine," he squelched a devilish grin. "Got to make certain they have the proper political attitude and don't get ideas, like hiding Jews."

Irritated, Mina tried another topic. "How's the fur business doing?"

"Everything is splendid, my dear Mina. Couldn't be better. I go to Leipzig as often as is necessary."

"Glad to hear it. But you should send us reports, Arno. You haven't sent any dividends either. It's specified in the will, you know."

"But my dearest Mina!" Arno exclaimed, jumping up. "I didn't realize you were short of cash."

"I am not!" Mina exploded, her pride punctured.

"My dearest Mina, you really had me worried for a moment. Come! It's a beautiful day and I'm dying to see your latest roses. Have you grafted new ones? You are so good at it. Whatever you touch, Mina, you turn into a work of art."

Arno bowed and gallantly offered Mina his arm. Internally, however, he was seething. It was a close call! It was Edgar's doing, he was certain. Edgar had written him a letter requesting the report and sent a copy to Mina.

I must get rid of that man, Arno fumed. But he smiled with the nonchalant charm of the con-man and took Mina's arm.

He sniffed the air, "Ah, the aroma of your flowers!"

Later that day, Arno's wife and son arrived. The Leuthold children were rolling marbles in the playroom. They had not seen their cousin in over a year. Wolfie was six, a year younger than Paul, but he had twice his self-assurance, and twice his bodily weight.

"Hello Wolfie," Rosi called cheerfully, when he entered the playroom. But Wolf did not respond. He looked them over like a field marshal—with wordless disdain. Then he anchored his hands on his hips, his feet apart, and announced, "You haven't got what I have!" Triumphantly, he stretched out his arm. An expensive gold watch gleamed on his wrist. He wore it over his sweater since it was an adult timepiece and much too large to fit the wrist of a six-year old.

His three cousins gazed in amazement, not sure what was more astounding, their cousin's bigheadedness, or his fine watch. They had never seen a child with a watch; even adults were often without them—watches could no longer be bought. Wolf, in the meantime, had noticed the marbles on the floor and taken a fancy to them. With surprising nimbleness he swooped down to pocket them.

"Not so fast," Peter shouted as he dived for the marbles to protect them, and so did Rosi. Wolfie let out a piercing scream for his parents; he was used to getting his way. But his parents were not in earshot.

"What a greedy kid!" Peter observed tersely after the guests departed, and Paul with a touch of envy added, "He's round like a butterball."

The Eastern Front

Those who cannot remember the past are condemned to repeat it —George Santayana

Maria hurried to the door to answer the bell.
"Herr Doctor!" she exclaimed, disbelieving her eyes. "Welcome home!"

Was it possible? The master of the house back from the front? A year had passed since his last brief furlough. Her face beamed welcome.

Leuthold placed a finger on his lips. "Let me surprise the Gnädige Frau."

Maria nodded eagerly. She softly closed the door and took Leuthold's coat, while he hastened with eager steps to the room Maria indicated.

The campaign into Poland and France had ended, and to the relief of the people Hitler had signed a non-aggression pact with the Soviet Union, making Russia and Germany allies. Peace was assured along Germany's eastern frontier.

Yet Hitler's desire for land and Lebensraum was far from satisfied. He hungered for the vast plains of Russia and for the oilfields of the Ukraine, and on June 22 of 1941, Hitler's secret Operation Barbarossa went into effect. Violating his Pact of Peace, his panzer divisions rolled across the border into the Soviet Union.

Hitler anticipated "another quick and glorious victory." He told his people: "We only have to kick in the front door and the whole rotten structure will come crashing down." While in prison in 1923, Hitler had written about Germany's need for Lebensraum, and that he intended to find it in the Russian plains. But few had read *Mein Kampf.*

When word of Hitler's latest invasion reached Churchill, he hissed two words: "bloodthirsty guttersnipe!"

With rapid steps Edgar traversed the hall and the ping pong room, smiling as he remembered the many happy ping, pong, ping, pong, ping. Then past the *Herrenzimmer,* his domain, where his friends used to smoke a cigar after dinner and where he played a game of chess with his men friends. Next to it was the *Damenzimmer* or parlor, Edith's domain, where she had her piano and her library of French and other foreign books. She spent much of her time there.

The other wing of the family's home had recently been divided off to create separate living quarters for another family whose home had been destroyed.

Edgar knocked on her door.

"Come in," Edith called, expecting Maria's loyal face.

"Edgar!" she exclaimed, flying from her seat, half fearing that the vision might disappear. During many sleepless nights she had worried and prayed for her man, who was fighting a war whose cause he did not espouse and for a leader he detested. She was already in his arms, holding him tight.

"How good to see you, Edgar," she whispered. "What brings you home?"

On the previous day, Edgar had received orders to proceed from Paris to the Russian front. Leipzig was on his route; therefore his unexpected visit.

"You're on your way to the Russian front?" Edith had turned pale at the grim news. She struggled for composure.

"You'd better take warm clothing," she stammered, trying to hide her fears.

Edgar nodded and held her tight. "My military transport will leave in two hours."

"Not even time to see the children," Edith replied softly. "They are in school." She, too, was thinking what Edgar thought: Will he ever see them again?

I must savor this hour, Edith kept telling herself, but it was not easy. Visions of indomitable Father Russia kept marring her happiness. Thoughts of Napoleon, once the undefeated master of Europe, kept crossing her mind. He, too, had taken his troops into Russia where the bitter cold and the endless plains of snow and desolation had defeated him.

"You must take my little compass with you," she urged him. The thought seemed to comfort her, and before Edgar could voice his objection, she flew to her desk and gently took it from her drawer. This exquisite, tiny compass, which Edgar had found for her in London, had accompanied her on all her excursions on horseback. "I won't be riding anymore," she added sadly. "Besides, I have Maxi to serve as a guide. Russia is vast. I want you to find your way home, Edgar." With a questioning look she indicated the pockets of his coat.

A small smile crossed Edgar's face. "I'll take it with me," he said to comfort her. "I'll carry it close to my heart." Carefully, he tucked it into the breast pocket on the inside of his coat.

"Is your whole regiment moving east?" she resumed.

"No, not the regiment," Edgar admitted. "I am the only one who was transferred." He quickly continued to distract her from the unsettling news, "My unit can't leave yet. We are in charge of keeping order among our troops in Paris. It's not an easy job. We allow no rape, no purloining, no excessive drunkenness. Nor does Hitler want his Aryan soldiers consorting

106

with French women," he mocked. "More importantly, we've set up an exchange program—we return French prisoners to France, while they provide us with male volunteers to work in Germany."

Edith had not heard a word. Her mind was running circles around the fact that he was the only one who was transferred. Why did they single out Edgar to fight at the Russian front? One man, why?

"If you are needed in Paris, why are they sending you to Russia?" she asked. She sensed an evil hand at work. "It makes no sense."

"I wish I knew. The general and I have been friends for years. I've asked him. He said he received a specific request for my transfer."

"Did he tell you who requested it?"

"The letter was signed by an unfamiliar name and had come through SS channels ... Edith, are you all right?" Edith had inhaled sharply. "You are suspecting someone, aren't you?"

"The same person you are, Edgar. He visited me a month ago, without calling first. He asked a dozen questions about you, what you were doing, where you were, which general you reported to. I was vague. I don't trust Arno, not after the Mathilde Riess incident."

"Did he say why he was visiting you?"

"He wanted to make sure all was well with me, or so he said. He even brought a few chocolates. You know Arno; he's the devil cloaked in charm. Frightfully self-important, yet evasive like a fox when I did the asking. He showed off the latest hits on my accordion and talked about his son."

She did not tell Edgar that Arno had pinched Maria. Her moments with Edgar were too brief. Besides, she did not want Edgar to write another fateful letter to Arno.

"Is Wolfie still the apple of his eye?"

"He adores the child." Edith answered absentmindedly. She had a weightier matter on her mind. "Edgar," she resumed, "Please don't send Arno reminders about the company reports. I don't care about the dividends. The money means nothing to me. You do."

"Yes, dear, no more reminders. Well, not until after the war," Edgar laughed.

The thought that Arno had caused Edgar's transfer cast a dark shadow over his short visit. Arno's poisoned arrows! The two hours flew by. Edgar joined his transport to the Russian front, and Edith, disconsolate, roamed the streets to find solace.

During the summer and fall of 1941, the German invasion into the vast Soviet Empire was marked by swift victories. It was the largest military attack ever launched—three million men, 750,000 horses, 3,500 tanks, and on and on. Within seventeen days they took 300,000 Russian prisoners, and pushed deep into Russia.

Yet the deeper the troops penetrated, the wider the front became. Soon it extended from the Baltic Sea in the north to the Black Sea in the south—over a thousand miles. In three short weeks, German panzer divisions had pushed 450 miles into Russia. They were within 200 miles of Moscow.

Hitler was exuberant. In September, he issued orders that the eastern infantry divisions be reduced in order to increase the labor force at home. He needed men to build ships and planes for his final push against England.

Most of all, he was eager to prepare for his grand attack on America. The naval ships on his drawing board were eight times larger than the largest ship ever built. They were to carry an enormous army to invade the American continent. He could barely contain his impatience to attack that rich land of resources. After that conquest, he would be the uncontested ruler of the world. It was his vision, his goal. He would settle down then and build his capital, the most spectacular city the world had ever seen, with monuments so grand that for millennia people would come to admire them.

In October, Hitler's press chief Dr. Otto Dietrich declared, "Russia is done with."

German troops had crossed the Dnieper River. Kiev, the capital of the fertile Ukraine, the food basket of Russia, had fallen into German hands.

"The Ukraine is ours; it is unable to resist any more," the radio announced.

Field Marshal Rundstedt's troops were pushing toward the rich oil fields in the Caucasus. When Rostov was taken, Hitler declared it the greatest victory in the history of the world. It confirmed his conviction that no greater conqueror than he, Adolf Hitler, had ever lived. From his underground bunker in Berlin, he ordered divisions from the Ukraine to march north toward Moscow. He wanted Moscow without delay before the Russian winter set in. He also wanted the oil fields in the South. And he wanted Leningrad, the capital of Tsar Peter the Great, a thousand miles to the north. "Wipe it from the face of the earth," he ordered.

Hitler's field marshals had achieved the nearly impossible. They could not be pushed any further. They began to object. They tried to reason with their commander in chief. They wanted to concentrate on one area at a time; not attack over a thousand-mile front. Their troops were exhausted. They were cut off from supplies and repair parts. In short, they were spread too thin over too large an area. Further advances would have dire consequences.

Hitler refused to listen. He knew better. He was in charge.

Several generals flew to Berlin to talk with Hitler in person. Yet Hitler wanted no discussions. He wanted absolute obedience. His orders were to be executed precisely as he gave them. He flew into violent tantrums during the meeting. His eyes bulged, his face flushed. His fist kept pounding the table while he roared at them like a man possessed.

"Slimy cowards you all!" he shouted at his generals. Possessed by his fantasy of greatness, he wanted Leningrad in the north, Moscow in the center, and the oil fields in the south. He wanted them now!

He wanted his greatness confirmed and the world awed by his might. He threatened to recall any general who dared to differ with his strategy, or who did not comply with his *Wunschliste*, as his generals called it, his list of wishes conceived in the safety of his Berlin bunker far removed from the realities of the battlefield. With iron willpower Hitler stuck to his guns—and more than one general lost his command for daring to differ.

Then came the first reversals. The Russian colossus shifted into gear and mobilized division after division to repel the enemy. They fought with unexpected resilience and with fierce determination. Hard-won Rostov fell back into Russian hands. Hitler, unwilling to accept the defeat, recalled Field Marshal Rundstedt, who led the southern advance. Hitler had stubbornly denied Rundstedt's plea for a different strategy, but Hitler wanted accelerated victories, not retreat and regrouping.

In the meantime, the rains set in and turned the Russian roads into quagmire. The Russians call it Rasputiza, the Period of Mud. Every vehicle, gun and tractors sank deep into the mud and could not be moved. The men had no cables to pull them out, nor replacement parts to make repairs. The weather turned colder. Yet the transports with winter clothing for the men were stuck hundreds of miles from where they were needed. In early December, a thousand soldiers froze to death. German supply columns could not advance—partisan units had sprung up everywhere and ambushed them, just as the generals had predicted.

Hitler's generals revolted.

To no avail.

Hitler, the World War I corporal, wanted it his way. He kept issuing orders to advance and responded to his generals' requests with counter-orders and insults. He alone was in command, and no one was to forget it. He intended to lick the Prussian Officer Corps single-handedly, that proud corps of century-old independence. *He*, Adolf Hitler, was the Head of State. *He* represented Supreme Justice. *He* was the Leader of the Party. *He* was the Minister of War. And most important, *he* was the Supreme Commander of the Armed Forces and the Commander in Chief of the Army. From his bunker in Berlin, he issued orders that forbade retreat. If he gave orders to advance, they'd better advance, or heads would roll.

"I shall take steps to strengthen my position," Hitler screamed at his staff and passed a new law that gave him greater power than any person had ever held: He pronounced himself the Leader **and** the Law with absolute power over life and death of every German, suspending every law that stood in its way.[34]

---

[34] "... The Führer must be in a position to force with all means at his disposal every German ... to fulfill his duties. In case of violation of these duties, the Führer is entitled after conscientious examination, regardless of so-called well-deserved rights, to mete out due punishment and to remove the offender from his post, rank and position without introducing prescribed procedures." Issued by the Reichstag on 4/26/1942. (1961-PS)

It seemed to work. Hitler's tenacity and unbending will drove German troops to reach the gates of Moscow. It was an incredible feat—won against all odds and at an enormous cost of lives.

It was December; the Russian winter set in. Victories reversed into crushing defeats. At the gates of the beleaguered city thousands of lives were lost. Soldiers starved and froze to death. While German troops had rapidly advanced into the heartland of Russia, the retreating enemy burned everything to the ground. There were no supplies, no shelter, no food, not even railroad tracks left to allow for transportation of the wounded back to Germany.

Hitler had read about Napoleon's campaign into Russia and his bitter defeat, but he snubbed its lesson. He chose to ignore the Russian winter, and the endless expanse of cold and nothingness. He himself never left the safety of his bunker to inspect the conditions at the front or to review his troops. He did not heed his advisors' warnings. Nor did he pay attention to his generals—he ridiculed them, condemned them, and dismissed them. When his Field Marshal protested the needless death of thousands of young men and officers during a battle, Hitler curtly cut him off:

"That's what young men are for," he said.

During that merciless winter of 1941, all military movement came to a grinding halt—Hitler's mighty Wehrmacht was caught as in a deep freeze. The tide had turned.

Eisling and his unit had pitched their tents near a clump of trees about a hundred miles southwest of Moscow. The quagmire had halted their progress. Now a sudden cold front was moving in.

Ahead of them lay a large open valley, but they lacked supplies and fuel to cross it. Leuthold had spent all day with his men trying to improvise shelter to protect the men, horses, vehicles and equipment from the bitter cold. They were low on anti-freeze, and the engines would not turn over. The day before, a snowstorm had buried everything under a blanket of snow. It was barely December. Winter had not yet begun.

Leuthold, hungry, cold and tired, could no longer ignore the grim reality—they had come to the end of their rope. He could see no way of getting the men out of their position alive, let alone advance against the enemy as Hitler kept ordering. They had no winter clothing, hardly any supplies, no fuel, and no repair parts. They were stuck, probably for the duration of the winter. And they were running out of food. How long would they be able to survive? On his way to the tent, a young lieutenant intercepted him.

"Herr Major, you are to report to the General, sir," he said. "I will take you to him."

The General was bending over a map when Leuthold entered. Slowly, he straightened, but his careworn expression remained.

"Ah, Leuthold. I don't like to lose you, but I got orders that you are urgently needed in Berlin."

"In Berlin, sir?"

"We desperately need more soldiers, Leuthold; we are fighting on too many fronts." The General sighed involuntarily. "The question is how and where to find more men. Berlin says you are an expert on German draft laws. Are you?"

"Not an expert, sir. I wrote my doctoral thesis on the topic."

"Well, they want you at headquarters. I'll give you one of our horses, can't spare any of the men. If you leave within the next fifteen minutes, you have a good chance of catching up with the medical transport that left earlier. It may be your last chance to get to Berlin before winter cuts us off completely. Good luck, Leuthold." As an after-thought he added, "Stop by on your way out."

As if on autopilot Leuthold proceeded as told. He confirmed his route and the point of rendezvous with the medical transport, gathered a few essentials, and stopped by the General's tent.

"A letter to my wife, Leuthold," the General said as he handed Leuthold the note he had written. "It may be my last."

The significance of the new assignment had not yet penetrated Leuthold's exhausted mind, only a vague feeling that the certain sentence of death may be lifted. Was he to join the ranks of the living again? While he and his horse headed west, Leuthold remembered Nobel's words of long ago:

"Get your Ph.D.," his prospective father-in-law had said. "It may come in handy one day."

As luck would have it, his professor had suggested the German draft laws as a topic for his dissertation. Nobel's words were strangely comforting to him while snow, night and enemy territory engulfed him. Nobel, he pondered—it seemed like an eternity ago—a wise gentleman. Honest. Hard working. Kind. One of the best.

His horse was shaking her mane. It had begun to snow again. In the darkness, the tracks of the truck were hard to discern; with more snow falling, they'd soon be invisible. These tracks were his only guide for finding the medical transport.

Maxi, his dog, could have detected them, but a horse could not. Edgar's confidence was ebbing. Surrounded by snow and unknown forest, it would be a miracle if he met up with the medical transport.

His horse shook her mane again. Edgar could sense her distress caused by the falling snow, the darkness and the emptiness in her stomach. He bent forward to wipe the snow off her mane. "You'd rather be in a dry stable," he said soothingly. "So would I." He tried to visualize the map and his route—the point of rendezvous was 55.9° 6' North, 34° 17' East, twenty-three point seven kilometers along these tracks. His hand shot to his breast pocket. Was it still there, the little compass Edith had urged him to take along? He could still hear her words:

"I want you to find your way home! Russia is vast."

On that same day, December 8, 1941, Mina in far-away Leipzig was studying her late husband's map of the world covering one wall of his study. She was visibly shaken. She had summoned the children and pointed at the small, greenish speck that was Germany. Then her hand swept over endless territories, enemy territories—England, Norway, Denmark, Holland, Belgium and the Netherlands, France, Czechoslovakia, Poland, Russia, and the North of Africa. She shook her head in disbelief, "And now we have added the United States of America to the long list of our enemies."

Mina was an admirer of the New World. She recalled the splendid voyages with her husband on the *Queen Mary*, the *Normandie* and the *Ile de France* when they visited his branch in New York. They had enjoyed much gracious hospitality there. She still marveled at American competence and enterprise.

She focused on tiny Germany again. Contempt and concern darkened her eyes, contempt for the greed and arrogance of its leader, and concern for the hopelessness of their future.

It was toward morning that Leuthold's horse collapsed, somewhere in the middle of Russia; he figured some two miles from his point of rendezvous. He felt the animal's neck, but his fingers were stiff and cold. He could not detect a pulse. Considering the hardships the poor animal had suffered, he was grateful she had taken him that far. Gently, he closed her eyes, patted her neck and rapidly continued on foot.

It did not take long for his pace to slow. He felt light-headed and overcome by hunger and fatigue. I must rest, his weary body wailed. How many months had it been since he and his men had seen a real meal? He could not remember. Their meager food rations had been cut again, recently. The weight of his six-foot, three-inch body had dropped to a hundred and fifteen pounds. Unless supplies reached the unit soon, the men would be running out of food.

I must rest, he thought desperately, rest for just a moment. Yet his trained mind told him otherwise. If you sit down, it reminded him, sleep and frost will overtake you. You'll never get up again. He reached into his breast pocket. Edith's compass! He tucked it into his left glove and concentrated on her words, "... find your way home." And like a robot he kept walking.

At 8:30, the General's phone rang. It was the commander of the medical transport. "Leuthold has not arrived. May we proceed without him?"

"The General will be back shortly," the aide replied. "He's saying a few words at Kurt's burial."

"Have him call me as soon as possible. We shall have to get going."

It was a shallow grave; the ground was frozen and rocky. The young soldier was a boy of seventeen, well liked by his unit. A wound from a sniper's bullet had caused an internal infection that festered, spread and killed the boy. They had run out of medications. The General himself had a son of seventeen, who was also fighting somewhere in Russia. At each burial the words became harder to formulate and more painful to deliver. With a heavy heart he walked back to his tent. How many more would he have to bury?

"Sir, the commander of the medical transport called," his aide reported. "Leuthold has not arrived. The commander would like to proceed without him."

"Get him on the line," the General replied as he sank into his chair.

"Commander," he said, when the aide handed him the phone, "Leuthold is needed in Berlin. He will come. Send someone to look for him."

The General was tired of the endless deaths. He had lost count of the many brave, young men fallen in action, men in their prime. Besides, he knew Leuthold. Leuthold could be relied upon.

O n that same day in the Erzgebirge, Edith with her children in tow and one of Maria's freshly baked loaves of bread in her backpack was skiing down to the Waldschlössl, the inn with the nearest telephone.

"Any calls for me?" she asked, trying to hide her anxiety. No one but Edgar and his office manager knew that number.

"None, Gnädige Frau," Ilse replied softly. "I promise to send someone to the cabin the moment we get a call."

"I know you will, Ilse," Edith smiled weakly. "Maria baked bread today. We thought we'd bring you a loaf."

Edith had not heard from Edgar in many, many months.

Barely fifteen minutes had passed, when the General picked up his phone again. "Leuthold has made it, sir," came over the wire. "He's delirious and on foot, but still alive. We're on our way."

Forty-seven days later the medical transport crossed the border into Germany. The jostling ride over the rough terrain had been torture for the wounded men. More than half of them did not make it. The men's moaning haunted Leuthold for months to come.

From his unit deep in the heart of Russia not one man lived to see another spring.

A Victim No More

Power corrupts; absolute power corrupts absolutely
—John Acton

The children's Christmas vacation came to an end, and the dreaded routine of school resumed. Their only bright moment was when Maxi joyously welcomed them home.

That Wednesday, though, there was no Maxi wagging his tail. Rosi and Paul rushed into the living room; Peter ran upstairs. No sign of Maxi.

"Maxi!" Their anxious voices resounded throughout the house. They stormed into the kitchen panic stricken, "Where is Maxi?" But Maria could not answer; she was blowing her nose to hide her tears.

"Where is he? What happened?"

With great effort Maria pulled herself together and explained. "They came and took him away. He'll be sent to the front to fight the war."

Speechless and heart-broken, the children collapsed into Maria's arms and sobbed. Their father was fighting at the front, and now Maxi, their beloved shepherd, too. The house seemed like a tomb.

To lift the gloomy mood, Edith invited three friends for a musical evening. The children, with somber faces, dressed in their best, turned the pages of the musical scores, while Edith and her friends played a Mozart Quartet.

Dieter, the violinist, with a head of curly hair and a twinkle in his eyes, was the children's favorite. He was a young medical student and a gifted artist. Whenever he visited, he'd pull out his notepad and to the children's delight drew an array of toys. As a peacetime luxury, toys were no longer manufactured, and Dieter's drawings were the next best thing.

Dieter drew a fine set of dominos. "Naw, no numbers," Paul exclaimed. "They remind me of school."

However, a ferocious-looking chimp had Peter enthralled, "Make it bigger," he cried, "so it can devour my teachers."

When Dieter drew a golden pineapple, they looked perplexed; they had never seen one.

"This is not for play," Dieter declared. "It's for dessert."

Paul looked quizzical. "It looks thorny and tough."

"But it is delicious inside, and sweet."

"You will find out after the war," Edith licked her lips. "One day, I hope, we can buy tropical fruit again."

Dieter had an uncanny gift of breathing life into his sketches and tales. Spell-bound, the children listened as he described the Iroquois Indians, while drawing a peace pipe, feathered headgear, and bow and arrow. Even Edith could not escape the magic of his words.

"Among these Indians," Dieter explained, "everyone is considered an equal and entitled to freedom and dignity—men and women alike. No one is considered better and no one worse. Before important decisions are made, they are discussed in open council until everyone agrees. There are no lower or upper classes among these Indians; and no one bosses anyone around."

"I like it," Peter murmured.

Dieter nodded pensively, "Before the white man arrived, they roamed over much of the North American continent. Maybe their customs inspired the white men to write a more democratic constitution than Europe had at the time."

Appreciatively, Edith exclaimed, "I've read their Declaration of ..." but suddenly stopped. If someone overheard and reported their conversation, they'd both be locked up in a KZ. Hitler did not believe in democracy, or in equality. Nor did he harbor respect for anyone. Life to him was a fierce struggle for survival where none but the most ruthless survived. Every German, Hitler had vowed, was to be tough as steel to earn his right to live.

Edith abruptly changed the topic.

"Dieter," she blurted, "tell me how is your training coming?"

"Better," Dieter grinned, realizing the cause of her discomposure. Dieter had been drafted eight months earlier to be trained for the medical corps.

"Better than what?" Edith looked puzzled. She had recovered her calm.

"Better than scrubbing latrines," Dieter mockingly raised an eyebrow. "After three weeks of medical training, I was reassigned to latrine duty. For the last seven months I've scrubbed latrines."

"What's a latrine?" Paul asked. A kick and a word from his brother gave him the answer.

"But Dieter, your had nearly completed your medical studies! Don't we need doctors?"

Dieter nodded calmly. "We do. But you know my background; my grandmother was Jewish. An informer must have needed some cash." Dieter's grandfather, a prominent doctor, had married a beautiful Jewess. Their son, Dieter's father, had followed in his father's footsteps and became a prominent doctor, too. Naturally, Dieter studied medicine.

Edith recalled Dieter's account of the Krystallnacht, when Göring, Berlin's chief of police, in a flurry of power ordered his men to burn Berlin's synagogues and smash the windows of Jewish stores. That night, three of Hitler's SS men had grabbed Dieter on his way home from class.

"You are a Jew," they yelled, but Dieter remonstrated that he was not.

"Pull down your pants," one of them ordered. "Let's see if you're circumcised."

Since Dieter wanted to live, he quietly obeyed. Not being circumcised saved his life.

"How did you get out of latrine duty?" Edith whispered.

"As luck would have it," Dieter beamed, "my last visit home coincided with a practice session of my father's chamber music friends. They were playing the same Mozart quartet we played tonight.

"The violinist happened to be an army man, and his first question was, 'How is the Army treating you?'

"I told him that I was cleaning latrines all day, and had no time to study. You should have heard him roar, 'We shall see about that!'

"A week or so later, while I was scrubbing, a lieutenant came running and told me I was wanted on the parade ground. That morning, an unexpected inspection had been called. When everyone stood at attention, the inspecting general told the

121

camp commander that he wished to see Medical Corpsman Dieter Bergman."

"Were you standing at attention, too?" Paul interrupted, trying to get a clear picture.

"No. I wasn't worthy of standing with the regiment. A parade ground is considered sacred soil. I was just a latrines man," Dieter chuckled.

"What happened?"

"The commander asked his second in command where I was; the second in command asked the next man, and so it went down the line until someone knew where to find me. He was sent to get me on the double. All the while, the general kept the camp standing at attention. When I arrived, the general, my father's violinist friend, cordially shook my hand." An amused twinkle played around Dieter's eyes.

"'Dieter, my boy,' he said in front of the whole assembly, 'I am glad to see you.' Then he turned to the commander of the camp, 'Do you have an office where I can talk with my friend in private?'

"The commander offered his own office to the general, also his finest bottle of brandy and his supply of cigars." Dieter paused.

His calm, gray eyes ever so slightly flickered with amusement as he pondered the foibles of men and the shifting winds of fortune.

"It's a funny thing," he concluded, "I haven't scrubbed a latrine since."

Dieter and the other musician departed, while Sigurd, Edgar's college friend, stayed behind. The children went to bed, and Edith turned on the record player.

"Have you heard from Edgar?" Sigurd asked.

"Not in many months," Edith whispered and changed the painful subject, "How are you doing with your new prosthesis, Sigurd? You are walking a little better." Sigurd had lost his right leg in the Polish campaign.

"Sylvia reminds me daily that I should be grateful. She says, it's better to be without a leg than among the dead, or to be still fighting in this ghastly war."

"A wise woman, your Sylvia. And how's my godchild, Susanne?"

"We'd like to send her to college after high school graduation, but her Hitler Youth leader is urging her to take up stenography or work in an ammunition factory. Everyone is needed in this wretched war. It may be ill advised, or, let's admit it, impossible to go against official advice."

"She's lucky to be given a choice. Shorthand may come in handy one day." Edith paused for a moment. "Sigurd, coming back to Dieter's account, weren't you also in Berlin during the Krystallnacht?"

"I was. A barbaric night! Like savages they smashed the synagogues and Jewish store windows. Even Hitler was furious. It got Himmler into the saddle."

"How come? I thought it was Göring's idea."

"It was. But Göring failed to get Hitler's blessings. Hitler may have approved of the general idea, but not of the way it was executed."

"What do you mean?"

"Hitler used to be outspoken against the Jews. Nowadays, he does not ever mention them. He has learned that it causes opposition among the people, especially among the educated and the upper classes. He can't afford that."

"True. I remember how outraged we were about the brutality of the Krystallnacht," Edith whispered.

"Hitler, too, was furious," Sigurd added quietly. "He needs the people's approval. After that night he removed Göring as Chief of Police and appointed Himmler. He also made Himmler chief of the Gestapo and head of the SS, his official bodyguard. I hear Himmler is the epitome of a yes-man; nothing but yes, mein Führer; of course, mein Führer; you are right, mein Führer."

"Edgar says it's the only response Hitler accepts."

Sigurd laughed. "You're quite right. Göring once tried to justify his action, he reportedly said, "But mein Führer, it's my job to eliminate the Jews and exterminate the politically unwanted. I don't care how my men do it." Hitler did not like that. He replaced Göring and sent him to the Air Force."

"Do you think Himmler will handle the job better?"

"Himmler is cunning, smooth and deceitful. He makes you believe that he could not hurt a fly. He uses subtler means, and more deadly ones. No one will ever know or even suspect what he is doing. Oddly enough, he's steeped in superstition and mysticism. He and his tall SS men in their black uniforms practice strange rites."

"Didn't he send expeditions to Greece and Tibet to trace the origin of the Aryan race?"

"Several expeditions, primarily to Greece. He seeks to prove Aryan superiority, which is the basis of Hitler's political thinking. Hitler and his Aryan master race!" Exasperated, Sigurd got up and paced the floor, painfully limping.

"Sometimes I wonder whether he actually believes what he wrote in *Mein Kampf.* It borders on the ludicrous. Let me quote him: 'It is the birthright of the Aryan race to enslave all other races.'" Sigurd was not a cynical person, but at that moment, contempt and outrage were written all over his face.

"Then he says, 'We must preserve the purity of the Aryan bloodline?'"

"Do you suppose this idea was behind his Sterilization Laws?"

Sigurd nodded. "Hitler wants nothing but pure, Aryan children to be born in Germany. Did you know that every member of the SS—over a million men now—has to get the Party's approval of the woman he wants to marry?"

"Get approval? What for?"

"To make sure she is of Aryan stock. Himmler estimates that in 120 years all Germans will be pure-blooded Aryans." Sigurd shook his head in dismay.

Edith found no words to reply, but her troubled look said plenty. She recalled those weeks when the government conducted rigorous physical examinations of every German citizen. In the process, some 40,000 people were sterilized, not only people with genetic diseases, but also alcoholics and criminals. Children with tuberculosis or other ailments were placed in state sanatoriums. Within a short time, a shockingly high percentage of these children died, supposedly from natural causes.

"Edith," Sigurd whispered before leaving, "don't discuss these matters with anyone; your children need you, and so does Edgar. We need to face it, we are powerless now. We should have been more vigilant and less gullible when Hitler was still the demagogue of the beer garden. After the unfortunate Versailles Treaty was signed, it was too late. People were too angry and desperate then to engage in reasoned thought."

Edith had hardly fallen asleep, when the high-pitched sound of sirens propelled her out of bed again. It happened every night. In seconds and in total darkness, she dived into warm clothing that lay in readiness, grabbed her bag and dashed off to the cellar like everyone else. There was no need to wake the children or urge them to hurry. The sound of the sirens and the fear of bombs were persuasive enough. Sleepy, cold and scared they huddled in the dark and humid cellar while overhead the bombers whined and underneath the earth trembled.

When finally back in bed, it was not easy to fall asleep. They lay in bed mulling over life's miseries. True, they had been spared another night. But they knew the bombers would be back within hours. The children's thoughts strayed to their classmates; had they survived the night? Had they lost their homes, their parents, or maybe some limb? It happened frequently now that a classmate's seat would no longer be occupied.

Was life nothing but suffering? It certainly was in Germany. Rosi restlessly turned. Was it not the same in England or in Russia or wherever a war was fought? They were expected to hate all these unknown enemies, but she couldn't. She felt their pain. Tirelessly, the government radio did its best to prop up the mood of the people—hardly an hour went by without news of yet another victory: "Five enemy planes downed, two enemy ships sunk, four hundred enemy soldiers killed!"

But weren't those soldiers human, too? The little girl tightly closed her eyes. Wouldn't their families feel the same pain as she would?

Doubt, gnawing doubt, haunted her. They were always hungry and shivered from the bitter cold. They suffered the callousness of their teachers and trembled at the thought of Nazi officials and the ever-present ears of informers.

Questions, unanswerable questions kept her awake.

Was life nothing but suffering and dying for the fatherland?

What would tomorrow bring?

More of the same? Or worse?

Would it ever end, this misery?

She wiped another tear from her eyes. Too much pain in this world, she thought, more than she could bear. Most alarming of all was the constant reminder of the government, the dreaded admonition relentlessly repeated at school and at Hitler Youth meetings, in newspapers and on the radio, the hideous warning: "We must be victorious! No German will survive a defeat!"

Victorious? Her head throbbed. She had asked her mother about the prospect of victory. But mother had evaded her question, "Maybe the Oracle of Delphi might know," she said, and then added, "But I doubt the Oracle would tell us."

To the little girl the solution seemed so obvious: enjoy life and let others enjoy it, too. Why make life miserable for one another? But adults seemed to have different ideas, strange ideas. This dark side of human nature was beyond her understanding.

How wretched, these sleepless nights, knowing that at any moment death and disaster could strike. She rolled over again. If only mother were here, she thought, and searched her memory for mother's consoling words:

"Dream of the happy moments of your life," she had told her. "You can choose your thoughts. Choose them wisely."

She tried. And tried again. It was not easy to conjure up happy times amidst this atmosphere of gloom. But mother had told her how to do it:

"Imagine yourself at the foot of a mountain. Climb it step by step. Admire the trees; each is so different. Look at the pine needles around your feet. Picture the clouds in the sky, some white, some gray. When you pass by the little pond, watch the ripples of the water and look for the little frog. Tell him your troubles, and you will fall asleep."

Three days later, bombs hit their immediate neighborhood. Horrendous detonations shook the earth, numbing their ears. The draft blew out the candle, leaving them in pitch darkness. Another detonation, and another, and another. "I hope Death will come quickly," Rosi prayed, trembling in her bones. But Death did not come. Not here. Not now. Death took Gretchen, her best friend, instead.

Three weeks had gone by, but Rosi's pain had not lessened. She was pale and withdrawn. Tears kept ruining the pages of her homework. Tears kept soaking her pillow at night. Gretchen kept crowding her mind. One night, she pictured Gretchen so vividly that she dreamt about her, a strangely wonderful dream. She saw Gretchen under her favorite tree with two other little girls, all dressed in white, talking, playing and laughing. But there was something special about them, something different. There was no strife, no anger, no meanness. They were genuinely happy, and without fear. Rosi awoke with a start. "This is it," she realized. "We need to be kinder to one another and rejoice more."

The shadows of the night no longer frightened her; they seemed to smile and gaily whisper:

"Look at the sunny side of life, and all that is beautiful.

"Look at the funny side of life and laugh.

"It is better to laugh than to bemoan the inevitable."

Comforting thoughts these were! They gave her the key to unlock her smile again. She was no longer a helpless victim of these wretched times. She had control over her life, not much, but no one could take it away: She could smile. She could be kind. She could be happy, and maybe make others happy, too.

The 'Enemy' — A Construct of Politicians

Liberty without learning is always in peril and learning without liberty is always in vain —John F. Kennedy

After December 1941, the intensity of nightly air attacks on the cities increased exponentially. No longer a mere dozen British planes were dropping bombs, hundreds of U.S. squadrons reinforced them.

It's suicidal to stay in the city, Edith realized. But to take children out of school and Hitler Youth meetings required a government permit. She quizzed her children about the Hitler Youth: they learned about their glorious leaders, sang marching songs, and knitted socks for the soldiers at the front. They were urged to work hard, do their duty, and be loyal to the Party. At government expense, they could learn most any sport or craft they desired. No youth was ever seen idle. Juvenile delinquency was unheard of.

Edith could not deny its positive aspects. Youngsters who have nothing to do, easily get into trouble. But she knew Edgar's feelings. He did not want his children exposed to Nazi dogma. Since not attending was out of the question, a remote location in the mountains provided an answer.

Edith tracked down her father's old doctor. He'd been retired for years, but was called up again to work at the local hospital.

The doctor remembered Edith well and was glad to help. After examining the children, he filled out health certificates and an urgent request that the children be sent to a higher altitude. Thanks to this document, Edith was able to escape with Maria and her two younger children to their mountain cabin.

129

Their only neighbors would be an old farmer a mile down the hill and a vacant hotel at the top of the mountain.

She planned to home-school her younger children, but Peter would have to go to boarding school. Her scant knowledge of physics and math, Latin and Greek were not up to the task. She did not share Hitler's bias against learning; Peter was to have a good education.

The ski cabin had served the family well for occasional weekends. Now it was to be their permanent residence, a big challenge! The cabin had no electricity. Candles, difficult to buy during the war, provided their only light. No electricity meant no radio and no news, since batteries were unavailable. They also had no telephone. In effect, they were cut off from the world. Visitors would be their only source for news. But visitors would be rare. Few people knew their whereabouts and those who did could not reach them unless they took the train and hiked five miles to their cabin.

The cabin also lacked gas. The only source of energy—for cooking as well as heating—came from the trees they cut down and chopped up for firewood, loads of firewood. During the long, cold winter, the upstairs bedrooms remained unheated. A glass of water in the bedroom froze solid by morning. Down covers and hot-water bottles made the beds tolerable, but getting ready for bed was another matter. The children would have gladly dived under the covers fully dressed, but mother came to inspect, and that ruled out this happy alternative.

There was no running water either. A small creek brought water to the house since pipes and insulation were denied to non-Party members, and Edgar still refused to join. When the creek froze during the winter, leaving them high and dry, they resorted to melting snow. This was no trifling matter. A pot full of snow produced barely a cupful in its liquid form, and water took on the value of gold, especially on Saturdays, the day of the weekly bath. A wooden sit-up tub would be moved into the kitchen, and from early morning, snow was melted and water heated. Edith got the first turn in the tub. Next, the children would be scrubbed. Then it was Maria's turn. And finally the laundry was soaked in it. The remaining brew was used for flushing the toilet. Precious drops of fluid gold!

A friend of Edith's in the Ministry of Education provided textbooks. Yet Paul and Rosi, elated to have escaped school and its dragons, hardly realized that their mother's informal lessons were a continuation of their education.

Every other day, Paul and Rosi skied down the hill to fetch milk and an egg or two from the nearby farmer, a crafty old man, who delighted in outsmarting "rich city folks." He would scribble an arbitrary figure on his blackboard on the wall. This, he declared, was what they owed him. Then he added current charges and demanded cash—otherwise no goods.

The children protested, argued and objected; they knew they did not owe a cent! But the farmer ignored them. He turned deaf and calmly went about his work. Not until he saw the money on the table would his hearing return. He carefully counted the coins, mumbled to himself, and filled their container. He played the same game every time they came, probably his way of surviving in the harsh climate where the soil was so poor that potatoes grew to the size of plums. Maybe a competitor or two might have changed his ways.

Incessant storms whipped up giant wind drifts that altered the landscape. For weeks on end, temperatures remained below zero degrees Fahrenheit—the sky a leaden gray. When on rare occasions the sun did break through the clouds, the snow sparkled like diamonds.

Once in a while a full moon lit up the night, and when it did, Edith took the children for a stroll on skis in this suddenly magical winter wonderland.

Lacking radio and television, they improvised their own entertainment. For holidays, the children wrote and enacted little plays. Parental garments served as costumes and were ingeniously pinned together, causing frequent bursts of hilarity. In the evenings they sang folksongs accompanied by Edith's accordion. She was a strong believer in the benefits of music. When they lifted their voices in song, she felt, the wounds of the day were soothed and a feeling of wholeness injected into their lonely world.

After the nightly singing, they gathered around the big table to play games.

"Doppelkopf," Paul announced, dealing the cards. "My turn to win." He did not like to lose.

"No reading, Rosi," Edith reprimanded. As often, Rosi was glancing at a book hidden on her lap. "One candle is not enough light to read by."

Candles were scarce. Only one at a time could be burned. During the long winter, darkness set in at four o'clock.

"Play! It's your turn."

"You'll lose if you don't pay attention," Maria added; she liked to win, too. Maria was part of the family here and shared in all evening activities. She dearly loved card games and often outwitted the others.

Later at night, they crawled under their covers, not just to keep warm, but also to muffle the distant rumbling of the air attacks in the valley below. They could not see the cities, but if the sky lit up toward the north, they knew bombs were falling on Chemnitz where Edgar had the main branch of his business. If the red sky hung to the northwest, it meant Leipzig was burning where grandmother Mina lived, and if the fiery sky stretched to the northeast, it would be Dresden, the city of art and beauty, where Peter was in boarding school.

The hardships of war! Every day. Throughout Europe. Would their leader ever have the courage to end this senseless war? Edith thought of her college roommate in London, who had a baby just before the war. And her friends in Prague and Warsaw; would they blame her for the war her country had caused? How about her friends in Copenhagen and Belgium, and her neighbor's daughter, who lived with her husband in Rotterdam? All enemies now? It made no sense. They were her friends; what did it matter where they lived?

Often, squadrons of enemy bombers flew directly overhead. On a clear day one could see them flying in perfect formation, majestic and beautiful, high above the fragile earth.

"It is a scary sight, but also ...," Rosi paused, she could not think of a fitting word. Awed, she held on tightly to her mother's hand as they watched hundreds of enemy bombers flying in perfect formation directly overhead.

"Can they see us down here?"

"I doubt it. They look like birds, magnificent birds of steel, don't they? They won't bother us. They have missions to fly, cities and factories to bomb. It's sad to know they'll cause death and destruction."

Rosi eyed the planes reproachfully—not birds of song, but predators of death. She remembered the eerie sight after the last air attack in the city. So much rubble; so many homeless, so many dead!

As she listened to the serene humming of the planes overhead, rebellious thoughts flooded her mind. There must be a better purpose for those metal birds in the sky. She had seen enough suffering to last her a lifetime. Why should young men kill other young men? Why should planes cause death and destruction? Why not fly for the fun of flying?

"It must be grand to soar like a bird! I would love to fly," she exclaimed, "but not enemy missions."

"So would I," her mother confided. "Did you know that Charles Lindbergh and the Wright Brothers were convinced that the invention of the flying machine would end all wars? They could not conceive of men using the airplane to kill their fellow men."

"Did they use planes during the last war, too?"

"During World War I? They did. Actually, the war spurred the development of the airplane." She gently scooped up a handful of freshly fallen snowflakes and blew them into the wind. They swirled and hovered and glided softly to the ground. She followed them with her eyes and added, "During the first World War, chivalry ranked high among the pilots. They respected the enemy pilot who braved the sky as they did, and rarely shot him down."

"They shoot them down now."

"Yes," her mother conceded sadly. "Respect has been replaced by fear; the fear of being killed if the enemy is not killed first. It's a fiercely competitive struggle."

The bombers were still droning overhead. Young men in their prime, Edith thought, feeling the pangs of a mother for her sons, bravely fighting for their country. One day they'll be victorious. I hope it will be soon.

She could not imagine how Hitler with his tiny, even though valiant, country could prevail much longer against a large world he had labeled his enemies. Deep in her heart she hid a traitor's thought. She was ashamed to admit it even to herself—yet she could not do otherwise: she considered the man who had caused this war as evil, and she did not want Evil to triumph.

She suddenly looked deeply somber. A terrifying thought had struck her. Would dictators and politicians own gadgets one day that could reveal the thoughts of their subjects? The idea was too preposterous to pursue.

They stood in front of their cabin, four feet of snow beneath their feet. Much like Russia, Edith thought. These days, her thoughts dwelled often in Russia where her husband was fighting. For a long time, mother and daughter stood deep in thought, both convinced that life was an impenetrable enigma with burdens for all to bear. When Edith found speech again, she sadly shook her head.

"War is not the answer," she said. "It is not human. No man or woman would willingly kill their fellow men unless they were taught to hate and fear them as *the enemy*."

She was not thinking of Göbbels, Hitler's mighty Minister of Propaganda, but of an American college friend of long ago. The friend had visited her brother's boot camp where he drilled to become a marine.

"Do you know what they chant?" her friend had told her aghast. "They chant Kill! Kill! Kill!"

She turned to her little daughter and wrapped an arm around her shoulders. "Many ugly things are said about the enemy. Be careful what you believe; discover the truth for yourself. Men and women in all parts of the world are much alike. We all have weaknesses; we all have strengths. We all suffer the same joys and pains, and have the same hopes and fears. We need to communicate and cooperate, not kill each other. We need to love instead of hate, and be compassionate!"

Temptation

Men are capable of every wickedness

—Joseph Conrad

The knock at the door sounded so urgent, that it compelled Edith to throw caution to the wind and open it. She had never acted that impulsively.

It was Ilse from the Inn, too breathless to speak. She had come to the cabin in great haste.

"Ilse, come in!" Edith exclaimed, searching the young woman's face for the gist of her visit.

"I had a call," she finally burst out, "a call from your husband! He's back from Russia. He'll visit you as soon as he can."

Edith collapsed into Ilse's arms, while rivers of tears began to flow, tears that had been dammed up during months of anxious waiting.

It was summertime at the cabin. All hands were busy pulling and pushing saws through the green wood of trees, splitting the logs to fit the stove, and filling baskets with blueberries to be canned for the winter. The mountain blueberry is minuscule, just like the small plant it grows on—barely six inches high. It does not measure up to the American blueberry that grows on bushes six feet tall.

Edith and the children scoured the woods for mushrooms, cleaned and cut them, and strung them like beads on a thread so they would dry for the winter. While hiking through the mountains, the children learned to recognize birds by their songs, and spent many happy hours climbing to the top of slender pines, chirping and warbling, and swaying in a wide arc as if they were swings.

In 1944, food shortages became critical, and Edith managed to acquire a goat to have milk for her children. Sitting on her little stool in the makeshift stable, Rosi came running in with a book in her hand and a question on her mind.

"Is yeast dead or alive?" she wanted to know.

"Yeast?" Edith carefully aimed the milk into the bucket. "Plant or animal?"

Rosi laughed, "It's not a plant and doesn't look like an animal." She eyed Alma, the goat. "But it does make bread dough rise." She looked to Maria for confirmation. Maria had just entered the stable with a bale of hay.

"So is it plant or animal?" Edith queried.

"The Encyclopedia!" Rosi shouted and ran off happily, while Alma kicked in her direction, nearly upsetting the bucket.

"But Gnädige Frau," Maria chided. "You explained yeast to me the other day!"

Edith laughed. "Maria, without you and your sourdough we'd have no bread! I gladly explain things to you, but Rosi has to learn that she can find out things by herself."

A couple of geese joined the menagerie—a hostile pair that hissed angrily, and with sharp teeth attacked any leg that trespassed into their territory.

It was rumored that deserters roamed the mountains. On Edgar's suggestion, Edith always carried a pistol.

One day while gathering mushrooms in the woods, Edith and the children heard slight rustling noises and noticed that two men were following them, hiding behind trees. Sensing the danger, they stayed close together. The men kept following them, carefully staying out of sight and getting closer.

"Arno's agents?" Edith thought in sudden alarm.

She stopped, looked pointedly back at her pursuers and cocked her Browning.

It was overcast. Arno had come to Leipzig for a few days. Viola's home was bombed and she needed help to find new quarters. Arno was good at handling these things; he wore the SS uniform, and had food and cigarettes to motivate people.

While in Leipzig he scheduled an urgent meeting with Hans, his SS buddy. Hans was a good friend to have; he could always be counted on "to act in the name of the fatherland." Obligingly, he had collected Edith's fur coats. He had taken away Maxi, their dog. Lately, Arno was nursing another grudge against his in-laws: their housekeeper. Maria had deeply wounded his feelings. She had slighted his manhood. She had haughtily rejected his approaches! Her look of scathing contempt when he had pinched her severely gnawed at him.

She needed punishment.

Besides, what entitled the Leutholds to have a housekeeper? Maria should be working in an ammunition factory—for the good of the fatherland. He called several times on Edith, but no one answered the door. Edith had told no one about their move to the mountains.

With her pistol cocked, Edith sternly eyed her pursuers. Slowly she fired a shot straight into the air—a warning to the men that she was armed. Then she turned in the direction she intended to take back to the cabin, took a deep breath and called with a strong and fearless voice: "Alex! Peter! Max!" as if these men were close by. She remained standing there, seemingly unperturbed, not budging, while watching with satisfaction the hurried retreat of their pursuers.

Later that evening, back at the cabin, there was a knock at the door. Maria jumped from her cozy seat by the big tile stove, a Tyrolean *Kacheloven* that heated the downstairs. It was made of beautifully hand-painted tiles and extended six feet along the wall and was six feet high. It had cushioned benches along two of its sides, where six people could sit in great comfort, leaning against the tiles to warm their backs. There was no better seat in the house.

"Stay there," Edith motioned to Maria. "I will go." Edith stood and thought for a moment. They could not pretend that no one was home. The light gave them away, also the smoke from the chimney.

"Talk loudly! With deep masculine voices," she told the children. They understood; they were to pretend that big, strong men were present.

Edith got her pistol and hurried upstairs. No one ever called in these isolated parts of the mountains. From the corner window she could see the front door and the person who had knocked. She saw one solitary man.

"Strange," Edith thought and scanned the nearby trees for others who might be hiding. The stranger knocked again. "I need to see his face," Edith realized, and noisily opened the window hoping the man would look up in her direction. And so he did.

"René! *C'est vous?*" she cried with great joy and relief, and hurried downstairs to open the door. There was much rejoicing. It was so rare they saw another human being! Maria brought food from the kitchen and all gathered at the table to hear the latest news. It had been many weeks since they had contact with the outside world.

"Are we still at war?" everyone wanted to know.

René nodded, his mouth full of food. Then he turned to Edith, "I was able to contact Edgar," he said. Ever since his return from Russia, Edgar had been assigned to the Draft Board in Berlin, and was able to look after his business, too,

139

which had been classified as 'war-essential.' Tiny, densely populated Germany had to feed its people entirely from its own crop.

"He is sending you his warmest thoughts." René continued. "He urged me to visit you. I have three days off. I brought you a French book."

René was a medical student from Marseilles. When the Germans occupied France, René was drafted into the S.T.O., *le Service Travail Obligatoire*, whose task it was to send young Frenchmen to work in Germany in exchange for French prisoners. Germany urgently needed workers. It gladly dispensed with its prisoners.

On the train to Germany, René had run into his college friend Pierre, whose mother had been Edith's classmate at *Le Rosé*, the Swiss boarding school. Through the college grapevine she had tracked down Edith's address and gave it to Pierre. The knowledge that her son would have a friend while in the country of the enemy gave her some peace of mind. Since Pierre was assigned to work in the far north, he passed on Edith's address to René.

René's assignment was as valet at the Marietta Hotel. He had a room of his own, ate in its cafeteria, took care of the luggage, and cleaned rugs and floors. He was well treated; in his own words, *ma vie, en fait, n'était pas mal* (my life, in fact, was not bad). After work, he was free to do as he pleased. He lost no time to contact Edith and quickly became a cherished member of the Leuthold household. The Gestapo would not have approved of Germans fraternizing with the enemy, but everyone was circumspect.

René loved poetry and literature, and like all Frenchmen, he had strong views on politics. In a hushed voice he occasionally shared them with Edith, but Edith preferred to discuss the

140

more pleasant aspects of life, such as books and philosophy, and René's future. He was going to be a doctor, René confided to her, and wanted a beautiful, lively wife and six children.[35]

When Edith and her children moved to the cabin, René came to visit them there.

"The irony of war!" René exclaimed. "I'm riding the enemy's train to spend my holiday with an enemy family."

"And you hiked many miles through enemy territory to get here. Were you singing *La Marseillaise?*" Edith teased him.

"*Non, non,*" he laughed, "But maybe I should learn to sing *Die Fahne hoch.*"

During his winter visits, the children taught René to ski. With five pairs of socks he managed to fill Edgar's boots, and huffing and puffing, he struggled up the mountain with them; Edgar's skis were heavy and long. On a particularly cold day, he turned to Edith and remarked, "Don't you think this is too tough for the children? They look positively frozen."

"We have no other challenges but the elements, René." Edith replied.

"But their lips are blue from the icy wind."

"Our winters *are* severe, but the children need to be outdoors. And they need to face problems. Sitting in a cabin all day is not good for them."

"But the long and arduous climb! Even I am exhausted."

Edith laughed, "And so am I, but it does them a world of good, René. They need to learn that they can handle the toughest effort and survive."

René could not counter this.

---

[35] He attained both. He married a charming, vivacious wife, who bore him six lively children.

"Life is not a bed of roses, René. Life can be mercilessly cruel. Who knows what life has in store for them, and us. One day the children will have to face life's hurdles on their own and need to be able to cope with them."

"*Vous-étez trés sage*, Edith, I bow to your wisdom," René murmured.

René was like a breath of fresh air, filled with youthful enthusiasm and joy. He never complained; on the contrary, he considered his stay in Germany as an adventure rather than a curse of war.

René was a reminder of a normal world. For Edith, he brought back memories of her happy year at the Swiss boarding school and he gave Edgar hope that there might be a future after all. René had no doubt that the war would end *bientôt*. For the Leutholds, it could not be soon enough.

Another month went by without word from the city or news of the world. Edith kept the children busy cutting and chopping wood and stacking it in neat, circular mounds to protect it from the weather. They read and studied. Another month went by.

And then one evening, there was a knock on the door, a happy, melodious knock, a knock that said I am glad to be here, I know I'll be welcome. They had just sat down for their evening meal when Edith heard it. She jumped up to open the door. She knew that knock. It had to be Edgar.

Maria hurried to the kitchen to get another plate. Edgar looked careworn and thin, not much better than the first time he visited after his return from Russia. And yet it seemed as if the sun had come out from behind the clouds and smiled again. It was good to have him home.

"How is Peter?" Edith wanted to know.

"Peter's boarding school has moved to its summer campus in the country." Edgar reported.

It was a great relief. Dresden had no industry and had never been bombed; still, war is war.

"I had dinner with Sylvia and Sigurd. Their presence makes Berlin nearly tolerable."

"Sigurd in Berlin?"

"Not even Hitler can send one-legged men to the front, though I bet he'd like to." Sigurd had lost his right leg during the Polish campaign.

"How about his practice in Vienna?"

"He closed it. Too unnerving to sit in judgment of his patients' sanity, he says. He's supposed to report them for sterilization, but can't do it. He's teaching now."

"Hitler's purity-of-the-race fixation!" Edith shook her head in dismay.

"On the more amusing side, his daughter Susanne recently shook hands with Adolf Hitler. She has a secretarial job at the Reichskanzlei. Ten of the younger and prettier secretaries were sent to Obersalzberg to be interviewed by Hitler."

"Did he need a secretary?"

"Apparently so. He had the girls brought to his bunker around midnight. After an hour's wait he shook hands with them and asked them their names and where they came from. And that was it. He had Borman put them up in his personal train until he would be ready to interview them. But nothing happened. Several weeks later—late one night—Hitler's men came to escort them back to Hitler's bunker."

"Weeks later?"

"So I hear. I'm sure the girls enjoyed their time off. Borman in person instructed them how to behave in Hitler's presence: 'Don't speak unless spoken to,' he said, 'and then say, *Heil, mein*

Führer,'" To the children's delight, Edgar's voice rose by an octave, while he curtsied with a girlish smile.

"Did Susanne get the job?"

"She didn't. Her friend Traudl Humps[36] did."

"Traudl, the dancer? I thought she was studying ballet."

"She took a part-time office job to pay for her lessons. When she passed her final examinations and gave notice, her boss told her she couldn't quit. New Reich regulations forbid employees to quit a war-essential job. Typing is war-essential, dancing is not."

"Hitler is interfering with everyone's life!" Edith protested, feeling pity for the young ballerina forced to be a secretary.

"Sigurd was certainly most grateful that Susanne did not get the job."

"I can imagine. You would be, too; but think of Susanne. She may have enjoyed the privilege of being chosen. I'm impressed that Traudl is such a good secretary."

"She isn't, but she's the only one Hitler interviewed."

"You said ten came for the interview?"

"All ten girls were asked to come back, but they were not interviewed. Hitler specifically asked for Traudl first, supposedly because she's from Munich, his favorite city. Her perfect Aryan looks may have helped."

A smile danced around Edith's eyes, but she did not comment in front of the children. "How is my mother?"

"Valiantly looking after her properties. There has been much destruction from the air in Leipzig, but fortunately no phosphor bombs as in Hamburg."

"Phosphor?" Edith asked, but Edgar changed the topic, and Edith understood. Some topics were not suitable to be dis-

---

[36] Better known by her married name, Traudl Junge.

cussed in the presence of children. Later, when the children were in bed, he explained.

"On impact phosphor bombs divide into millions of burning blobs that cannot be extinguished. People who are hit by even a small fragment die of excruciating pain. They can't wipe it off or get rid of it. They slowly burn to death. On the train to Berlin, I ran into a college friend of mine who just came from Hamburg and had seen it. He said the horror of phosphor bombs defies description. One of the soldiers in his regiment had been hit with it. In desperation, the man shot himself."

"Good God! Why do we do this to each other?" She covered her eyes to block out the image. "Are we using phosphor, too?"

"Thank God, Germany has no phosphor and it's too expensive to make."

"Aren't people fed up and tired of the war?"

"They are, Edith. But we have no choice. Anyone who complains will be taken into custody, and you know what that means. People are afraid. A few people still believe in Germany's victory, but they are getting fewer. And remember, Göbbels' clever propaganda machine is constantly reassuring us. The radio never mentions the unpleasant facts of war. It only reports Hitler's triumphs."

Edith knew and folded her hands. Her knuckles turned white from the pressure. Resignedly, she asked, "Is mother doing all right?"

"Arno is bringing her coffee from time to time."

The thought of mother getting her coffee brought a smile to Edith's lips. Mina dearly loved her cup of coffee. And yet, the idea that so many suffered, while others, like Arno, gained from the situation in shameless, selfish ways, annoyed her.

"Do you think it's his SS-uniform that gets him coffee, chocolates and eggs? What position do you suppose he holds? When I asked him during his last visit in Leipzig, he was most evasive."

"No one really knows, except that he is posted in Latvia. He's boasting grandly about his importance to your mother. Creations of his imagination, I suspect. One fact is certain, he knows how to use the uniform to his advantage."

"How can Viola love that scoundrel! He is the embodiment of Joseph Conrad's words: Men are capable of every wickedness."

Edgar did not approve of wickedness, but there was much truth in Edith's words, whether he liked it or not.

"Viola and her son just returned from a two-week holiday in Switzerland," he said.

"Switzerland? How can they leave the country? No one else can!" Edith thought of her own children and how desperately they needed food. Hungry Germans referred to neutral Switzerland as the land of butter and honey.

"Arno is a wheeler and dealer. Nothing is beyond his reach, no matter how dishonorable," Edgar replied wistfully.

For a moment, Edith was overcome by an intense desire for food. Just once to have a stick of butter again, a jar of honey, or a chicken for dinner. Not really for herself. Food was a means to a healthy body, not an end in itself. But her children were growing. They needed food. Her heart was aching to see them hungry, weak and undernourished. She was sick of serving them skimpy meals and having them leave the table hungry—day after day after day.

She looked at Edgar. He dealt in seeds. Seeds were highly in demand. They were like currency among the farmers. But she banished the thought. She knew her husband too well. Even if she had asked him to deal in the black market, he could not and would not have done it.

She realized that some people are just not capable of committing dishonorable acts. Her Edgar was one of them. It was not in his nature. He was born and raised in the tradition of honor and integrity—it was in his genes, an inseparable part of him. In her mind's eye she could see the early Christians when persecuted for their faith—afraid, and yet unafraid—marching to their death.

She reached over and squeezed his hand. She admired this honorable, steadfast man. It was easy to succumb to temptation—the pressure under the National Socialists was high. And so were the rewards. It was tough to resist. She thought of the SS-official who had taken her fur coats for his personal gain, and of Arno who used the power of his uniform to rob the innocent and helpless. Power! It brings out the worst in people who are selfish and weak.

A Happy Interlude
Love is Eternal —Irving Stone

Rays of the autumn sun penetrated the somber atmosphere of Edgar's office when the telephone rang, and a shy voice at the other end asked for Maria.

"It's Otto, isn't it?" Edgar asked with a smile on his face. He remembered the young gardener from next door and the furtive glances Maria and Otto had exchanged. He remembered well that wonderful feeling of being in love. "Are you in town?"

"I am. I've got a two-day furlough. We are being shipped out to the eastern front on Sunday morning."

"And you wanted to see Maria?"

"I do."

147

"The family is no longer in the city. They are in the mountains for the duration of the war."

There was a long and heavy pause, "Maria too?"

"Maria too." Edgar sighed feebly, feeling the pain that his words had inflicted.

There was no reply, but Edgar did not have the heart to hang up. "You would like to see her, Otto, wouldn't you?"

"I sure do," came the hopeful answer.

"Maybe we can work out something." Edgar broke into a happy grin. "I am driving up to the mountains tomorrow morning. If you like, I will take you along. We can get you on the late-afternoon train, and you will be back in the city by Saturday night around 20:00. How does that sound to you?"

An overjoyed, "Really?" was all that Otto could muster.

"But there are strings attached, Otto. If you don't mind, let me tell you." Edgar took a deep breath. He hated to do this to the young man, but he knew he had to. "Maria is like a daughter to us, and we have to look out for her. I know she likes you, too, but we don't want her to get pregnant, not until after the war, when she's married. An unwed mother is a dreadful stigma for a woman, and an even worse one for the bastard child. I know you wouldn't want that for Maria or a child of yours." Edgar paused after his long and moralizing speech. Then he quickly added, "Think it over and let me know if you want to come."

"I do want to come!" came the happy answer, "I'm glad you're looking out for Maria."

Edgar nodded approvingly. He liked the young man.

"Good. Where do I pick you up?"

It was Saturday mid-morning when Edgar arrived at the cabin. There was great rejoicing and Edith was pleased to

148

see Edgar looking less distraught than usual. He seemed to be in a most cheerful mood.

"Maria," Edgar called into the kitchen, "I left an important envelope in my car. Would you mind getting it for me?"

"Glad to do so, Herr Doktor," Maria dried her hands on her apron and smiled.

"You can take your time, Maria. We'll have a late lunch today. No hurry."

"I'll come with you, Maria," Paul offered. He liked the idea of an excursion down to the inn where the car was parked. Maria was good company.

"No, Paul," Edgar intervened. "I'll need you here. I have an important task for you." And while Maria went to the kitchen to put on her shoes, Edgar bent down and whispered to his son, "Undo Maria's apron. She won't need it on her errand."

With a glint in his eyes, Paul took off for the kitchen. He sneaked up behind Maria, undid the bow, and tickled her. Then he pulled away the apron like a trophy and triumphantly carried it off. Maria jumped up with a squeal and pursued the little villain, but stopped in her tracks. Her employer had appeared in the doorframe. Embarrassed, she put on her other shoe.

"Paul," Edgar did not raise his voice, but it was compelling, "Take Maria's apron upstairs and place it neatly on her bed." He turned to Maria with a smile, "If that is alright with you, Maria?"

Relieved, Maria nodded and left, while Edgar took his wife into the garden to tell her about the surprise waiting for Maria in his car.

"How good of you! Maria will be thrilled." Edith was overjoyed. "Maria deserves a break. I often worry about her. It is very lonely up here. No one to talk to but us. No young men. Nothing but trees. I would hate to lose her."

"I know. It's a comfort to me, too, that you are not alone."

"She's a fine young woman. Do you think she'll be safe with Otto? Paul might have been a good chaperone."

"Don't worry. I won't let her come to harm. Otto and I have a gentleman's agreement. He's an honorable young man."

"Edgar, are you placing candy in front of a young man with a sign: Don't touch?" she smiled chidingly, yet greatly relieved.

An hour and a half later, a blushing, beaming Maria returned—not with an envelope, but with a happy Otto in tow. Lunch turned into a joyful celebration of life. No one spoke of war. Happiness seemed to engulf everyone.

Otto had never been in the mountains before, and as soon as everyone had folded their napkin and placed it in their napkin ring, Edgar sent the two young people off to explore the woods, but not before he had put his hand on Otto's shoulder and met the other's gaze. Otto nodded, and satisfied, Edgar sent them off.

"Wouldn't mind to dance at their wedding," both Edgar and Edith thought, as they strolled hand in hand across the meadow, savoring the warm glow of young love.

A Bomb in Hitler's Bunker
Pride and Self-Hate are one Entity —Karen Horney

The day dawned hot and humid—the day Hitler was to be assassinated.

Why did it have to fail?

Its success would have saved thousands of lives!

In the Erzgebirge, it had been drizzling all week—perfect conditions for mushrooms to burst forth. Edith and the children found loads of them and cleaned, cut and strung them like beads on a necklace to dry for the winter—seven feet long, a record for the summer.

In far-away Berlin, the attempt on Hitler's life, the *Putsch*, was about to take place. Hitler had recently moved from his bunker in Obersalzberg to be closer to Berlin. The war was going badly. He wanted to be near the capital to exert greater control. The *Wolf's Lair*, his new underground headquarters, was hidden in the forest near Moysee. It was made of impenetrable, sixteen-and-a-half-foot steel and concrete, covered with flat roofs of grass and shrubbery.

It was hot and humid. The guards wore netting over their faces; hordes of ferocious mosquitoes haunted them.

Hitler had visibly aged. He had lost weight and was more irritable than ever. He could no longer bear to be alone; he needed the company of others. It forced his indomitable willpower to take command and to insist on certain victory.

Yet the enemy kept advancing. His staff and visitors were riddled with fear and despair. They depended on Hitler's optimistic presence. They wanted to be reassured that his secret weapons were to be launched at any moment.

They did not see Hitler when he was alone, when he fell apart. Hitler abhorred his own company. He could not sleep at night. He was dependent on his worshippers to prop him up— worshippers he could deceive and manipulate.

Ever since childhood, Hitler had but one raison d'être—to dominate others, to pretend he was better than they. He manipulated his mother. Ruthlessly he bullied his classmates. It soothed his feelings of inferiority, his inner loathing of himself.

During his Vienna years he added hatred to his arsenal— intense hatred toward everyone. In 1914, his antipathy toward the Jews and Slavs compelled him to enlist in the German army. After Germany's bitter defeat, his hatred intensified and drove him to express it in fanatic, rebel-rousing rhetoric against the allies and the government.

Later, his deep-seated resentment of educated and knowledgeable persons drove him to ignore his military advisors and to countermand the counsel of the German Officers Corp. He wanted to be in sole command; he alone knew best; he alone was all-powerful. As ultimate confirmation of his power he elevated himself above the German law.

Yet in spite of his supreme power, or maybe because of it, he loathed himself. He despised himself more than his enemies. Was he aware of his life-long charade?

The rapture and worship of the once desperate masses had died away—his people were suffering more than ever before. His once victorious armies had been slain—his battered, scattered soldiers were retreating. His goal of world domination was crumbling before his eyes—the end was approaching with unalterable certainty.

Nothing, not even his iron willpower could alter the bitter fact: The world had enough of the evil he had caused. It was determined to stop him.

Hitler kept up his victorious front, but it took a heavy toll. The thought of defeat gnawed at him like a venomous viper. Nor was his pretense cheap. During the twelve months preceding the attempt on his life, Hitler spent 92.6 million Reichmark to purchase 881 paintings. With big fanfare, he donated them to the city of Linz, his hometown by choice. Linz was to have the finest museum, outshine Vienna, and become *the Cultural Center of the Greater German Reich*.

Unable to face the world and haunted by anxiety, Hitler sought distraction in nightly tea parties held in his underground bunker. He needed diversion more than ever. Not a night passed without a gathering. *Demand invitations* brought him reluctant guests. No one spoke of war. They strained for amusing anecdotes to cheer their impenetrable leader, who reclined on his sofa stretching his legs.

"We shall see victory. Absolute victory," was his unalterable stance. "Soon we shall take revenge." Revenge was one of his favorite words. He savored it as a vulture savors blood.

Hitler's midnight tea parties were the quintessence of stress. They lasted until the first light of dawn, but not even then, not even to his closest associates, did Hitler reveal the fear he felt; not even to Eva Braun, his mistress, who had suffered Hitler's ill treatment year after year.

Poor Eva Braun! Hitler scorned her, neglected her, used her, kept her hidden and never paid her the slightest courtesy. He forbade her to smoke, sunbath and dance. She lived in poverty for years. During the war he permitted her to live with him in his underground bunkers. Her diaries express deepest unhappiness. One of her entries reads: "I wish the devil would fetch me! I would be better off with him than here ... today I waited three hours in front of the Carlton for him and then had to watch as he bought flowers for Ondra and invited her for dinner ... He wants me only for his needs."[37]

Among his regularly summoned midnight attendees beside Eva Braun and his four young secretaries were Hitler's early supporters from the streets of Munich. They held top government positions now.

Himmler headed the secret police and the infamous SS. At Hitler's tea parties Himmler gallantly kissed the ladies' hands. Always anxious to please Hitler, he talked in a soft and gentle voice, telling of his efficient, friendly way of running his detention camps, and how he personally taught the inmates to be

---

[37] *"Hitler, Eine Biographie"* by Joachim Fest, pp. 744-745.

useful. One of the inmates, he recounted, had set fire on four occasions. So Himmler put him in charge of the fire watch.[38] It was a brilliant move, Himmler modestly commented; the man has turned into a competent inmate.

In Hitler's presence even the much-feared Borman became as docile as a lamb. He knew what his ruler demanded—absolute subservience. Life and career were in jeopardy if one differed with his views. "Jawohl, mein Führer," was Borman's standard answer to anything Hitler said.

Joachim von Ribbentrop, the winemaker, was summoned, too. Hitler had appointed him to be Germany's Minister of State—to the embarrassment of many Germans. When sent to Great Britain to attend the Coronation of George VI, Ribbentrop greeted the English Monarch by raising his arm, clicking his heels, and saluting him briskly with "Heil Hitler!"

Göbbels' presence at the midnight teas provided at least some spark of amusement, usually at someone's expense. Göbbels was a man of wicked cleverness with a tongue that could cut through steel. One day, Hitler's Reich Press Chief mentioned that he got his best ideas while in the bathtub. Göbbels promptly retorted, "You should take a bath more often, Dr. Dietrich."[39]

On July 20th, 1944, a meeting was scheduled in Hitler's conference room to discuss the Allies' landing on the beaches of Normandy. Hitler had dismissed the Allies' attempt as foolish and doomed to failure. The successful landing came

---

[38] "Until the Final Hour, Hitler's Last Secretary" by Traudl Junge. Copyright © 2002 by Ullstein Heyne List GmbH & Co. KG, München. English-language translation copyright © 2003 by Anthea Bell. Published by Arcade Publishing, New York, NY. pp. 124-129

[39] Ibid. p. 95

as a horrendous shock. It convinced Hitler's generals that the war was lost. They knew the dismal state of their exhausted troops and the lack of supplies. They had seen the destroyed cities and hard-suffering civilians. Hitler had not. He had not left the safety of his bunkers since the beginning of the war. It was a wake-up call for the generals. They realized that Hitler's hypnotic talk of victory was nothing but deceit. Worse, they understood Hitler's utter lack of concern for his people. He would drive them until none were left alive.

Every one of the generals had sworn a sacred oath of loyalty to Hitler; they were ready to break it. They wanted to stop this useless bloodshed. Yet they knew Hitler did not. A peace treaty could only be negotiated over Hitler's dead body.

Colonel von Stauffenberg volunteered for the job. At the July 20th briefing in Hitler's bunker, the Colonel carried an explosive device in his briefcase. He placed the briefcase carefully against the leg of the conference table, barely six feet from the spot where Hitler stood, and the device went off as planned.

At that precise moment, General Bodenschatz leaned forward to point out a detail on the map, and it was his body that took the brunt of the explosion. Hitler's male secretary and several others were killed; Keitel and Jodl were injured, and others, like General Schmundt, were severely burned and died later in the hospital. Two men were hurled several meters, and the conference room collapsed. Yet Hitler remained unharmed, with nothing but minor injuries to his eardrums and his arm that he carefully hid from everyone but his doctor.

Of all the ironies, the failed putsch turned into a grand triumph for Hitler. It reenergized him. It provided him with an excuse for his military setbacks—they were the obvious result of his generals' conspiracy. Above all, it proved that God and Destiny were on his side. They had protected him so that he, "the Chosen One, could lead Germany to ultimate victory." His confidence and optimism rose to an all-time high.

The people, listening to Hitler's captivating speeches after the putsch, felt hope again. Göbbels exploited the putsch for every ounce of its propaganda value: "Our Führer's survival is proof of his God-given invulnerability," was heard everywhere. To Hitler, this was not a myth; it became a reality, an obsession. Destiny had chosen him to rule the world, and he wanted the world to know it.

Now that this "criminal clique," as he called the conspirators, "has been exposed and brought to justice," he had great hopes for the future and his ultimate victory. "The putsch," he said in a radio speech, "may have been the most fortunate event for our future."[40] Hitler's wrath toward the assassins was merciless. "I shall make an example of those criminals, ... I shall make sure that no one else can keep me from victory or do away with me."[41] Göbbels hunted down not only the conspirators, but also several hundred others whom he merely suspected or did not like, and brought them to a cruel end.

Visitor from Dresden
Dresden is the Venice of the North —Reiseführer

An icy snowstorm blew around the cabin, creating giant snowdrifts. It was the last day of February 1945. In the mountains, isolated from the world at war, one day was like the next. The weather provided the only variation. But it never served as an excuse to stay indoors. No matter how cold or

---

[40] *"Inside the Third Reich"* by Albert Speer, p. 393
[41] *"Until the Final Hour, Hitler's Last Secretary"* by Traudl Junge, pp. 124-129, p.134

stormy, by late morning, their studying done, the children donned their outgrown clothes and braced for the daily outing.

It was tough to climb to the top of the mountain, considering their empty stomachs, the threadbare jackets and the solitude. There were no other skiers, no lifts to carry them uphill, no snow machines to smooth the slopes for their descent.

Skis were heavy and long. They were made of hickory wood and measured to the tip of the outstretched hand. Leather straps served as bindings and wrapped around the boot.

Before most outings, they had to wax their skis, rubbing vigorously the stiff paste onto the skis. Otherwise, the snow would stick to them like a sack of cement. Well-waxed skis, of course, had a habit of sliding back when climbing up, but they gladly lived with that.

Frequently, strong storms swept down the hill, turning the outing into a battle with the elements. Each breath had to be wrested from the wind, while the icy snowflakes hit their faces like a thousand pins and needles. The descent was not easy either. The snow was deep and often crusty, eager to catch a tip of their skis and propel the skier flying through the air.

Nonetheless, the worse the weather and the tougher the climb, the cozier it felt to be home again. Even the monotonous food—potatoes, peas or cream of wheat—tasted wonderful when famished from the exertion. The physical challenge had refreshed body and soul.

Returning from the slopes one afternoon, they noticed footsteps by the door. Their father had come for a visit, and with him an old friend, the Countess Westarp. They found the lady sitting in their living room, mute as if in shock.

Her home—no, the whole city of Dresden, "the Venice of the North" with its winding river Elbe and its historic castles, ancient churches, picturesque bridges and art galleries, was no more. The most devastating air raid of the war had demolished the city and burned it to the ground.

For centuries, the city of Dresden had been the seat of kings. It had no industry and had never been bombed. Throughout the war, it had served as a haven for thousands of children and refugees.

Then on February 13, 1945, three months before the war ended, the Royal Air Force launched an air attack on Dresden never equaled in the annals of war.[42] It covered the city with 700 tons of high explosives and phosphor bombs. Within hours, the city turned into a raging inferno.

Thousands of planes returned the next day to drop more bombs. The intense fire spread throughout the city and depleted its oxygen, causing thousands of people to die of asphyxiation.

On the following day, the Flying Fortresses of the 8th Army Air Force dropped an additional 700 tons of explosives on the city.

On the next and fourth day, planes returned for a last time. This time not bombers—there was nothing left to be leveled— but single-engine P-51 Mustang fighters that targeted civilians who had survived and were fleeing from the raging fire.

During those four days and nights an estimated 150,000 to 250,000 civilians, mostly women and children, died, many of them burned alive or suffocated to death.

Allied reports state that it was Churchill's attempt to demoralize the civilian population to hasten the end of the war. Unfortunately, civilians had no influence on Hitler's policies. Nothing mattered to Hitler but power and victory.

---

[42] According to John Keegan and other historians.

The Countess had spent that fateful week in Leipzig visiting a friend, and survived. But she had lost her family, her neighbors, her friends, her home, and her capacity to laugh.

Magnificent parks once graced this splendid city. Not a tree was left. The houses where Schiller had composed his *Ode to Joy* and Carl Maria von Weber wrote his *Freischutz* were leveled to the ground. And so was Dresden's famous *Frauenkirche,* a prominent cathedral of the Protestant faith dating back eight hundred years. In the eighteenth century it became a Catholic church when the Protestant King of Saxony had a chance to also be crowned King of Poland if he converted. So overnight, his subjects became Catholic, too. They were not asked. The choice of religion, just as the decision to send men into battle, was at the pleasure of the sovereign.

"Will you be staying with us, Countess?" Edith asked while pouring a cup of tea for her friend.

"No," Edgar explained, looking at the mute lady, who sadly shook her head. "She will drive back with me on Sunday to return to her friends near Leipzig, whom she visited during the fire."

The Countess nodded slightly, sipping her cup of tea, looking vacantly at the window laced with delicate patterns of frozen flakes of snow.

Wickedness

If you wouldst live long, live well; for folly and wickedness shorten life —Benjamin Franklin

Far away in Latvia, Arno stretched contentedly in his bed. He enjoyed his post in the Baltic. He had a fine Latvian house and plenty of liberty. As a member of the occupying forces, and wearing his SS uniform, he felt seven feet tall.

A Latvian girl was snuggling in his arms—Nadia, a local girl with good connections. She was not beautiful, but she was knowledgeable and discreet. And that was important. The German military strictly forbade fraternizing with the local girls.

On the floor next to Arno's bed was a pile of official death notices. Arno had requisitioned them and scrutinized them nightly in his bed—leisurely and with keen anticipation. He was searching for a particular name. It was not an easy task, because the names of dead soldiers were printed sometimes by rank, sometimes by date, but never in alphabetical order. Arno had skimmed thousands of names, but he did not tire of it. It gave him immense pleasure. He was sure one day he would come across the name he was looking for—the name of his brother-in-law Edgar listed among the casualties.

"A brilliant idea to have Edgar transferred to the Russian front," he prided himself. "Why should I share Nobel's estate when I can have it all. I know Edith won't contest it."

He chuckled and pulled Nadia closer.

"When will you marry me, Arno?" Nadia rubbed her head against his shoulder.

"Nadia, darling, you know I want to marry you. But I am bound by SS regulations. The SS has to approve whom I pick for a bride."

"Am I not good enough?" Nadia pouted.

"I think the world of you! You know you are better than anyone. But you are Latvian; you don't have a chance to qualify right now. Let's wait until this bloody war is over."

"Will it ever be over?"

"Don't you worry, honey. The world changes every day. I could marry you without approval, but I'd be shot. You wouldn't want that, would you, honey?" He rolled on top of her and smothered her with passion.

"Things will be different after the war," he consoled her. He stroked her hair and glanced at his watch, "Nadia dear, I mustn't be late. I have to be at the Commander's house at 20:30. I'll drop you off on the way. We'd better hurry."

Spring was in the air, but it lacked the pre-war mood of carefree happiness. It was 1945, the most devastating stage of the war. Arno took Nadia to her apartment and returned to his house. He had no meeting with the commander; he wanted privacy to listen to the news from the BBC. He locked his door and swiftly set up his short-wave radio; he had confiscated it from a Latvian. It was nearly nine o'clock, time for the news from across the Channel.

Hitler strictly forbade the possession of short-wave radios. He and Göbbels, his minister of propaganda, fabricated their own version of the news—news that did not necessarily coincide with the true state of affairs. Arno had heard rumors that Russian troops were rapidly advancing. German newscasters did not mention that fact; they still promised victory.

Anxiously, Arno tuned in to the BBC. The news of the British Broadcasting Corporation was not encouraging: "German defenses have collapsed; Allied troops are recapturing Normandy and France; the Soviets have regained lost territories and are nearing the Polish border."

The Polish border? They will be liberating Latvia within days! Arno intended to be far away when the enemy rolled in. He listened intently, his heart pounding. His truck was ready, loaded with the treasures he had accumulated, including a set of civilian clothes, and, thanks to his good connections and a hefty bribe, new identification papers omitting his SS membership. He would leave in a day or two, he decided. The details of his *strategic retreat*, as he called it, had to be carefully planned.

161

The screeching sound of breaks interrupted his thoughts. Adrenalin shot through his arteries. He jerked the electric cord from the socket, hurried to the closet, and tucked the radio into a large box. For all eventualities, the box was labeled, *To be taken to the SS Office of Investigation, (content: misc. items recently confiscated).* The box stood in the darkest corner of the closet with the label facing the wall. A long coat hid the box. However, if the box were to be found, it would gain him nothing but praise for his obvious loyalty.

Arno could hear swearing outside, and his face lit up. He had a local man dig up the walkway to the house, so it would be treacherous and slow to traverse in the dark. It prevented prowlers from sneaking up to the windows. Frequently, he scattered a few pieces of broken glass. In enemy territory such nuisances had to be expected. A hard fist banged on his door. Arno reached for his pistol and peeked through the window. He caught a glimpse of a uniform.

"Who is it?" he called.

"SS-Gruppenführer Müller," came the reply.

Arno hurried to the door, grinning. A brilliant idea had hit him. "Müller, good to see you." He warmly shook the other's hand. "Let me get you a glass of beer. How about a bite to eat? I'm quite good at fixing a sandwich."

"No food, but I can use a beer," Müller replied, settling himself into an armchair. He pulled a map from his briefcase and unfolded it on the coffee table.

"The enemy is coming closer," he mumbled, looking nervously toward the open kitchen door. "No one's in the house, is there?

"Not a soul but us, Müller. Do you really think that the front is moving closer?" Arno enjoyed feigning ignorance.

"Probably just a temporary setback. I'm banking on Hitler's new weapons."

"I'm not so sure, Arno. I think we need to get ready to defend ourselves. The locals may give us trouble when they hear they're going to be liberated."

"The enemy can't be that close. Do we know where he is?"

"We haven't a clue."

"Can't we communicate with our people at the front?"

"That's the problem. All lines have been cut."

"But we've got to know where the enemy is, Müller. It's crucial," Arno scratched his head and then exclaimed in disbelief, "You mean we have no contact at all?"

"None."

"We've got to find out!" Arno rubbed his chin. Then he turned to Müller, "You are right Müller, absolutely right. That brilliant mind of yours! I will do it. I'll reconnoiter. Somebody's got to do it. We can't prepare unless we know where the enemy is. I know the area pretty well, Müller. We have no time to lose. I'll leave within the hour." He folded the map, but stopped short, "I'll need a pass for my secret mission."

He got a sheet of official stationary and handed it to Müller, who scribbled the words that Arno suggested. Müller was still baffled about that brilliant idea he supposedly had. But if someone thought him brilliant, Müller wasn't going to argue. Arno, never at a loss for words, kept talking until the front door closed behind the visitor, and Arno was alone again.

With a broad grin Arno folded Müller's "Letter of Authorization" and tucked it into his billfold. It would be most useful for getting gasoline, passing checkpoints and avoiding inspections. This official pass would get him back to Germany.

He made two calls before he left, one to his secretary and one to Nadia. He wanted them to know about his secret mission. It would give him time to gain distance from Latvia before they asked questions regarding his whereabouts.

Then he took the receiver off the hook. He wanted to talk with no one before he left, especially not with Müller, who might have second thoughts and call the mission off. A quick trip to the kitchen completed his preparations. Barely 35 minutes had elapsed since Müller's departure. Arno was ready for his *strategic retreat.*

With a smug grin he climbed into his truck and headed west, widening his distance from the Russian front. The mere thought of enemy soldiers made him jittery. Thanks to his uniform, his letter of authorization and his fertile imagination, he passed all checkpoints without being questioned. His black-market cigarettes bought him hot meals wherever he went. He avoided hotels; they were under government surveillance. Yet he did not forgo the comforts of a good bed. He slept in farmhouses. Civilians were terrified of SS officials and didn't dare to turn them away. Thus, he made it back to Leipzig in four days and in acceptable comfort.

He was still ahead of the Russians. But for how long?

The Russians had crossed the border into Germany—in spite of Hitler's threatening tirades. Nothing could stem that Russian flood that Stalin had set into motion, least of all Hitler's Home Defense, consisting of untrained, unarmed seniors and children.

In the city of Leipzig, Arno's progress slowed to a crawl. Bomb craters and rubble blocked many streets. Would he be safe here from the Soviets? He doubted it. They were already fighting in the streets of Berlin. Leipzig, located in the center of Germany, was on the same longitude. To be safe, he needed to flee farther west. Nadia's friends had heard about unimaginable cruelty of the victorious Slavs.

164

"We have no time to lose. The Russians may be here by tomorrow," he urged Viola minutes after his arrival. He had not seen her for nine months. "I want you and Wolfie to drive to Frankfurt within the hour."

"How about you?"

"I'll get another truck from the company, and follow when it's loaded."

"I can't drive a truck!" Viola wailed aghast.

"Nothing to it," Arno tried to brush aside her fears, "I'll show you how. Remember, anything we leave here, we will never see again."

It was a strong argument, but Viola, an intimidated subject of Hitler's police state, was not convinced. "No way," she protested. "I'm not driving an army truck. I'll end up in prison."

She had a point, and Arno drove to his office to get a company truck for her. He strode into his office with a hearty smile, warmly shook hands with his secretary and accountant, and secured the keys for the company's largest vehicle.

Ernst, the company's only remaining male employee, was resting his weary bones by the small stove. He was too old and infirm to be drafted.

"Ah, Ernst, you look fit as a fiddle," Arno greeted him jovially. "Help me transfer the items from one truck to the other. Brought you a fine bottle of whisky and some cigarettes." The old man's face lit up and he set to work with a will.

When the two men returned to the apartment, Viola was preparing food for her Wolfie. He wanted his meals when he was in the mood for them, not when it was mealtime. Since the two men had plenty of work before them, Arno saw to it that Ernst, too, got something to eat and a beer to wash it down with. Then he turned to his son.

"Wolfie, I've brought you a few things," he said, and produced a lovely little radio he had confiscated from a Latvian. Wolfie studied it carefully, "It's not new; it's been used."

"What do you mean!" Arno exploded. "Thousands of people would be thrilled to have it."

"It has a scratch."

"Where? You mean this tiny scratch? It's barely visible. If you don't want it, I'll keep it," Arno stormed and reached for it. But Wolfie was quicker.

"It's not yours; you just gave it to me," he replied haughtily. "What else do I get?"

He's too smart for me, Arno thought proudly. "Here, everything in this box is for you. I'd better help your mother."

Viola, accustomed to obeying her husband, had gathered things in frantic haste. If the Russians were to occupy the city, she knew there would be rape and violence. She was willing to leave, but not alone, not in a truck, and not without proper preparation. She sobbed and yelled sporadically.

"I must say good-bye to mother before I leave," she wailed.

"No good-byes, Viola. There is no time," Arno shouted. "The Russians are north of the city. They may be here by tomorrow."

As a last resort he promised to bring Mina with him to the West, though it was not on his agenda. "Hurry, my dear. Here is a list of places for you to stay and of people to contact, so I can find you."

After anxious instructions in driving the truck, she was off into an unknown future, her son wailing at her side.

Arno heaved a sigh of relief and with Ernst returned to the Nobel firm. The warehouse yawned with emptiness. Barely a score of furs remained.

166

"Let's load the best ones into the truck," he ordered. When done, they returned to the apartment to add practical items and valuables. Everything was expertly stacked, not a square inch wasted. The most important treasure was yet to come.

At the Leipzig Museum of Fine Art, in its underground air shelter, Nobel's valuable collection of art was housed. If Arno desired an opportune moment to get his hands on that collection, it was now, during the bloody chaos of the Third Reich's final hours.

Next morning, at 9:00 AM sharp, Arno with his most ingratiating smile approached the curator of the Leipzig Museum: "Frau Nobel has sent me to take her art collection to the West before the Russians carry it off to Moscow."

The curator was a small, delicate intellectual with a whimsical sense of humor and a shrewd mind. Nobel had liked the young curator and taken him into his confidence. Thus, the curator knew that after Mina Nobel's death seventy percent of the artwork was to go to the Museum.

For a moment, the curator hesitated and studied Arno's face. Should he release those priceless works of art to Arno, an irresponsible good-for-nothing?

No, he decided, a thousand times no!

It was risky to refuse the wishes of the SS. Yet he decided to take the risk.

"Why certainly," he said. "Very wise of Frau Nobel. I just heard the news, though. The radio assures us of certain victory. You don't seem to think so?"

Arno was not prepared to discuss politics. "Of course we shall be victorious," he replied edgily. "It's just a temporary setback. But since the Russians are close, Frau Nobel wants to take all precautions."

"I quite understand. A wise precaution. Where will you take the paintings?"

It's none of his business, Arno thought angrily, getting hot under his collar.

"We are wasting precious time, Curator. Where shall I take my truck so it can be loaded?"

"Let me see," the curator rubbed his chin. "The keys to the vault are held in trust by the Museum's director. With a written statement from Frau Nobel, however, I am quite sure the director will let me have them." He held out his hand for the document.

A lengthy debate ensued, both men straining their wits to achieve their ends—Arno to get hold of the art, the curator to preserve it for the Museum. In their first round, the unflappable curator prevailed. Arno had no choice but to back off. He needed to find Mina and persuade her to give him a written request.

It was a long drive to Mina's house, which gave Arno time to simmer down and plan his strategy. He knew she would strongly object to her husband's art leaving the sacred halls of the Leipzig Museum. On the other hand, he had a way with her. He had a way with all women.

Mina had just finished lunch and the sight of her favorite son-in-law put her in a most pleasant frame of mind.

"Don't tell me the Russians are coming. Do something about it," she reprimanded him.

"I plan to, dearest Mina. I plan to save your dear husband's fine art collection."

"Don't worry about the art, Arno. It is very safe were it is."

"I really should be thinking of saving my family's belongings first," Arno replied plaintively. "But when I realize how

168

much these paintings mean to you and your beloved husband, I can't let them fall into Russian hands. It's my duty to the family. I know you want me to take these treasures to the West before the Russians take them to the Hermitage."

For a moment, Mina hesitated. The Hermitage? Not a bad place for these works of art. She was a great admirer of the Hermitage. It would be a safer place for her husband's art than handing it over to Arno.

Arno stepped behind her and gently massaged her neck. "Nothing better than a bit of massage in these stressful times," he said sweetly, and Mina banished her thoughts. Arno, after all, was running her husband's company. He was her favorite son-in-law. He had brought her coffee. Nonetheless, the art would stay in the Museum where her husband wanted it.

Arno never conceded a battle unless he got what he wanted. His eloquence was formidable, and his delivery irresistible. And in due time Mina signed what Arno had typed. But the moment she put down the pen, she realized her mistake. Her backbone stiffened. But it was too late. Arno, quick as lightning, whisked away the letter and took off. He remained deaf to her frantic words and hurried out of the house with Mina in pursuit. He jumped into his waiting vehicle and drove off. He never looked back.

Arno returned to the Museum bursting with glee. Mina's letter would place a huge fortune into his hands, and—most gratifying—assure his victory over the obstinate curator.

With intense pain, the curator watched as crate after crate with paintings of the old masters was carried from his vault. One glance at Arno sufficed to tell him that the Museum would never see these treasures again. He could visualize Arno selling them to black-marketers for a fraction of their value. They probably would end up at garage sales one day, or be forgotten in someone's attic. Among them were sixteen priceless etchings, crafted in the sixteenth century by Alfred Dürer. The very thought made his soul ache. But he was helpless.

The curator was not an emotional man, but as he watched the gloating profile of Arno, dressed in his SS uniform, giving orders to Museum personnel to carry away this priceless art, he succumbed to an emotion of intense fury.

That black Schutzstaffel uniform, he suddenly realized, must have been the inspiration of the devil in person. Tall men clad in sinister black, adorned with impressive insignia, and given excessive authority to intimidate the world around them! These men were the devil's henchmen, he thought, and his fingers twitched. A strong impulse to strangle Arno overcame him.

He stared at the man, visualizing the crime. Arno was a good fourteen inches taller than he was, and twice his weight. He glanced at the security guards and the workers, all members of the Nazi Party. He could not count on their support.

Helpless and deflated, he turned and disappeared into his beloved Museum. The odds were not in his favor—he, as so many others, was impotent against the force of evil.

On his long drive to Frankfurt, Arno had leisure to think. He carried millions of dollars worth of art in his truck. It gave him a sense of immense wellbeing. He felt a warm kinship to Göbbels, his hero, who also had garnered great riches.

There was one damper, though; Mina knew that the art treasures were in his possession. Legally, they belonged to her. After her death they would go to her three daughters and the Museum. Yet the idea of sharing had never found favor with Arno; he wanted it all. His prolific imagination would have to wangle a better solution.

Indeed, even before he entered the Autobahn, he had devised a scheme. He would store the crates in a safe place where Mina could see them whenever she came to visit. In the meantime, he would sell their contents in far-away places—Brazil, America, or South Africa—repacked in new crates, of course. The empty crates would be carefully closed and retained.

He had pressured the curator into providing him with a list of the paintings and a photo of each. This would facilitate selling them. Once the paintings were sold, he would invite Mina and the three heirs to open the crates. They would have a festive dinner with wine and a speech by him about his daring and courage to save the art. He chuckled at the thought. We shall all be profoundly shocked and dismayed to find the crates empty. It will be child's play to dissuade Mina from investigating the unfortunate theft.

Elated with his plan, he whistled the Horst Wessel march. As to the furs, they would keep him and his family in luxury and food for years to come. Arno could think of no greater pleasure than to do business in the murky arena of the black market.

Or could he?

His mind was never at a loss when imagining pleasures. His pulse quickened as he thought of Katrina. She lived not far from where he was. Ah, he remembered her well—as if it was yesterday, not fifteen years. That voluptuous body of hers, her hot temper and fiery passion! He would have married her, but she didn't have much of a dowry. He had lived with her for nearly two years. Wonderful years. She had just been divorced from a well-to-do, elderly husband, and had relished the amorous attentions of Arno, a vigorous young man. Arno inhaled deeply; he could smell the fragrance of her body and feel her smooth and silky skin.

She lived some twenty-five kilometers east of the highway Arno was traveling. He was certain she hadn't moved; no one moved unless bombed out. And he knew she still loved him passionately. All his girlfriends did.

One little detail had slipped his mind. He had promised to marry her. To Arno, marriage was simply something you promised a girl. He had tried to put off the wedding as long as he could. As he explained to her, he was waiting for his sizable inheritance to clear the courts. He had told similar tales to his other women friends, and it had kept them happy and patient. When he could no longer postpone the wedding, he quietly left her, without an explanation, without a word, without a good-bye.

It was on the day of their engagement party. He had taken her to the hairdresser and promised to pick her up two hours later. Arno did not pick her up. Two hours later, he had cleared out his belongings and left town—in her car.

Too much pressure to tie the knot.

In spite of his great fondness for women, Arno never bothered to understand them. He ignored the old tenet, that "Hell hath no fury like a woman scorned."

A scorned woman! That is exactly how Katrina felt.

Weeks after he had left her, she could still feel her fingers itching to wring his neck. If she ever got hold of him, she swore, she would teach him a lesson he would never forget. For many months she had to suffer her family's patronizing sermons and her neighbors' meaningful glances. She did not forgive or forget.

Arno pulled over to the curb and studied the map. He remembered well where she lived. It was a scant forty-minute drive. No distance at all, considering that five days and nights had elapsed since he'd held Nadia in his arms. His pulse quickened, his face flushed. He burst into his favorite song, a song he could well identify with.

> *La Donna e Mobile, qual piuma al vento.*
> *Oh wie so trügerisch sind Frauen Herzen, ...*
> Fickle is woman fair,
> Like feather wafted,
> Changeable ever.
> Constant, ah, never!

Yes, it described him to perfection if "woman fair" read "man debonair."

Smartly, he brought about his truck and headed east instead of west.

K atrina was sitting in her tiny room rubbing her thigh. During an air raid, the walls of her home had collapsed and a beam had pinned her leg to the ground. She had lain there for many painful hours. Her leg had given her trouble ever since. She could stand again, but barely walk.

She still looked beautiful, too thin perhaps, but her eyes still had the old fire and her long hair the deep luster in spite of her lack-luster life. She had married again, and was thrilled when she found herself pregnant. But she lost the child in her eighth month when running for the air shelter.

Two weeks after that dreadful day, her husband was transferred to the eastern front, and two months later he was reported as missing in action. The letter arrived just before a bomb leveled her home and she lost all she owned. Nothing but her underground shelter remained, four windowless walls, a bunk, a closet and a stove. She was living there now.

Two days earlier she had lost her job. The Nazi official, whose assistant she was, had taken off. She, too, wanted to flee.

But how?

Public transportation had come to a standstill. She had no car of her own, and no valuables or money to barter with. Worst of all, she could not walk. She was stuck, left to the mercy of the Russians.

Katrina's chin rested heavily on her fists. She sat at her little table, brooding, her thoughts engulfed in gloom. She did not hear the truck or the steps that were approaching. It was that voice calling her name that snatched her from her dejection.

A familiar voice!

She recognized that voice and it struck her like a thunderbolt. Her heart raced and her fingers twitched to seize a dagger. Revenge at last!

She jumped from her seat, but the sharp pain in her thigh brought her to her senses. She slumped back into her chair and rubbed her thigh. Today a rogue at my door, she agonized, and tomorrow the Russians.

The thought of Russian invaders sparked her brain into action. She had prayed fervently for days to find refuge from the Russians. Perhaps this was the answer to her prayer. She closed her eyes to collect herself, but only for an instant.

She was ready to receive Arno.

Arno still owes me a car, she thought bitterly. He will not leave me behind this time. With a sweet, sphinx-like smile full of promise she called his name, "Arno, Liebling, is it you?"

Arno has not changed, Katrina thought. A few pounds heavier, but otherwise the same charming chatter, the same bright promises and the same endearing demeanor. Indeed, Arno insisted on taking her with him further west.

"Where did you park your car, Arno, dear?" she asked with concern.

"Right in front of your door, as always," he replied smugly.

"Not a good place, dearest. One of the police officers considers this his personal spot. Let me show you a safer place."

She threw a few items of clothing into a pillowcase and guided him out the door, leaning heavily on his arm.

They drove around the block, and parked across the street.

"What time shall we get up?" she asked him sweetly when they settled for the night.

"How about 6:30?" he proposed. "Or is it too early for you?"

"6:30 is fine," she replied, trying to divine his thoughts. Did he mean 6:30? She doubted it.

Arno awoke toward three in the morning. He could hear rumbling in the distance. Enemy guns that close? I should have left at 2:00 in the morning as I intended, he agonized remorsefully. He wanted to leap out of bed and leave, but that would awaken Katrina.

Nervously—inch by inch—he worked his way off the bed. He had carefully arranged his clothing on the chair, so he could find it in the dark and get dressed quickly. He groped for the chair. Ah, there it was.

And his clothes? Where were his clothes?

Not on the chair.

He got to his knees to feel the floor.

Nothing.

He crawled to the little table, and the other chair.

Nothing.

Maybe in the closet. He had noticed Katrina hanging up her clothing. She probably hung up his uniform, too. Carefully he fingered his way along the wall. There it was. Slowly, slowly he opened its door—old closets tend to creak.

The sound of the distant, high-pitched artillery fire was grating on his nerves. The darkness did not help. Where was his confounded uniform with the keys to his truck? He felt something, but no, it was his SS cap—the last thing he wanted. He groped with both hands, but he found nothing.

Then it struck him. Where were Katrina's clothes? They were hanging there last night.

His heart skipped a beat. Perspiration clouded his eyes. The closet was empty.

He stifled a scream.

Had she left? It couldn't be.

He felt his way back to the bed, and fingered the covers.

Nothing but a pillow under her blanket.

"Light," he howled, "I need light!" He searched for the candle and the matches they used the night before—her only source of light. He found the candle, but not the matches. Feverishly he felt every surface. Nothing! He grabbed the stool and smashed it against the floor, once, twice, a dozen times until only part of a leg remained in his hand.

"My truck," he winced, and lunged toward the door, stubbing his feet on the debris on the floor. Swearing profusely, he found the knob and yanked it hard. But it did not give way. The door was locked.

He remembered the deadbolt lock. He had praised Katrina for her prudence.

"Katrina," he yelled. "Katrina!"

No one responded.

"I'll break down your door," he yelled, "and then your neck!" The door was a heavy, fireproof steel door.

"My truck," he screamed. "I've got to get to my truck." He kept hitting the door, stark naked.

176

He was trapped below ground in perpetual darkness. No food, no clothes, no chance of escape. His only possession: an SS cap and a stolen watch. Half crazed, he collapsed on her bunk and sobbed.

Cannon Fodder

Fight for the glory of the Fatherland —Hitler

"What's the sense of it all?" Peter thought despondently, as he surveyed the bicycles neatly parked in front of the post office. He poked his fist into his empty, growling stomach; his boarding school should be feeding him lunch at this hour.

"Steal a bicycle!" he muttered in dismay. He disliked the idea. Common thieves did that sort of thing, not he. And yet, that was the plan he and his three friends had agreed upon.

"What are we living for anyway?" He could not think of an answer. A few months earlier, his friend had asked that question at a Hitler Youth meeting.

"For the glory of the fatherland," they were told.

Pompous nonsense, Peter thought at the time. It's more likely they feed us to the enemy as cannon fodder. He realized how close his surmise had come to the truth as he was waiting that noon for the signal from his friend to get a bike.

It was spring of 1945. American and Russian forces were rapidly advancing on Berlin. Hitler's Germany, which was to last a thousand years, was about to collapse. Yet Hitler, like other dictators before and after him, was not prepared to give up. If his people did not win him a glorious victory, they did not deserve to live. Hitler would not surrender. He would rather see total destruction.

Just before Germany's total collapse, Hitler ordered schools to be closed and all boys to report to their nearest Civilian Defense Post. They were "to take a stand against the enemy."

That morning the principal of Peter's school had called a meeting to read these order.

"What shall we fight with?" one of the youngsters asked; the boys were fifteen and younger.

"We have neither weapons nor uniforms for you," the principal admitted, wiping his brow. He, too, had pondered this question.

"You may have to pick up a gun from a dead or wounded soldier," he counseled. "The Russians are only a few miles away." He looked at the paper in his hand and repeated, "We must defend the fatherland. Everyone proceed at once to the Civilian Defense Post in Dresden! They may have an answer."

With these words the boys were herded through the gates of their school into a hostile world.

Take a gun from a dying soldier? End life as cannon fodder in the last moments of a senseless war? It was not an enthralling prospect. Peter and his three friends agreed on that point and made their own plan.

First of all, they needed some sort of transportation. Without it, chances were high that they would be caught and possibly shot for desertion—they were easy to spot, wearing the school's uniform.

They decided to go to the post office where people parked their bicycles—none locked. With a bicycle, they had a fair chance of escape.

Nervously, they scattered about. They had to act simultaneously, before post office patrons got alerted. Uneasily, Peter looked at his friends. There was the signal. Yes, he did want to live. He got a bicycle and scurried away—not east to meet the enemy, but west to get home.

Peter made it to the city in good time, faint with hunger, but glad to be alive. The house was still standing and the key still in its hiding place, but the place were deserted. They must be at the mountain cabin, he figured, and early next morning, he bicycled to the train station to catch a train.

Having no money to buy a ticket, Peter searched for the person, who collected and sold tickets on the train. "I want to get home," he pleaded with the old man, "but I don't have a penny. Will you take my bicycle in trade?" Beseechingly he searched the other's eyes.

The conductor, a grandfather of eighteen little ones, shook his head. "Can't do that," he declared sadly, looking at the skinny boy. "But I can lock it up for you until you come back."

Together they walked to the conductors' warming room and left the bicycle there. "You come and see me, when you get back," he said. "Let's hope it will still be there." He locked the door and turned to Peter, "You'd better get on that train, son. It may be the last one."

"Thank you, sir!" Peter beamed, and after a moment's hesitation he added, "That bicycle—you can keep it. I won't be coming back." Peter was glad to get rid of the bike now that he was safe. Contently, he hopped onto the train to get home.

It was pouring when Peter started on his six-mile hike to the cabin, but he did not mind the rain. He preferred it to Russian bullets.

Night had fallen when he arrived. It was pitch dark, and so was the house—not the tiniest flicker of a candle. Yet the door was unlocked. He called, but no one answered. "Spooky," Peter thought as he entered.

The house was deserted. Peter lit a candle and found the kitchen stove still warm. He was tired, locked the door, ate some cold soup, and went to bed. In minutes, he was asleep.

In the middle of the night, a bizarre sound crept slowly into his consciousness. It sounded like a pebble bouncing against his windowpane. "Pingggg." There it was again. Drowsily, he turned over. Another "pinggg." Now he was awake and got up to take a closer look. It was dark and raining heavily. There; another pebble. He waited and watched.

Someone leaned forward from behind the tree and took aim again. Peter recognized him. It was his father. Peter waved and hurried downstairs to open the door, while Edgar went to get the rest of the family. They were waiting further back in the trees, hungry, tired, cold, scared and soaked to their bones.

On the previous afternoon, women and children came up from the village to hide in the forest. They stopped at the cabin and told them that Russian troops were approaching. All resistance had collapsed. Russians, they heard from other refugees, were looting every house and raping every woman. The road, on which the Russians were advancing, was about a mile from the cabin. Edgar took no chances and with his family went into hiding, too.

Toward four in the morning, after a wet and miserable night, Edgar returned to the house. He was glad to see it still standing. But was it occupied? He quietly turned the doorknob, but found it locked. He had left it unlocked on purpose, so the foe could enter without breaking the door. Obviously, someone was inside. It could be villagers; it could be Russian soldiers. With luck, it would be his son Peter. He decided to find out and looked for pebbles to throw at Peter's windowpane.

III. Aftermath

Woes of the Vanquished

History is written by the victors,,, with little interest in the woes of the vanquished —Paul Kennedy

The Russians did not come that night or the next. The villagers went home and Edgar returned to his duties in the city. He took Peter with him and placed him with a farmer friend in the country where he would be safe, have food and wholesome work until the war was over. The enemy seemed still far away. The radio was still promising victory.

Edith, Maria and the children went about their daily life as usual, cut off from the turbulence of the world. It was May 1945. They had just sat down for lunch, when shots were fired right outside their door. One, two, three, ... a dozen shots. Had the war come to them? Rosi flew upstairs to her bedroom to fetch her few items of gold jewelry. She crumpled them into a scrap of paper, stuffed the paper into her pocket and raced back downstairs. Just then the door crashed in and a dozen soldiers pointed their guns at them.

"Hands up . . . Line up against the wall!" the men ordered.

Edith, Maria, and the two children did as they were told. They stood against the wall, staring blankly at the gun barrels pointed at them. One of the men searched Edith's pockets and removed her wristwatch. Another glanced at Maria. She wore a summer frock and a kitchen apron, her neck and arms were bare of adornments. Obviously, she had no treasures. And the children? They were of no interest to the soldiers, who were eager to search the house.

Three of the soldiers stayed behind, guarding the vanquished. Two Czech soldiers spoke German, and Edith began a quiet conversation with them as if it were the most natural thing to do. She offered them lunch. Not that there was food for so many, but the gesture reassured the children and calmed the young soldiers, too. They were Czech soldiers, they said. The war had ended, and Czechoslovakia was reclaiming the Sudetenland. This was Czechoslovakia now; the German border had moved a few miles further north.

While standing against the wall, they heard the soldiers rummaging about upstairs. Was it five minutes or five hours? It seemed like an eternity. Time stands still when facing guns.

The children stood wide-eyed and motionless, Maria moved her lips as if in prayer, and Edith calmly talked with the men. She asked them about the recent happenings in the world, and about their lives and their plans for the future now that peace had returned. Imperceptibly, the strained enemy confrontation eased into a friendly conversation.

At long last, the search party crowded into the room again. Czech phrases flew back and forth. They were deciding the family's fate.

One of the soldiers motioned with his gun for Edith and her charges to precede him out of the house. By the front door hung two tattered little jackets that Edith quietly handed to the children to wear. Wordlessly they put them on, little knowing what significance these jackets would have for their future.

Silently, they followed the young soldier down the mountain. Rosi's mind was racing. Was he going to shoot them? Maybe not—more soldiers would have come along. On the other hand, he had a rifle—they didn't stand a chance against him. As long as Mother remains with us, she reasoned, surely all will be well. What was it that Hamlet said? "To be or not to be, that is the question"—too sinister, she decided, and struck it from her mind. She was not ready to think of dying.

They came around a curve on the mountain path, where the highway came into view, a highway packed with thousands of refugees, pathetically dragging bundles of belongings. It suddenly struck the young girl what horrors befall a conquered nation. To be shot was no longer so frightening.

As far as the eye could reach, the highway was crowded with refugees. They were barely moving. They had come from the Balkans where Germans had settled for centuries, from Hungary, Bulgaria, and Yugoslavia. They had formed German settlements there and had preserved their customs. The victorious Russian army had driven them away.

The bundles they carried were all they had left. At the border, Czech soldiers would search them first and keep what they pleased. Then it would be the Russians' turn to search and abuse them. Eventually, they would reach Russian-occupied Germany, where the struggle for survival would begin in earnest.

Would they be joining the fate of these refugees?

Edith, with motherly interest, chatted with the young Czech soldier. She asked him about his family, his life and his aspirations. He no longer was the enemy; he was a human being again. They walked through the fields not far from the road where the endless throng of people was waiting. The crowd would have stoned them for passing, had it not been for their armed escort.

They were getting closer to the checkpoint now. Frightening sounds filled the air, soldiers shouting, women screaming.

Dante's inferno, Edith thought. Young and old alike were stripped and searched for valuables before they were allowed to move on. The meadow around the station was littered with treasures the soldiers fancied to keep.

Edith and her little group had reached the checkpoint. Their escort exchanged a few words with the Czech border guard, and then with one of the Russian guards. It took only moments. Then he handed Edith a loaf of bread and waved her across the border. A loaf of bread? It was worth its weight in gold. Where had it come from? They did not know; it happened so quickly.

They had crossed the border! Stunned, they hurried away, afraid they might be called back and searched. As they gained distance, it slowly dawned on Edith that a miracle had happened, a miracle of kindness in the shape of a young enemy soldier. He had spared them from hours of misery, from search and rape; he had whisked them swiftly across the border, and given them a loaf of bread.

They headed for Oberwiesenthal, where the Leuthold's visitors used to arrive and depart. It was a ski resort, but during the war the ski lifts closed and tourists stopped coming. Edith planned to stay a few days. She nursed strong hopes that they might be able to return to their cabin; uranium was being mined close by. Surely, the Americans would not relinquish an important uranium mine to the Communists.

They entered the first inn on the outskirts of town. The old innkeeper looked them over guardedly. A bedraggled lot, she mused. Two women without a purse, and not a single piece of luggage.

"Are you refugees?" she asked.

"We are," Edith replied. "We had a cabin on the *Keilberg,* We were forced to leave."

"I don't take refugees. Besides, the inn is full." She pointed to the door.

"I do have money," Edith assured the woman, but the innkeeper's face did not soften.

"Give me a moment," Edith explained as she sank into a low, creaky chair. She untied her shoe and took it off. Gently she extricated several layers of shoe inserts that she herself had cut out of cardboard, and carefully examined them. Everyone watched in suspense.

"Here it is," Edith exclaimed, pulling out one hundred marks.

"Well," the innkeeper mumbled, and reached for them. "I'll take them. You can stay for a few days." But Edith was not inclined to let go of her treasure.

"What are your rates?" she wanted to know; she disliked the woman's greedy attitude. The woman did not reply; she sulkily eyed the bank notes in Edith's hand.

Edith placed the bank notes gently back into her shoe and leisurely put it back on. Then she took Paul's hand and turned to the door.

"I think we'll have some food first. We can discuss your rates later," she said.

Paul heaved a sigh of relief when the door closed behind them. "I am glad we didn't stay," he said. "She's a nasty woman, grumpy and mean." Maria nodded and squeezed his hand; little Paul had put it in a nutshell.

"We'll go to the pretty Mountain Inn." Edith encouraged him. "I don't like its location. It's in the middle of town, but they know us there. They will be civil."

The owner of the Mountain Inn, Frau Hanns, was more than civil. She found two adjacent rooms for them, conjured up a little toy for Paul, and brought them soup. Before long, the children lay in bed. They had no pajamas, no toothbrushes, no comb and no soap, but they had two towels thanks to the kindness of the owner, who brought two of her own. Hotels no longer provided towels or soap.

Tears were running down Paul's cheeks as he lay in bed in his underwear. "Why did we have to leave?"

"The region belongs to Czechoslovakia now. It belonged to the Czechs before the war; we bought our land from a Czech owner. I don't blame them for claiming back their big and beautiful mountain," Edith explained and paused. "Let us thank God for the many good years we've had in our cabin, and especially for His protection today. We were very fortunate."

Rosi, who was half asleep, opened her eyes in surprise, "We were?"

"We were! Think of the enemy soldiers who came with their guns today—yet they did not shoot us. There were twelve of them, twelve enemy soldiers. We were only four, two women and two children—yet they did not harm us. Think of the kind soldier who gave us a loaf of bread. There is much kindness in this world." She smiled. "If that soldier had not taken us across the border, we would be standing on that highway right now, and probably be standing there for days. Someone looked out for us."

Maria, who like Paul had been bemoaning their fate, furtively wiped a tear from her eyes and folded her hands.

Edith did not mention what she was most grateful for—the soldiers had not raped or harmed them, nor had they touched her daughter. Rosi was only thirteen, but she was tall and in the eyes of Slavic soldiers might well have been considered an adult.

Nor did she mention another bit of good fortune—the children's old and tattered jackets. What if the soldiers had refused to let the children put them on or had examined them? Those old little jackets hid substantial family assets, bank notes, and valuable pieces of jewelry. It had taken her many days and much secret effort to sew them into the lining so no one would notice the hidden treasures. She had never sewn before and disliked needlework, but she had done it, and her plan had worked.

Early next morning, Rosi woke up with a start—the war had ended! Chills went down her spine. She tried to remember the previous day; there was no doubt in her mind that it was true, the soldiers clearly told them that the war was over. Anxiety raced through her slender frame. She had heard the government's admonition not once, but a thousand times: "We must be victorious. No German will survive a defeat." Germany had been defeated. They would have to die.

She had grown up sheltered and isolated from the world, without radio and TV, and lacked an adult's sophistication. She did not know that politicians' words have nothing in common with truth or fact. She took the admonition literally as just another cruel aspect of war. They would have to die.

But when and how? This When and How took on sinister imaginings. It had to be soon, she figured; the war had ended.

It was puzzling, disturbing and frightening.

But life went on. Day after day.

They stayed at the Mountain Inn for several weeks. The streets were not safe; they were all confined to their rooms. Edith managed to secure a Russian grammar book and intensified her studies. If she could follow the Russian broadcasts, she might learn of their chances to return to their cabin.

In the meantime, they needed food, toothbrushes and clothes. They needed blankets and towels. The stores were empty; absolutely nothing could be bought. Reluctantly, she decided that the children would hike back to the cabin, pretending to be looking for mushrooms. For days she agonized over the plan and would have preferred to go herself, but what if her children ended up motherless. Nor could she send Maria, a young girl in her prime.

The most urgent reason for going was to leave a message for Edgar. He had no way of knowing where they were. It was impossible to contact anyone. And Edith was certain that he would be looking for them. If the Czechs were to capture him, it would spell certain disaster for him. The children knew the woods well and would easily find their way to the cabin. If it was empty, they were to pack some of the necessities into a knapsack and return.

The children were thrilled about the plan. The hotel room was like a prison to them. They wanted to roam the woods again, and have a chance at adventure.

They set out early one morning equipped with a basket for mushrooms. It was cold and gray and they walked briskly until they reached the woods. They breathed easier under the green canopy and started to enjoy their outing. Dutifully, they searched for mushrooms until they had a dozen.

Then they hurried to their house. When they saw it—their cabin—they felt a sudden and profound love for it, more than they ever had before.

Until that day, they had taken the cabin for granted. Now they realized what they had lost—not just a roof over their head or a place to live. No, it had been their home, their haven from schoolteachers and Hitler Youth, and their refuge from air raids. They stood quietly for a long time, both deep in thought, remembering. Who might be living there now, they wondered.

Not a sound could be heard. Not a puff of smoke rose from the chimney. They took a deep breath and ventured closer.

"I'll peek in the downstairs bedroom and you in the kitchen and living room," Rosi suggested. "Then we'll try the front door."

Everything appeared to be just the way it was when they had left. Even the front door was unlocked.

"Look at this," Rosi called, who was the first to enter. The soldiers had thoroughly searched the place and dumped the contents of all drawers onto the floor.

"What a mess! I wish Maria could see this," she laughed.

"My room was never *that* messy," Paul added with great emphasis.

As instructed, they distributed the various notes for their father and gathered the necessities. Toothbrushes and pajamas were still in their accustomed place. Paul pocketed a pack of cards, and Rosi added mother's French book and Maria's sewing kit and purse. They had found all the items on their list. Paul checked the pantry for anything edible—nothing but Maria's last loaf of bread. It was hard and moldy, but he took it. It was better than nothing. Then they were on their way.

Rosi's heart pounded as they left the cabin.

"I feel like a burglar," she confided. "You too?"

"Don't be silly. Have you ever heard of a burglar stealing his own toothbrush?" her brother muttered, his heart racing just as wildly.

"I wish we could sing," he added. "But we'd better not."

Quietly they moved down the mountain, keeping their eyes and ears alert for strangers. They were glad that it went downhill. Their big knapsacks and bags slowed them down. All went well; they encountered no one. On the outskirts of town, they knocked on Magdalena's door. Frau Hanns had arranged that they could leave most of their baggage with her. Walking through the middle of town heavily loaded would call unwanted attention. Their booty would be transferred to the inn in small increments.

The children were thrilled with their success and could not wait to visit the cabin again. It provided an exciting escape from the dreary confinement to their hotel room.

Yet the second trip went not as well. A group of Czech soldiers surprised them on the trail. A sharp bend in the mountain path had muffled the sound of the approaching soldiers.

When they suddenly did hear the men's voices, they dropped their bags under the first clump of trees and jumped behind the next. A grave error, they quickly realized. But it was too late. The bag with the pots and pans had clattered noisily. The soldiers heard it and approached with rapid steps, their guns ready to shoot.

When they found the children's treasures, they gingerly picked them up as if they contained explosives. For an instant, a smile crossed Rosi's face, eight armed men afraid of two children and a bag of pots? The soldiers did not know the weakness of their hidden enemy.

Rosi's tree was hardly twenty feet from where the soldiers stood, its trunk barely five inches in diameter, too slim to hide her. She could see them clearly, and felt almost certain they saw her, too. She did not dare to move, not even her eyes to look for her brother. She barely dared to breathe. Only one thought raced through her head: if they were to notice her, she would not let them catch her alive. They would have to kill her first. She seethed with the primordial fear of a cornered beast.

The guns pointing in their direction were mesmerizing. The end was clearly in sight. Like lightning, Paul's short life passed

before him. Why are they hesitating, he wondered. They out-
number us.

A word suddenly caught Rosi's attention. The soldiers were
talking about Marscha, a much-dreaded bloodhound kept at the
Inn a mile away. They had heard dreadful stories about that
dog. She was used for capturing people.

As unexpectedly as the soldiers had come, they left again,
taking the children's bags with them. Panic-stricken, Rosi and
Paul stumbled off through the underbrush. There was no time
to lose. Marscha had to be avoided at all cost. In frightened
frenzy they hastened down the mountain. They wanted to get
back across the border, away from the soldiers and their ferocious hound. They wanted to get home to the inn.

The faces of those soldiers remained clearly etched in the
children's memory, as did the intonation of their voices, and
the startled expression of their eyes. Yet that the soldiers failed
to see them remained a mystery. The children did not go back
to the cabin. They had toothbrushes now, and pajamas; and
they had left the messages for their father.

At the inn, they watched from behind the curtain of the
window as Russian soldiers herded German men and women
along the street. Why were they taken away? Would they be
sent to Russia? What was to be their fate?

The soldiers rounded up people quite at random. Anyone
who happened to come along was pushed into the column.
Some of them, it was rumored, were taken to dismantle factories and hospitals that were to be shipped to Russia. Nobody
really knew.

"Don't allow the children to stand near an open window,"
Frau Hanns urged Edith one morning. "Have them look motionless from behind the curtain."

"I will tell them," Edith assured her.

"This morning, my accountant's friend was shot while he was shaving himself, using the open window as a mirror."

"What a savage world we live in," Edith murmured, and added, "Any word from my husband? Any traveler going to the city to carry another message?"

"No word yet, and no travelers today. I'll keep looking."

Edith had asked several strangers to carry word to her husband in the city. But no word had come back to her, and she feared that no message of hers had reached him either.

In July, the Allied Powers met in Potsdam to discuss the details of peace, and Edith's hope of returning to their cabin rekindled. But it quickly became clear that the major decisions had already been settled at Yalta, where Stalin had prevailed. The Sudetenland would remain in Czech hands. There was no reason for her to stay in Oberwiesenthal any longer.

Master of our Fate

Temptation and provocation are invitations to trouble

Edith wanted to join Edgar in Chemnitz as quickly as possible now. The question was how. Would they find transportation, a place to stay, and food while en route? Without transportation, it would be a long and perilous walk. She intended to leave her travel plan with Mrs. Hanns in case Edgar would be looking for them at the hotel. She still had not heard from him, a constant source of worry.

Edgar had returned to the city to be near his business during these perilous times and protect it as best as he could. Now the area was under Soviet occupation. She was certain he would be looking for them, and every time someone knocked at her door, she'd jump up, hoping it would be him.

A brisk knock at her door interrupted her thoughts. She was poring over a map that Frau Hanns had lent her.

"Come in," Edith called, vaguely disappointed that again it failed to be Edgar.

"I have good news," Frau Hanns beamed. She was treating Edith like a daughter.

"Come and sit down," Edith smiled, "You've been so good to us. What would I have done without you!"

Frau Hanns waved a hand. "I may have a ride for you. As much as I hate to see you go, I know you want to get home to your husband."

She thought for a moment. Then she continued in a whisper. "That new guest we have, the man with the car. He mentioned that he'll be going to Annaberg on Friday."

"That is half-way to the city," Edith exclaimed. "Will he take us? I'll be glad to pay."

"I've asked him. He had noticed you and was pleased to give you a ride. He was not happy when I mentioned the children and Maria. But he'll come around."

Edith was quiet for a moment. "What do you think? Should we go with him?" she asked partly alarmed, partly determined not to let this opportunity slip by.

"It's not without risk, but life is risky. He is tall and looks tough; he has not gone hungry. He drives a nice Mercedes. I would suspect he's been an influential Nazi. He has a brusque, SS-like manner about him."

"We've had plenty of practice putting up with them. Maybe he'll share one of his extra sandwiches with us." Edith laughed about this unlikelihood, and continued more seriously. "It would be good to get a ride to Annaberg."

"You would be wise to take it; we rarely get guests who have a car these days."

"And gasoline no longer available. Do you think we will have to push him?" Both women laughed at the thought of an SS man in his Mercedes being pushed by women and children.

"It is mostly downhill." Frau Hanns reassured her.

"We will take the ride." Edith decided. "It certainly is better than walking." The streets were not safe—too many soldiers lusting for adventure.

"Promise to be careful," Frau Hanns urged. "Tell the children and Maria never to leave you alone, not for a minute. He's not the kind of man I would trust."

Edith nodded. "I shall leave a copy of our route with you. From Annaberg we will go to Hainichen."

"Why not directly to Chemnitz? Hainichen is quite out of the way."

"I feel safer taking the longer route. We can spend a night at the Singer farm, one of Edgar's clients. They are good people and will have food for the children. In Hainichen we can stay with Edgar's stepmother, Kate, who is like a mother to him."

"It is nearly twice as far. You will be walking three days."

"I know. I just studied the map again, but I know the area well; we have driven it often. Somehow, I like the route to Hainichen; it seems safer. It's a funny thing, I feel uncomfortable taking the other route."

"Then follow your instinct. Take the Hainichen route." Frau Hanns was a strong believer in a woman's intuition.

Friday arrived and they met Mr. Fritz. Edith had expected him to be taller. But he made up for it in arrogance, just as Frau Hanns had described him. Edith introduced Maria as her sister-in-law—the close bond between the women meant more power. Besides, she wanted him to treat Maria with respect.

Edith had grown up sheltered and chaperoned, and was a strong believer in the goodness of mankind, but she was not

194

naive. She had read Balzac and Baudelaire, and was aware of the thoughts that lurk in the minds of men. She had given the trip much thought and discussed certain points with Maria and the children. She felt that undesirable behavior in others could be forestalled by one's actions, precautions and expectations.

Frau Hanns saw them to the car, a black Mercedes just like Edgar's that the SS had taken away. Mr. Fritz unlocked the door, and Edith and Maria nimbly slipped into the back seats, pulling the children with them.

"No, Gnädige Frau, you must sit in front," Mr. Fritz ordered, visibly annoyed.

Frau Hanns looked at the man and could envisage his meaty fingers exploring Edith's thigh. "Much too dangerous," she exclaimed. "The first Soviet soldier will stop your car if you have a woman at your side." Then she turned to the passengers in the back. "Be sure to duck your heads low and out of sight whenever you see soldiers or police."

Fritz looked miffed; he was used to being obeyed, not being told. Before he could protest, Frau Hanns put a motherly hand on his fine car and explained: "The new police up here and the soldiers take great liberties. You've got a beautiful car, Mr. Fritz. It's best to play it safe and not provoke them."

Fritz had momentarily forgotten that he'd been stripped of his black uniform and divested of the power that went with it. That power had passed on to others now, and he was not certain to whom. Without another word he got into the car and started the engine. Frau Hanns waved good-bye, murmuring a fervent prayer.

They drove silently through town. The women in back were kneeling with their heads on the seat. The children were lying down and glad to do so; it was 5:30 in the morning.

"We are out of town; you can sit up." Fritz announced.

"Thank you," Edith responded. "You are most gracious to have offered us transportation. No trains are leaving from Oberwiesental these days."

"Is Annaberg your final destination?" Mr. Fritz asked.

"No, Chemnitz is," Edith explained. "My husband is expecting us there. We sent him word that you kindly offered us a ride." This was not true, but it seemed prudent and excusable.

Fritz abruptly turned his head. The words had sharply affected him. "How did you do that?" he demanded. "There's no telephone service anywhere."

"A friend offered to wire it for me from the police station. Some wires must still be intact. Is Annaberg your home?" she asked pleasantly.

There was a long pause. "No, not really. I was bombed out. My sister lives in Annaberg."

"She will be happy to have her brother home. Annaberg is a beautiful city. I'm a great admirer of the Annenkirche and its intricate cobblestone construction."

"I was married in it," he announced, more animated now. "It is magnificent. Have you heard its Walcker organ play? There's nothing like it."

"I've seen it, but not heard it. I've climbed to the top of the church tower and enjoyed the magnificent view of the Upper Erzgebirge. It was one of those fine clear days. The church must be quite old, isn't it?"

"It is," Fritz replied with pride; "four hundred and fifty years."

They passed through a small village and the passengers ducked low again. Fritz stole a glance at Edith's legs as she crouched on the floor. Good-looking legs, he fantasized. His hands were twitching. He wanted her next to him in the front seat, within easy reach.

He thought of Göbbels, Hitler's Minister of Propaganda, his idol ever since he joined the Party. Göbbels was shorter than he, not handsome, and had a clubfoot. But he always got what he wanted. He had a fine wife and six children. Yet when he was away from home, he saw to it that every night he had a pretty girl at his disposal. Fritz remembered attending a musical with him. During intermission, Göbbels had turned to him and said:

"Fritz, see to it that the manager has the sixth chorus girl from the left in my hotel room by 11:30 p.m. sharp." It was not a request. It was an order.

He took another look over his shoulder. She shan't get away, he thought, and licked his lips. He planned to invite them to spend the night at his sister's. Better yet, he'd ask his sister to insist on it. He was sure they'd accept. If not, he'd tempt them with a good meal. Mothers, he knew from experience, would do anything to feed their hungry brood.

As to his sister, she was a dear. She didn't like his style of life; *sordid* she called it. But she'd cooperate. She had done so many times before when he had brought a pretty girl. She didn't approve, but what did it matter—as long as she did as she was told. After all, she depended on him for food. He had brought her black-market supplies throughout the war.

He snickered quietly as he thought of the pretty brunette he had taken home three weeks earlier. She proved to have quite a mind of her own. She screamed and kicked. He finally had to stifle her with a pillow to keep the neighbors from calling the police.

Behind him, little Paul was coughing, which diverted his thoughts to Maria and the children. He chewed his lip. What to do with them? Luckily the house was large. He would put them up in the attic room on the far side of the house. Once the children were in bed, he would have his sister ask Edith to help her translate a letter downstairs in the study; he had seen Edith with a Russian book. She couldn't refuse a request made by her hostess. The study was right next to his bedroom. He would take it from there. In anticipation of the evening he whistled one of his favorite tunes from *Die Fledermaus*.

Edith was glad she did not have to talk. His occasional hungry glances had not escaped her. More than that, she could sense his ignoble intentions. Nonetheless, she believed in the basic goodness of human beings. If she appealed to his better instincts, he surely would respond accordingly. No man or woman was perfectly good or totally depraved. It was a matter of degrees.

Men, she figured, have a sensual side, but they also have a reasonable one. She felt sorry for Herrn Fritz, and was sure he had some good qualities, too. Undoubtedly, someone's unscrupulous example had corrupted him. We all tend to follow in the footsteps that precede us. She faulted Hitler, the man at the top, and those who surrounded him. Their speeches focused on honor, duty, and obedience, but did they practice those virtues? Edgar was certain they did not. Hitler and his advisors had only one goal: to manipulate the masses as a means for achieving world domination. The means did not matter to them.

"I'm glad my sister has a large house," Mr. Fritz interrupted her deliberation. "I'm sure she will want you to stay the night. You will like her." With a glance at the children he added, "She is a very good cook."

"Soldiers ahead! Heads down," Maria shouted. She hadn't seen any, but she knew that Edith would not want to respond to his invitation.

Mr. Fritz looked right and left and in the back mirror.

"Where?" He grunted.

Maria muffled into the seat, "Over there, in the side street." By then, they had passed the street.

Edith was grateful for Maria's diversion. Even if his house were the Taj Mahal, she had no intentions of staying there. She preferred the open sky. Why tempt fate, Edith reflected, or more precisely, Mr. Fritz? The problem was, how to take leave of him. She could sense that he would insist on their staying at his sister's.

Annaberg was a charming small town. It had no industry and remained untouched by the war. It provided a safe topic for conversation.

"Does your sister live right in town?" Edith asked after they had discussed the town's history.

"She has a big house on the other side of town. It's my house, actually; but she is living there now. I often stay with her."

"Your parental home?"

"No, my parents passed away. I bought the house." Fritz remembered the tiny basement they had lived in, his father out of work as thousands of others. He recalled his nightly route of garbage cans that he combed for food. Hitler brought them work and salvation. He'd never been hungry since.

They stopped at a small gas station just outside of town.

"Let me pay for the gas, Mr. Fritz," Edith offered, jumping out of the car while giving Maria and the children a compelling glance to do likewise.

"Stay in the car," Fritz ordered alarmed. "I'll be only a moment; just a brief chat with my friend."

Edith smiled graciously, "You have been most kind to bring us that far, Mr. Fritz. We still have many hours of daylight and shall be on our way. It'll do the children a world of good to walk for a while."

"But you must spend the night at my sister's. You need to have food before you leave!"

All very tempting, Edith thought, but she remained firm. Slowly and with dignified gentleness she extended her hand, "It has been a great pleasure for us to travel with such a fine gentleman. Perhaps, one day, our paths will cross again. Thank you for your kindness."

Fritz grimaced with disappointment. He wanted his reward. Yet her words had strangely affected him. She had called him "a gentleman." No one had ever called him that before. A lady calling him a gentleman! The end of the Nazi rule had been a severe shock to him. It had stripped him of his status as an SS-man. He could no longer wear his uniform. He had lost his identity and his power.

"A fine gentleman." The words had a wonderful ring! It certainly was better than being a nonentity—a nobody. Personally, he had never considered himself a gentleman. It was something quite out of his league. But it sounded grand. He had made much money during the war; he would be a wealthy gentleman. He drew up to his full height and made an attempt at kissing Edith's hand.

"If you want to stretch your legs, walk ahead, down this road," he offered grandly. "I'll catch up with you shortly and will take you right to the road that leads to Chemnitz."

Then he hurried toward the little building behind the station. He was glad to have privacy for tapping his secret source of gasoline. It had been a good day so far and was bound to get better. She had called him a gentleman, and gentlemanly he had offered her a chance to stretch her legs, her good-looking legs. But what pleased him most was his clever ruse of promising her to take them to the road toward Chemnitz. Over the years, he had become a master in the use of persuasive words. Soon, he would have Edith in his car again and take her and her brood directly to his house.

"Let's leave quickly before he comes back," Edith murmured to Maria and took Paul's hand. But her son was hungry and about to protest—Mr. Fritz had mentioned food. "Quickly through the fields and toward the woods," she urged him. "His car can't reach us there."

"But he promised us a good meal, and I am hungry," Paul objected, close to tears.

"A cornfield," Maria whispered to him and pointed.

"Wow," Paul whispered back, surveying the large field close-by with its infinite supply of corn. His reluctance was forgotten; he hurried ahead. They had reached the cornfield in minutes.

"Let's walk gently and keep out of sight. We don't want anyone from the road to notice us," Edith urged. When they reached the far end of the field, they sat down and had their meal. "We are eating stolen corn," Edith shook her head. "Let us at least give thanks to the farmer whose corn it is. May God repay him."

"I can leave him my golden bracelet," Rosi offered, fishing in her pocket for her treasures. "The corn is really good."

Edith smiled and nodded to her daughter, "I would gladly leave him something, too. But it would never get to the person who should have it. We shall thank him in our prayers."

Paul stuffed an extra corn into his pocket and they got on their way. They walked for many hours, but did not reach the Singer's farm as Edith had hoped. Darkness was approaching. They returned to the road where progress was faster. If Fritz would be looking for them, he would be searching the road to Chemnitz, not Hainichen. They were about to cross a bridge when Maria hoarsely uttered, "Soldiers!"

201

"Under the bridge!" Edith whispered. Each woman seized the hand of a child and dove under the overpass. They found a beam on which they huddled close together, straining their ears for the voices of the Russian soldiers. There was no doubt they were coming closer. Had they seen them taking refuge under the bridge?

They were overhead now, about a dozen of them. Just then Paul started to cough. Edith grabbed his head and buried it into her lap, while Rosi leaned on top of him to muffle the sound. No one dared to breath. Did the soldiers hear him? If they didn't hear Paul cough, Maria agonized, they will surely hear my heart pound. She ardently folded her hands.

The bridge was quiet again, the soldiers' voices trailed off into the distance. For a long time no one stirred. When they recovered from the fright, Edith and Maria held counsel. They did not dare enter the village. Obviously, it was occupied.

"We'll wait until it's dark," they decided. "Then we'll return to the woods and spend the night." Edith patted her son's head and added, "Tomorrow, we shall look for the Singer's farm. You will get a good meal yet."

It was not easy to get comfortable on the forest floor. It was too dark to find a smooth spot, and they lacked blankets. The early morning cup of tea that Mrs. Hanns had brewed for them was the last liquid they had drunk. Their throats were parched. They lay close to one another, the children in the middle. Maria worried about ants and other crawly beasts, and Edith about wolves that roamed the area and the trip that lay ahead. At least it did not rain. Soon the children were breathing softly, but the women turned restlessly all night. They were glad when the first light of dawn renewed their hope.

"Today we shall get food," Edith encouraged everyone, as they started on their way. "We'll stay up here in the forest," she added, her throat aching for liquid. "We have a better chance of finding a creek." But they found none. They came across a few blueberries, yet the scant berries were just enough to stimulate their stomach juices, making them hungrier than before. They walked close to the edge of the forest, so Edith could see the horizon and watch for the handsome church steeple she remembered overlooking the Singer's farm.

And there, at last, it was. The farmhouse had to lie below it in the valley.

In spite of the sleepless night, Edith's steps quickened. Like a young girl she bounded down the meadow. Maria could hardly keep up, while the children, affected by their mother's change in spirit, hopped and skipped like on a Sunday outing.

"Frau Leuthold," Maria shouted, "Look! Look over there!"

Maria pointed, and Edith let out a scream: "Peter," she cried, tears of joy rolling down her face as she ran down the hill—she had spotted her oldest son. "Peter," she murmured, as she held him tightly. "What blessing to see you."

"I knew it. I knew you'd be all right," Peter kept repeating. "Father was beside himself when we found the cabin deserted and your toothbrushes still there. He was determined to go to the Czech authorities and demand to know what had happened to you." He picked the dirt off his hands. "I had the hardest time talking him out of it. I knew you'd be all right."

"And where is he now?" Edith could not hide her anxiety.

"He has brought me here. I am working on the farm," he wrinkled his nose and looked at his dirty hands, "never again. But the food is good," he admitted. "There's no food in the city, no water, nothing. Just ruins."

"No Soviets here?"

"Not a one. The closest village is eight miles away."

"And Father? Where is he?"

"He said he would go to Hainichen and then back to Chemnitz hoping to find you there."

"Let's go to the house and meet the Singers and then decide what to do next. Your brother is starving for a meal. So are we, and thirsty."

Peter went to a shady tree to retrieve his canteen bottle of water and passed it around. Then the five of them strolled happily toward the house.

"Mother," Peter looked grave, "Herr Singer has not come back from the eastern front. Frau Singer is running the farm. I think she's still hoping he'll come home."

"How is she coping?" Edith asked, her voice barely audible.

"All right, I think."

"She has several children, doesn't she?"

"She has a twelve-year old son and a fourteen-year old daughter. They both help in the fields. Her other son, the sixteen-year old, was drafted just before the war ended. He didn't come back either."

Everywhere the same story, the same heartache. Most of the men were gone—gone forever.

Frau Singer had aged twenty years, it seemed to Edith. I probably have too, she thought. Yet she was as kind as Edith remembered her. She brought them food and offered to take them in for the night.

"We have an old Diesel truck that takes the milk to the Central Milk Station on Monday morning. It's not far from Hainichen. You can walk from there," Frau Singer suggested, and Edith gladly accepted.

"It's not a comfortable ride, but better than walking."

The children rejoiced to have nourishing meals and roamed fearlessly about the farm. They had not played outdoors since they left their cabin. It seemed like an isle of peace

204

in a cruel and hostile world. For them, Monday morning arrived all too soon. A few more hugs for their brother Peter and they were on their way.

The truck had no windows. It was pitch dark and the floor hard, except for the straw that Frau Singer had added for their comfort. They drove over narrow, rough trails between the fields, bouncing and jolting, and arrived at the Milk Station after what seemed an eternity, glad to continue on foot.

After a strenuous, three-hour march they reached Hainichen. Edgar had grown up in this town, and Kate, his stepmother, still lived in the big old house. His own mother had died shortly after he was born.

With immense relief the tired travelers saw that Kate's house was still standing, unharmed by the war, and joyfully climbed the familiar stairs to the front door. They longed for a friendly welcome and a safe place to spend the night.

Paul eagerly reached for the bronze knocker, already tasting grandmother's good cooking, when Edith suddenly snatched the boy's hand. In panic she pulled the children down the stairs and hurried down the street. Maria looked at her perplexed, but did not speak. Maybe a premonition, she thought, and followed them.

"Let's knock at the neighbor's door first," Edith whispered to her and hurried toward a small house further down the street. An old lady peaked through the window. When she recognized Kate Leuthold's daughter-in-law, she came quickly to open the door.

"Come in," she said briskly, and anxiously bolted the door behind them. Then she embraced them warmly and found chairs for them to sit. She had known Edgar since he was a baby, and Edith since their marriage, and from Kate's warm accounts.

"We had to flee from our mountain cabin, Frau Johans," Edith explained. "We are on our way to the city where we hope to find Edgar. I don't know why, but I was suddenly afraid to knock at Mother Kate's door. How is she? Is she still living there?"

"My child!" the old lady exclaimed in alarm, tears welling up in her eyes. "God in his mercy has protected you!" While saying so, she jumped up from her seat, and hurried to the window that opened toward the street and closed its curtains. "Two or three dozen Russians have taken over her house. They would have gladly taken you in, but they would have never let you leave. You were lucky they did not notice you passing by. No woman dares to go near that house."

Edith, too tired to fully grasp their narrow escape, was still focusing on Kate and repeated her question, "Where is Mother Kate? Is she all right?" She dearly loved her mother-in-law.

"She's fine. She found a small studio not far from here."

"Is it safe to visit her; I mean, for us to go there?"

The old lady hesitated. "No one is safe. Not in the streets, nor in their homes. And women least of all. The Soviets are unpredictable. Let me heat a kettle of water. We'll have some peppermint tea."

"We would love a cup of tea, Mrs. Johans. Do you still grow your own mint?" Edith inquired.

The old lady nodded and got up. She took the children with her to the kitchen, gave them something to eat and made them comfortable in her bedroom above. Then she returned.

"It's better we talk in private," she explained. "Before you see Kate, you should know what has happened to her. The strain has aged Kate."

More bad news, Edith thought. Will the nightmares never stop? She was too weary to think.

"It's about Kate's daughter Irene. You know that a year before the war ended, the SS sent her to camp Ravensbrück[43] for special training. Then they placed her in the picture-frame factory to supervise its workers. The factory was off-limits. No one knew what was going on behind its gates."

"I thought Irene was a nurse at the local hospital, wasn't she?"

"She was; and we assumed Irene would be the factory nurse. She was not allowed to talk about her work. It was on condition of absolute confidentiality that she was allowed to go home at night. Not even Kate knew what her work involved.

Apparently, the factory had been converted to produce wooden frames for machine guns. Since no manpower was available, they brought in 500 Jewish women from various detention camps. It was Irene's job to supervise them and to prevent sabotage. It must have been living hell for the poor girl. Kate says that Irene couldn't bear to see all the suffering going on there and twice tried to commit suicide. Whenever I saw her, she would ask me for extra underwear for the workers. I later learned from Kate that she would wear an extra layer when she went to work. Then, in the factory's bathroom, she would quietly pass it on to the women who didn't have any.

"The supervisor of the factory was a callous and cruel woman. She mistreated the workers. She actually beat them. Worse, she stole their food rations.

"When Fred, the owner of the factory—I know him well, he's a good man—heard about the watery soup they were being fed, he sent his own cook to prepare their meals. So once or twice a week they'd have a good meal. Then it was watery soup again. He was a decent man, but he was not allowed on the

---

[43] Part of camp Flossenburg

production floor because production was under direct SS supervision; they supplied the workers and the supervisors.

"Fred had plenty of his own problems with the SS. They regularly overcharged him for the workers—they charged him for extra days, and for more women than actually came to work; and they charged him for the many hours the workers spent in shelters because of air raids. Fred disliked and distrusted the SS. Yet what could he do? We have to follow their orders or suffer the consequences."

"Where is Edgar's sister now?" Edith interrupted, anxious to get to the point.

"I wish we knew. After the war, the factory closed and Irene went back to work at the hospital. They urgently needed her. The hospital was badly understaffed and overcrowded. Shortly after the Soviets occupied the town, they scheduled a meeting of all hospital personnel, including doctors and nurses. From that fateful meeting no one ever returned!" She stopped, tears trickling down her hollow cheeks.

"We have heard that they loaded them onto trucks and took them away. The sick and wounded were abandoned. Relatives and friends picked up some of them. A couple of weeks later, the hospital was dismantled and trucked away, too." She stopped again, overcome by the memory.

Edith and Maria sat in stunned silence.

"Let me tell you about Edgar's brother-in-law Nick," the lady continued. "Nick was there when the Soviets kicked Kate out of her house. They let her go, but they kept Nick. We have lost so many of our best citizens," she swallowed, her eyes filled with tears. "The Soviets get hold of them, and we never see them again. They are not war criminals or Nazis, mind you. They are academicians and lawyers, people with money and education. The Communists consider them a serious threat.[44] Many of my younger friends are among them. I'm still alive because I'm old. At my age you are no longer a threat to anyone."

"How do the Soviets know who is a threat?" Maria asked.

"They don't know anyone here." She was thinking of the Jewish church members, who had been betrayed by their own church.

"That is the saddest part of all, Maria. Does the name Kurt W. mean anything to you, Edith?" Edith shook her head and Mrs. Johans whispered, "He is our current mayor. Before the war he was some sort of health practitioner, who secretly performed back-alley abortions. Since he was not a doctor and in serious violation of the law, the Nazis locked him up. After the war the Soviets liberated him. He became a fervent Communist and was made mayor of our town, busy turning our best citizens over to the NKVD.[45]"

The teakettle whistled. It was a welcome relief. Mrs. Johans and Maria went to the garden to get mint leaves. Maria sorely needed a cup of tea. The misfortunes of this little town deeply affected her. An avalanche of trouble seemed to have crushed through its friendly gates.

She thought of her own family. Were they still alive? She and Edith had tried to find out. But it proved impossible. It could be months before telephone, mail and bus services would be restored. She had to get there somehow and see for herself. She would do so as soon as they got back to the city.

---

[44] In all Communist-occupied countries, the educated and the wealthy were systematically exterminated. According to reports from the Red Cross, some were forced to sign confessions and were executed. The majority was left to die.

[45] Short for *Narodny kommissariat wnutrennich djel*, meaning Soviet secret police in East Germany.

The three women settled into their chairs, each clasping her mug, each wrapped in silence, each wishing that the tea's refreshing aroma could wash away the miseries of war.

At long last, Mrs. Johans spoke again. "I think it is best that you spend the night here, Edith. I have no beds, but I have blankets and the living room floor. It's not much, but it is more than Kate has. I shall ask the neighbor's little boy to let Kate know that you are here. It is safer for her to meet you here than for you to go to her place. And then we'll figure out a way to get you safely back to Edgar."

Edith pressed her hand. "May God bless you for your kindness, Frau Johans," she murmured.

Kate arrived early next morning. She brought a small bag of food that Edith half-heartedly refuse.

"You will be going hungry for a week if we take part of your meager rations," she chided.

Kate shook her head, "The children need it more than I do." Then she told Edith the good news, "Edgar was here again last week looking for you. He gave me this letter for you. Read it, then we will talk."

A millstone of worries rolled off Edith's shoulders. She jumped up eagerly and took the folded sheet. It was without an envelope, reminding her that Kate, too, had left home with nothing but the clothes on her back, just as she had. Unfolding the sheet, she hurried through the kitchen and out the back door.

Sitting on the staircase that led to the garden she read Edgar's words. His handwriting, always immaculate and beautiful, betrayed signs of great nervous stress. "Stay off the main roads," he urged her. "They are not safe. Go to Nöller's farm. It is fourteen miles through the woods. You will be safe there. It is out in the country. I shall be looking for you there."

A map! I need a map, Edith thought, as she hurried back to the living room.

Kate had anticipated her need, "Edgar is very concerned that you take a safe route. A friend of mine gave me a map and marked it for you. If you leave soon, you will get to Nöller's before nightfall."

"Let us visit for an hour. Then we shall be on our way," Edith replied, moving next to Kate on the sofa, while Frau Johans took the children to the kitchen to prepare a snack for the journey.

For a long moment the two women sat in silence. Like a tidal wave, painful events had inundated their lives and had not yet receded. Danger was all around them. Where to start?

To talk about their pain would mean reliving it.

"The horrors of war," Kate sighed, expressing the anguish they both felt. The war had ended, and yet conditions were worse than ever before, the devastation of the cities, the loss of their loved ones and of their worldly possessions, and now the vengeance of their victors.

"Why do we have to fight wars?"

Edith's eyes were glazed from unshed tears. She put her arm around Kate's shoulder, "Too many wars fought to gratify one leader's greed for glory! Hitler lost his war and took the easy way out, while we, his people, have to suffer the consequences."

"We will have tough years ahead—our Communist victors are not known for reason and civility."

"Just think of the millions of young men in the prime of their lives who fought and died in this war! Think of the lonesome women and fatherless children left behind, with nothing but the pain of their losses!" Kate protested, tears wetting her pale cheeks. Her three brothers had fallen at the front; it was too painful even to mention. Cautiously, both women skirted the calamities of their lives. It was easier to speak of pain in general, and of the anguish of others, than to reopen their own wounds.

"Why do our own people add to our misery?"

Kate thought of two people in particular: Supervisor Kratz who had tormented her daughter and the Jewish women at the factory, and the Communist mayor who caused more suffering in town than six years of war had.

"Why is mankind so cruel?"

"A government of women may be better."

"But think of Irene's supervisor."

"Education may be the answer—education in government, and in decency and compassion. It should be a must for anyone entering public service."

"I'd advocate that for everyone. Still, I think most people are good like your Irene. What courage to bring clothing to the Jewish women while SS-men were watching! We, too, were lucky. A kind enemy soldier got us safely across the border."

At last the dam had broken. They talked rapidly now about the events that had stricken them. For Kate, worse than the loss of her brothers, her daughter, her home and all she owned, was to watch the suffering of her grandchildren who had lost their fathers.

When they tired of talking about their fate, they turned to the creative aspects of their present lives, the everyday tricks of survival that their world of devastation necessitated.

Stranded in an impoverished world with nothing but the summer frocks they wore, both had to call on their imagination to survive. They eagerly exchanged ideas on plants and herbs that could be used as medicines; the kind of beans to roast for brewing a breakfast beverage; about grasses that were tough enough to twine into shoelaces; on making their own clothing by turning curtains, napkins or pillowcases—if you could get them—into something to wear. Time flew. Kate kept a watchful eye on the clock. She was eager for the young travelers to reach their destination safely and in daylight.

When a little blond youngster of nine peeked in from the kitchen, Kate rose.

"You had better be on your way, my dear Edith. Your guide has arrived; come and meet Hans."

Edith warmly shook the boy's hand.

"He will take you to the woods. Are you good at climbing over back yards fences, Edith?" Kate chuckled. "They tell me it is safer than walking in the streets."

Edith could not suppress her tears when she hugged her kind mother-in-law and whispered goodbye. She had an uneasy premonition that it would be their last farewell.

Kate and Frau Johans waved from the back porch until the travelers disappeared.

"You need not worry, Kate," Frau Johans assured her friend. "Hans knows all the people along this route. He has taken several people safely out of town."

Rosi and Paul greeted the back yard adventure with great fervor, more so than Maria and Edith, who hadn't climbed fences in years. Paul enviously counted the apple trees they passed. If only one of them were mine, he fantasized. When he spied a ripe, red apple on the ground, he whispered to Hans, "Is it all right if I take this one?"

Hans laughed, "Sure, there are plenty on the tree; take one for each of you."

They arrived in the woods, and after a reluctant good-bye they were on their way. Alone at last, Edith's steps slowed, her shoulders slumped. They had spent fourteen hours in Hainichen, but it seemed like a century—so much painful news. One in particular was hitting Edith now, an item in Edgar's message. She glanced at his letter again:

"... Nöller did not returned from his last mission. His sister is running the ranch. I visited her. She was confident that her brother was alive and would return. Her optimism is of some comfort. I fervently hope she is right."

Toward noon heavy drops began to fall and soon turned into a downpour. They found refuge under a dense clump of trees and decided to eat their food before it got soggy. Then fog closed in. Edith studied the map, then the terrain, and the map again, and was struck by the truth of Edgar's words: "A map is not the territory." It decidedly was not, especially when in a forest wrapped in fog. They would have to look for a farmhouse to inquire where they were.

They found two women working in the fields who advised them to take the small country road. It was good counsel, their progress was faster, and before nightfall they knocked on Nöller's familiar door. It seemed like an eternity had passed since Nöller had demonstrated Max Schmeling's straight rights.

"Do you remember the evening of the dinner-dance?" Paul whispered to his mother—he and his siblings had sneaked out of bed that evening to watch from the upstairs balustrade—"we saw Uncle Nöller take a flip through the air to ask you for a dance."

"In his elegant tuxedo!" Edith smiled, recalling his stunt.

"There's no one like him," Paul added, and Edith nodded, gently squeezing his shoulder.

His sister Anna was young and pretty, but sorrow and hard work was casting a shadow over her fine features. Like most German women, she, too, had been widowed during the war.

She warmly welcomed the weary travelers and refreshed them with food and drink, while recounting the story she had learned from one of his pilots. During the last days of the war Nöller's plane was severely damaged by enemy fire. Nonetheless, he managed to bring it to the ground, though behind enemy lines. Nöller, he speculated, had most probably been taken to a hospital; but no one knew.

Early next morning, the travelers set off on the last leg of their trip. On Anna's insistence Edith and Maria wore headscarves, the type field workers use. She also handed each of the two women a walking stick. "When in the city," she said, "lean on it heavily so you look like ancient grandmas. And smear some dirt onto your faces." She turned to the children, "don't forget to call them grandma and auntie. It is vital. You don't want to catch the attention of Soviet soldiers!" She embraced them all once more and they were on their way.

Edith kept a brisk pace that day. Maria and the children found it hard to keep up. "If we hurry," Edith held out as enticement, "we'll be sleeping in our own beds tonight, with a roof over our heads. And we'll be together with father."

They made it to the city in good time. But the deeper they penetrated toward its center, the more discouraged Edith became. She thought she knew the city well, but she had not anticipated the extent of the devastation. All around them was nothing but ruins and rubble. She had no clue where they were or where to go. All prominent buildings had disappeared, no landmarks were left to guide her. She was tired and anxiety was about to overwhelm her.

How would Edgar find his way, she thought in despair. He is so good at it. The answer came almost immediately: Establish the main direction and follow it. To reach the city's northern suburb, they had to proceed north-northeast. The sky had cleared and the sun was low in the sky. It should be easy to keep the evening light directly behind them.

But it was not easy to pick their way through the rubble. The pavement was like a sieve of potholes. At times, the street was blocked by debris. It would be impossible to maneuver the streets in the dark. They anxiously hastened forward, barely looking right nor left.

When a dead dog blocked their path, half buried under a heavy beam, Paul burst into tears, and Rosi sank to her knees to pat the animal. Edith caught her hand just in time. Who knew when they could wash again their hands.

"He reminds you of Maxi, doesn't he?" she murmured. "Me too."

They turned into another street. Two women were searching in the rubble further ahead and Edith asked them for directions.

"You would be better off if you followed the main road," one of them said. "It will take you all the way to the Kasselberg. You can't miss it. It's been cleaned up somewhat."

With the last light of dusk and their last ounce of energy they reached home. Part of it was still standing and looked inhabitable. Yet the windows were dark as if the place were deserted. Perplexed, they looked around them and realized that the entire city was in darkness—no more electricity. Their hearts pounding they looked at each other. Would father be home? Or would they find strangers? Or Russians?

They had no key.

Maria was the first to speak, "Why don't we knock and call?" Since no one objected, she pounded on the door and shouted, "Herr Doctor, we are home!"

Rapid steps came toward the door. Edith knew these steps. Edgar was home. They were together at last.

A Woman Scorned

Hell hath no fury like a woman scorned —W. Congreve

Five weeks had passed since Katrina disappeared from her shelter. That evening, she had lain on the edge of her narrow bunk straight as an arrow, motionless, barely daring to breathe. She was waiting for Arno to fall asleep. A tinge of remorse troubled her womanly soul. Should she take off in Arno's truck and leave him stranded?

Yes! A thousand times yes, she told herself, and overruled all qualms. He used me, lied to me, and scorned me. He lived with me for two years and never contributed a dime. Yet he talked grandly about the big inheritance that would make him rich—make both of us rich. He never lifted a finger; he cleverly charmed me into waiting on him. And on the day of our engagement party he took off in my car. He left without a word, without a good-bye.

She still smarted from her family's disapproving sermons and her neighbors' reproving glances. She was certain he would leave her behind again, or ditch her somewhere along the way. She was no asset to him now.

At last! Arno's regular breathing signaled that he was asleep. She slipped into her clothes. Now the keys to his truck; she knew exactly where to find them. She had watched Arno closely when he tucked them into the upper pocket of his coat.

She found his jacket, but not the keys.

Their eyes had met when he slipped the keys into his pocket. He must have removed them and hidden them elsewhere. Nervously, she groped through his other pockets. But no keys. She would look later. She was anxious to leave before Arno awoke. She stuffed his uniform into a pillowcase, found the matches and tiptoed toward the door.

217

Her heart pounding she cautiously closed the door, but not cautiously enough. It creaked and then clicked. Panic stricken, she locked the door. She could not face Arno now.

Pain was shooting down her leg and up her back. Biting her lip she limped across the street. The night was pitch dark. No moon, no stars, no streetlights. But she could make out the truck. Its dark bulk loomed like a monster. On the previous night, Arno had pulled her up to the truck. Would she manage those steep steps alone?

She searched his pockets again, and found a handkerchief, a comb, a wallet, some folded papers, cigarettes, but no key. She groped again, her hands turning clammy. Again the same items—the comb, the wallet, she stopped and slipped the wallet into her pocket. Had she missed a pocket? She fingered the cloth, first the outside, then the inside. At last, in a small, inside breast pocket she found the keys.

He had not trusted her, a sign that he could not be trusted either. She stuffed the uniform back into the pillow and tossed it as far as she could. Then she tackled the steps. A sudden detonation upset her balance. She tried again and again. Finally, she got hold of the door handle and pulled herself up.

Her fingers trembled as she tried to find the ignition; she had never driven an army truck. In the distance she discerned the sound of artillery, and suddenly it dawned on her—the Russians were coming and she would not be here. She had transportation! Euphoric, she focused on the job at hand. She had watched Arno intently the night before when he started the engine and worked the gearshift.

The truck jerked into motion. Jumpy at first, but it moved.

As she gained distance from her bunker, she began to relax. Before long she turned into the Autobahn to Frankfurt. The traffic intensified and soon slowed to a crawl. Everyone who had a car seemed to be on the move. With the first light of dawn she became aware of other trucks like hers, army trucks. She was driving a military vehicle! To be caught in a stolen one would have dire consequences.

She kept driving—one hour, another hour, until the traffic came to a standstill. Just ahead of her, a railroad crossing had lowered its bars. Panic seized her, and an infinite loathing of Arno and his army truck. She felt trapped and needed air. She climbed off the truck and limped toward a tree not far from the railroad tracks, an old oak tree, sturdy and protective. She leaned gratefully against it. If the train moved slowly enough, she pondered, she would try to get on it.

The morning was chilly and she buried her hands inside her pockets. Her fingers brushed against something slick and unfamiliar. Arno's wallet, she recalled, and was about to fling it from her, when the rumbling of the approaching train brought her back to reality—train conductors evicted penniless passengers. The train's rumbling suddenly turned into high-pitched screeching—the train was trying to stop. Anxiously, Katrina searched the sky. Sure enough, enemy planes were closing in. Moving trains were a favorite target.

Rather dead on that train than caught by the Russians or Nazis! Katrina stepped closer to the tracks. The screeching wheels of the train paralyzed her with fear. One, two, three passenger cars zoomed by.

She watched them as in a trance.

The impatient honking of the cars behind Arno's truck startled her back into the present. Her vehicle was blocking the lane; they wanted her quickly to return. She crossed herself, moved closer to the train, and reached for its railing. The ground jerked away from under her. Her legs dragged for several feet, and then, with supreme effort, she pulled herself onto the lower platform of the train. She lay there numb with pain, clinging to the moving train.

A brutal blast shook the earth and a blinding flash lit the crossing. Instinctively, Katrina covered her face. *Don't let go of the railing,* she agonized. Too late; in horror she slid off the train. The first bomb had hit the highway just missing the train. Arno's truck was no more.

Commanding Respect

One person with courage makes a majority

—Andrew Jackson

Three weeks had passed since Mina signed the letter for the museum, and Arno made his escape. She was still furious. He had manipulated her, and she resented that. For the first time she realized that her husband and Edgar were right—Arno was a con artist. Charming, but a con artist. She would not let him get away with it. She would have him return the paintings to the Leipzig Museum.

For the present, she decided to stay at her summerhouse by the lake. It was more peaceful than in the city, and much gardening needed to be done. Her 73-year old gardener had been called up to defend the fatherland and not returned.

It was a busy month for Mina, tending three acres of garden. She was pruning her roses one morning, when she heard Russian jeeps rolling up her driveway. Two dozen soldiers leaped out with their rifles, and bolted up the stairs to her house.

Without a moment's hesitation, Mina hurried after them. She caught up with the soldiers in her living room. "Knock, before you enter someone else's house," she demanded indignantly, "and clean off your dirty boots!"

She was still holding her garden scissors in her hand and a bunch of dead roses. She was short like Napoleon, but like Napoleon she commanded respect.

The soldiers stopped, perplexed. A conquered German daring to bark orders at them? A little, gray-haired lady at that; a fearless, bossy babushka who reminded them of their own grandmothers back home. You do not trifle with them.

Their spokesman gleefully pointed out that the house was theirs now. Thirty-two of them were going to live in it. "We are going to take a look at it now," he declared. "You had better stay down here!"

They inspected the house and searched every nook and cranny. When they returned, they commented on the beautiful flowers throughout the house and asked who arranged them.

"I do," Mina replied sternly.

"Will you do them for us? You can stay if you do," their spokesman offered.

Mina agreed and moved into the guesthouse.

Her resident Russians had come from far beyond the Ural Mountains, a primitive and poor region, where they rode horses and lived in tents, where they prepared meat by sliding it under their saddlecloth and rode until it was tender. To them, Western civilization and modern appliances were like phantoms of fantasy. They were strangers to modern technology, and that included water-flushing toilets, not common outside the Western World. In 1940, even in the United States, forty percent of all homes had no indoor plumbing.

Mina's Russians had never used a Western toilet and figured it was a contraption for washing potatoes. When you bought a pound of potatoes after the war, a good four ounces of it was caked-on mud. So the Russians dumped the potatoes into the toilet bowl and flushed to get them clean. That is not what happened. The smaller potatoes disappeared and the toilet overflowed.

Furiously, the soldiers summoned Mina and accused her of sabotage. Mina arrived, irate to see her toilet clogged and the floor flooded, and, in no uncertain terms, gave them a piece of her mind.

A few days later, the Russians discovered that the lake was full of fish and decided to catch some. Unfamiliar with the Western art of fishing, they designed their own method. They gathered hand grenades, lots of hand grenades, and threw them into the lake. It caused quite a detonation, and in a sad way their scheme worked. The explosion burst the lung of every fish in the lake, and their little dead bodies floated to the surface of the water.

The Russians scooped up what they needed and left the rest to rot. The grenades did a thorough job—five decades later the lake was still without fish.

In the evenings, Mina's Russians indulged in vodka and song. They also fancied target shooting. When it was too dark to shoot rabbits and birds outside, they used inside targets— Mina's fine paintings on the walls. When Mina discovered her walls and paintings riddled with bullet holes, she did not mince her words. Thirty Russian soldiers did not intimidate her! But the Russians had the last word. They told her never to set foot in her house again.

So Mina returned to her apartment in the city of Leipzig, determined nonetheless to visit her house regularly and attend to its upkeep. Her house and garden deserved better than mindless abuse.

Many years earlier, Mina had planted beautiful wisteria vines around the house that over the years had grown to the top of the gable. They flowered for weeks, giving off a refreshing scent. Since they needed frequent trimming to keep them clear of the windows, Mina came often to do so.

One day the unforeseen happened. The Russians took care of it themselves. They chopped off every vine near its root, and before long, Mina's beloved house looked as if it were in mourning, covered with the dying vines.

Mina was speechless when she saw it, and fled to her neighbor's house. She felt in dire need of a soothing cup of tea and a friendly ear. The residence belonged to Mr. Reclam, the publisher of Reclam books, and an ardent fisherman, who had often shared his succulent catch with her.

Walking toward his house, Mina noticed a strange transformation of his grounds. The once impeccable lawn and flowerbeds were crowded with black-market booty of every description—pipes, concrete blocks, lumber, crates and other items long unavailable to the public. She knocked at the door with considerable vigor, and before long, Kurt, Mr. Reclam's handyman, opened the door.

"Looking for Mr. Reclam?" the man grinned. "He ain't here any more. He's run off to the West."

Mina resented the man's patronizing smirk, but her curiosity was piqued.

"So you are taking care of his place, Kurt?" Mina asked with an even voice.

The man's grin broadened. "Takin' care of his place? Naw. It ain't his place anymore. It's my property now. Mine. Kurt Gasse. Mr. Gasse, owner of Grossteinberger Lake #47." He stretched smugly to his full height.

Mina felt like whacking him one, but thought better of it. First, she wanted to hear his story.

"Why, Mr. Gasse," she said, "Congratulations. You must tell me all about it. Will you make me a cup of tea?" Saying this, she walked past him into the living room. Her own problem suddenly seemed trivial.

Kurt Gasse was stunned by the unexpected honor of being called by his last name—no one had ever done so—and he hurried to offer her a seat. No one had ever joined him for tea and gratified he brewed his best. While sipping tea, Mina listened to Gasse, who with great animation told her of his cunning and conniving to become the owner of his employer's property. His secret? Right after the war he became an ardent Communist.

"A great concept, this Communism," he exclaimed. "Everyone has a right to share in the riches of this world."

Mina nodded, she could see the appeal of his concept: What's mine is mine. And yours is mine too.

"So you are a big politician now, Mr. Gasse?"

"If I may say so," he grinned and nodded proudly.

So ardent a Communist, Mina thought, that they made him the owner of his employer's property; but she did not say so. Her eyes wandered through the large bay window that offered a fine view of the garden, and scanned the pipes and beams and building materials Kurt Gasse had amassed. They spoke volumes about politics and enterprise, greed and opportunity, and about the changing winds of fortune.

Dear Mr. Reclam, Mina sighed to herself. I hope you will find better fishing in the West than we have here.

Across the Rubble

The battle is not to the strong alone; it is to the vigilant, the active, the brave —Patrick Henry

Edith and the children were glad to be home. Nearly three months had passed since they left their mountain home.

They were glad to rest. Not so Maria. She stood by the window with an aching heart and surveyed the neighbor's house. Two lonely walls remained. No hope of seeing her Otto. The garden had received no care in months. The hedge where she and Otto exchanged timid glances once had grown a foot. Where was her Otto? Had he returned from Russia? Was he still alive? He had promised to write, but only two letters had come, a long, long time ago. She desperately wanted to visit her family now that she was close to home. Had her parents and brothers survived those last months of the war? She fervently hoped they had heard from Otto.

"Give me a few days to find a safe way for you to get home," Edith urged with genuine concern. A young, attractive girl like Maria was not safe anywhere. Five days later, opportunity knocked. Edgar came home from his office with exciting news. Nöller was home!

"If you don't mind, I shall leave in the morning," he beamed. "I cannot wait to see Nöller. Besides, he will need seed for his fields. My first stop will be at Maria's parents to drop her off. It will be a worthwhile trip, the last one until I find a source of gasoline."

Maria's parents were glad to have their daughter home—they had lost both their boys during the last days of the war.

By late morning, Edgar reached the Nöller ranch. Profound joy filled both men when they embraced.

"It's a miracle to be still among the living," Nöller grinned.

"Few of our friends are."

Both had matured beyond their years. Still, with unchanged fervor they delved into their memories of the light-hearted, un-encumbered years before the war. It was more comforting than the recent past or the uncertainty of the future. So much had changed! Anna shared with them a leisurely lunch, forgetting for a spell the hardships of war.

A car or two seemed to be driving up, but they paid no attention. The bond of their warm friendship and the memories of youthful abandon were like a beacon of light in the grim reality of the present.

Together they had climbed the Matterhorn, where an icy snowstorm surprised them; but they survived. They double-dated at college, hiked the Bavarian Alps and spent many glorious hours on horseback. Happy, carefree days!

Harsh voices came from the entrance hall and before they knew it, eight Soviet soldiers crowded the room.

"We want you for questioning," they told Nöller. "You come with us."

Incredulous, Nöller shook his head. "I've just been released from the hospital, I have been home barely two days."

"We know," their spokesman replied. "You are home now. You come with us."

"Why would you want to question me? I'm a rancher. Never been a Nazi. Never been involved in politics."

"You are a spy," the soldier countered and opened a notebook. "You visited German consulate in Moscow on June 25, 1923, and two weeks later, consulate in Leningrad."

Twenty-two years ago? Nöller marveled at the exactitude of Soviet record keeping and searched his memory. It was true. He did travel in Russia and did visit the consulates with letters of introduction as was the custom then, but not as a spy. He was a student then, eager to see the world. Apparently, the members of the young revolutionary Leninist/Communist movement had blacklisted him at the time. They figured if Nöller had connections to the consulate, he had to be a spy. If he were not a spy, he obviously belonged to the moneyed intelligentsia. In their eyes, that was even worse.

"I know he is a farmer," Edgar jumped to his defense. "I just brought him seed for his fields. He grows wheat and alfalfa, and breeds livestock. He does not have time for politics. Come and take a look at his farm."

The soldiers were not interested in agriculture; they wanted their man. "You come with us, too," their spokesman shouted angrily, pointing his gun at Edgar. "Show me your ID."

Trying to gain time and inspiration, Edgar kept searching his pockets. But no useful thought came to his aid. He handed over his ID.

"Dr. Edgar C. Leuthold," the Russian read, and cocked his head, "You a doctor?" Germans place the *Dr.* in front of the name instead of a *Ph.D.* after the name.

"Yes," Edgar replied, not explaining that a "Dr." does not necessarily mean a doctor of medicine.

The Russian hesitated for a moment. Medics, he must have reasoned, were a useful category; different from the dangerous intelligentsia they had orders to exterminate. He handed Edgar his ID and left without him.

Edgar collapsed into a chair. He would have done anything to save his friend, but what? One single man against eight armed soldiers? He did not stand a chance. He sat in shock for a long time. Nobel's words crossed his mind again, "A Ph.D. may come in handy one day," he had said. Who would have foreseen this strange turn of events? His Ph.D. had saved his life again—once in Russia, when he was called back to serve on the draft board, and now for the second time. But his friend Nöller! He was unable to help his friend! The soft touch of a hand on his shoulder brought him back to the present. It was Anna, standing in front of him.

"What happened?" she asked softly, tears in her eyes. From Edgar's expression she guessed the tragic event.

"Will we ever see him again?"

Edgar was too shaken to speak. He got up and walked to the window to regain his composure, "I hope so," he finally said, returning to her side. Yet he felt painfully certain that Nöller's chances of escape were next to nil. "I'm glad you stayed out of sight," he said, taking Anna's hand. "Be sure to wear something old and ugly and pretend you are 98 if they ever come this way again."

The Valley of Death
"Better to die on one's feet than to live on one's knees."
—Albert Camus

Edgar drove back to the city, clutching his steering wheel as if it were Stalin's neck, but it did not lesson his pain.

He could not face Edith with the tragic news. He needed solitude, or work to numb his sorrow, and presently found himself in front of his office. During the last weeks of the war, bombs had hit his warehouses again, but two offices were still usable.

He was about to park when he noticed two Soviet jeeps out in front. Had they come to take him for questioning, too, like Nöller? They certainly did not pay social calls. His heart pounding, he stepped on his gas pedal and headed home. If the Soviets did not find him at his office, they would be looking for him at the house. Every minute could spell the difference between life and death.

At the house, Paul was pleading with his sister to play a game of chess. At age eight he was an excellent strategist and usually won.

"I can't," Rosi whispered, lying pale and tired on her bed. "I'm too hungry and ..." she broke off; she could not tell her younger brother that she was scared. But she was. Being back amidst the ruins was a daily reminder that they had lost the war and therefore the right to live. They had survived six years of hunger, deprivation, air raids and Hitler's iron dictatorship. What a nightmare it had been, Hitler's vise-like grip on his people and his army of secret police and informers. But now they were doomed.

"Do you mind if we play later, Paul? Right now I need to think," Rosi whispered.

Ever since the war ended, one question kept haunting her: "When are we going to die?" Hitler said they would if they did not win the war.

Rosi dug her head into her pillow. "How will it end?"

In the meantime, a merciless tide of soldiers from the East had flooded the country. They engulfed the land and enslaved the people. Like a pack of hungry wolves they ravaged the country.

The world came to know it as Communism.

Not a man, not a woman, not a child were safe—not in their beds, not hiding in their attics, not walking in the streets. Randomly, people were shot, raped or sent to Siberia. Hitler had robbed them of nearly everything. Now, they lost what little was left.

When will we die? Rosi's head throbbed. Life was complex and cruel.

"Father is here," Paul called from the window where he was watching for the water truck that occasionally brought water; the city's water mains were broken.

Paul pointed to the street, "Father is in a great hurry."

Indeed, swift steps came flying up the stairs, two at a time, and their father's panic-stricken face appeared in the door.

"Get in the car! Hide in the back seats," he called hoarsely.

Maybe we'll escape death after all, Rosi thought, as they both raced to the car.

A moment later, their mother threw a dark blanket over their heads to keep them out of sight. Soldiers would stop the car if they noticed women or children in it. Edith hopped into the front, duck her head low and off they were. It had taken less than two minutes.

They left home never to see it again.

A mile or two before they reached the train station, they ran out of gasoline. They abandoned the car and continued on foot, Edith with Paul a few steps ahead, Edgar with Rosi behind, as if they were strangers. The streets were deserted. Ruins everywhere. They rose into the gloomy sky like eerie phantoms. Some buildings were sheared off as with a razor blade, baring the bowels of the deserted apartments. Pictures still dangled from the walls. Unmade beds gave quiet witness that someone had slept there before a shell knocked off the other half of the room. A boot balanced precariously on a ledge. Here and there in the rubble yellow covers hid unburied bodies, an official precaution to warn the living: danger of typhoid. Somewhere a dog wailed, forsaken, hungry and scared.

At last, the station came into view, but their hope was short-lived. The platform was packed with hundreds of other pitiful refugees and fugitives, some sleeping, some crying, most of them numb with misery—waiting. No one knew if trains were still running. It was rumored that the tracks had been blown up. Hitler had given Albert Speer, his architect and minister of armament, instructions to destroy everything and burn it to the ground before the enemy approached. They came to be known as the *scorch-the-earth directives*[46]. Nothing was to fall into enemy hands.

This was not all; his people, too, were to be doomed. "If the war is lost, this nation must perish," Hitler wrote. "It has proved to be weak."

Had Speer carried out these orders?

No one knew.

Edgar and his family settled on the gray asphalt near the tracks. They remained there all day and all night in mind-numbing wretchedness. By early morning, a rumbling sound brought life into the crowd.

A train! Feverish panic gripped the crowd. To get on that train became a matter of life and death.

"Hold on to our hand or to our clothing. Do NOT let go!" Edgar warned his children. "Your life will depend on it."

It did indeed. The crowd stampeded like cattle to get on that train. When the train pulled out of the station, they saw an angry crowd that had remained behind.

At the next stop, Russian soldiers boarded the train. The air was tense, stuffy and hot. For days, few passengers, if any, had bathed. Tempers were on edge, but stifled by fear. A pocket watch chimed eleven o'clock. It was Edgar's, a beautiful heirloom given to him by his grandfather.

"Gimme!" a Russian standing nearby demanded eagerly and held out his hand.

Edgar looked aghast. "It belonged to my grandfather," he pleaded. For Edgar, the watch was an heirloom and a symbol of

---

[46] On March 19th, 1945, Speer was given orders, titled *Demolitions on Reich Territory*, also known as the *Nero Decree*. Nero, the Roman Emperor, supposedly engineered the Great Fire that in *anno* 64 burned down two thirds of the city of Rome.

a civilized world. It was a link to his past—a tangible reminder to keep striving.

The Russian wanted no sentimental argument; he wanted the watch. He whipped out his pistol, shoved it into Edgar's ribs, and shouted:

"You gimme. You come with me."

Deadly silence gripped the compartment. The Russian poked Edgar harder to get him moving. No one stirred, except Edith. Gently she took her husband's watch, and with a conciliatory smile and a few Russian words handed it to the soldier. She showed him how it worked and what it could do.

The Russian, pleased to hear his mother tongue and delighted with this exquisite toy, forgot about Edgar's arrest.

The tense train ride came to an end in the small border town of Falkenstein. In the distance, Edgar surmised their destination—the American Sector of Germany. It lay beyond a five-mile wide, off-limit zone, called "no-man's land." Trespassers were shot in that terrain or captured.

Edgar found a guide who was willing to take them across the border. But at the appointed hour when the family came to his door, the guide refused to go.

"Impossible to cross right now," he explained. "Three people have been shot and several captured."

Yet Edgar had no alternative. They could not return home, nor could they stay in the border town. They had no place to hide, no food to eat, no place to sleep. With or without a guide, they had to risk it. The guide drew a map and gave them a bowl of soup that they gratefully ate. Then, on that rainy September night, they set out to reach freedom.

Around six o'clock that evening they crossed the road that took them into no-man's land. Edgar took a close look at the road marker nearby. The bold numbers carved into the stone read **153**. Gently rolling woods and meadows lay to either side. They walked this way and that, getting wetter and wetter. Uphill and downhill. Trees everywhere. Soon total darkness. Now mist. Then rain. They walked and walked.

Every crackling branch or rustling leaf made their hearts pound faster. Suddenly they heard sounds of heavy boots. They stood rooted to the ground. Chills shot down their spines. It was pitch dark, impossible to see. They didn't dare to breathe. The sounds came closer, then grew fainter, then disappeared. They changed direction. Hours passed. They had no knowledge of the terrain, no map.

Suddenly shots rang through the still air; there was shouting and muffled screaming. Peter and Rosi sank to the ground frightened and exhausted. Would they be next?

"Let's end it now," Edith pleaded with her husband. To be captured seemed inescapable now. The very thought of it was agony to her. It would mean death or separation, rape or torture, Russian work camps or Siberia. Death, sweet solace, flashed through Edith's mind. If they were captured, that chance might not come again.

A year earlier, two of her teen-age cousins had been ordered to join Hitler's SS. Both boys were tall, blond and good-looking, the attributes that Hitler idolized but lacked. On the train to Berlin, both boys hanged themselves by their belts. To them, death was more honorable than joining Hitler's SS.

Suicide and honor—they make strange bedfellows! Yet the dividing line blurs when the only alternative is membership in the SS, Hitler's Schutzstaffel, a group known for its atrocities.

"We have shoelaces and belts," Edith whispered. "And we have plenty of trees."

But Edgar would not hear of it, nor would the children.

Their mother's words had renewed their tenacity to live. They recoiled from the idea of hanging from a tree. They were young and optimistic. The idea of capture had no meaning to them. They wanted to live. They were back on their feet and doggedly trudged on, hour after hour.

Daylight was approaching. Ahead in the dense mist they saw a road. They hurried forward. There! A few steps to the left was a road marker. It had to be the West!

They gazed at the numbers speechlessly. They read **153**, the very same marker they had passed twelve hours earlier.

Stunned beyond words they stood rooted to the ground when out of the mist a bicyclist emerged. They should have run. But they could not stir. They stood as if turned to stone.

The man bicycled closer. He will shoot us, Rosi thought, but she was too tired to care. He kept coming. Then stopped. Edgar reached into his pocket and handed him something while explaining their predicament.

"Go this way and that … " Edith heard him say. "Eventually, you'll come to a large meadow with a creek. You'll have to cross both. On the far end begins the American Sector. The soldiers guarding the area have orders to shoot. So run fast. Good luck."

It was full daylight when they reached the meadow, a vast, forbidding place. Uncertain, they stared at its vastness. There, at the other side, they saw their goal, the Western Sector, the free world! They could see it clearly, but they were too exhausted to feel its promise of hope; the night had been too long. They stared at the meadow, then at their father, and for an instance they perceived a hopeful, encouraging flicker of a smile and a tiny nod. It signaled go.

They ran with pounding hearts. They ran for their lives. They dared all to reach freedom.

IV. Eternal Hope

A New Beginning
Freedom is not for the Timid —Vijaya L. Pandit

When their fear and tension subsided, they became aware of hunger and exhaustion. Not a house was in sight to ask for directions, or a creek to squelch their thirst. They trudged along, hoping to find some habitation. Food and rest was all they wanted. When they reached a village, they found it crowded with refugees. They knocked on many doors trying to get a room. But no one wanted refugees.

Edith was growing faint and feverish and when at last a kind farmer pointed to his barn, they gratefully curled up in the hay and sought refuge in slumber. A worse nightmare awaited them the next morning—Edith's fever had worsened. There was no doctor, and anxiously, they watched over her day and night. They took turns trading their meager possessions for nourishment. And miraculously, Edith pulled through. She must have sensed that she could not desert her family in its darkest hour.

They soon learned that they needed a Permit of Residency if they wanted to stay in the American Sector. Without that permit they could not obtain coupons to buy food or apply for work. As everywhere, food was scarce, and authorities staunchly denied permits that would add more hungry mouths. "Go back to East Germany," was their point of view.

Some thirty miles from the town in a deserted, dead-end corner of the American Sector, Edgar discovered a small inn, the Falkenstein, located amidst the Thüringer forest on a road that led north into the Russian Sector. Since the border was closed, no one ventured into that area, and Edgar was able to lease two rooms, a great improvement over the barn.

They were the only guests at the inn. Right below their window was the American border station—a small guardhouse with a rail across the street; sixty feet further up was a large Russian post. It seemed like an ideal spot, except for the proximity of numerous Russian soldiers, casting a menacing shadow. No one could venture into the woods.

In contrast, the American post and its two soldiers conveyed a most friendly atmosphere. American soldiers were known as the *sunny boys* and Paul did not hesitate to visit them. He spoke no English and the soldiers no German, but they had no trouble communicating.

Paul: Wow, leftovers! May I eat them? I'll clean the dishes.

The Americans: Sure. Go right ahead.

It established at once a splendid relationship.

To Paul's delight, the soldiers were excellent chess players, and he spent many happy hours playing with them.

The family took their meals at the inn. For breakfast the innkeeper served them bread and mint tea, for lunch and supper potatoes and cabbage, or soup.

Edith and the children picked dandelions and other edible grasses that Edith prepared to supplement their meager meals. Dandelions are bitter fare, but they were too hungry to be choosy.

The innkeeper referred to his daily pot of soup as the "Hitler Menu." During the winter of 1943, when Germany suffered crucial defeats, Hitler decreed that the German people must live more frugally. They were to eat *Eintopf* (a one-pot meal, or soup) for their Sunday dinner, and the German people obeyed.

They knew what was good for them—Hitler's informers were roaming the streets, sniffing like mice.

Hitler's cook also served *Eintopf* on Sundays, much to the dismay of Hitler's guests. Though docile yes-men, they did not share Hitler's passion for frugality. They relished good food and drink, especially on Sundays, and Hitler's dinner guests stayed away. Hitler did not like this; he wanted an attentive audience at all times, and from then on issued demand-invitations for his Sunday dinners. Hitler himself was a strict vegetarian, hoping this would prolong his life. He ate sparingly and detested delicacies. An admirer brought him a pair of beautiful lobsters one day. "Such things should be outlawed," Hitler stormed, and had them removed.

Christmas Day of 1946 dawned cold and white. Edith and the children decorated the room with fir branches and pinecones, nature's generous contribution. No candles or skis. Nevertheless, a special treat awaited them: a Christmas dinner promising carrots, a small piece of chicken AND all the potatoes they wanted to eat.

"I ate seven potatoes," Rosi happily confided to her brother. "For once, I'm not hungry."

Edith surprised the children with a pair of ice skates; the type that fastened to regular shoes, so either child could use them. Paul did not think much of skating; he preferred to play chess. But Rosi loved the sport and gladly took sole possession. About 500 yards from the inn, hidden in the woods, was a little pond that froze solid during the winter. With a homemade gadget she cleared away the snow, and the pond became her stage and the trees her audience.

It was early in January; a chilling day she would always remember. A Russian discovered her haven of joy.

"Woman, come here," he shouted, when he spied her through the trees.

Rosi looked at her coat at the other end of the pond, closer to the soldier. She could not abandon her coat—it was an irreplaceable necessity. Her heart pounding, she skated toward the Russian, who delightedly repeated:

"You come here, woman."

Rosi reached her coat, swooped it up and turned to flee in the opposite direction.

"Come back! Now!" the soldier shouted and started running after her.

Like a rabbit pursued by a hunter, Rosi fled through the forest and toward the inn, the Russian in eager pursuit. He was gaining on her. The skates on her feet hindered her speed. On the ice they came off frequently, but for once they clung like barnacles.

She had nearly reached the inn. It was not far to her mother's room, just one flight up the stairs. But climbing stairs with skates on her feet? The Russian was bound to catch up with her. And then? No, she decided. She did not want a Russian soldier near her mother.

She headed for the American post instead. It was farther than the inn, but the American border guards would know how to tangle with the Russian. Without knocking, she flew through their door, which luckily wasn't locked. The Russian stopped short, barely ten feet behind her.

She slammed the door shut and whispered: "Russian soldier," pointing terror-stricken through the little window. With trembling hands she took off her skates, watching the Russian through the window until he was out of range. With a timid "thank you" she raced home to the inn and collapsed on her bed in tears.

"Good bye, little pond, good bye," she sobbed. She knew she could not go to her pond again.

That evening, when the family headed for dinner—a short walk along the outside of the inn—a Russian fired a shot at them. The family dashed for the entry. When safely at the dinner table, Edgar took off and examined his hat. The bullet had left two holes in it, barely missing his head. He squeezed his daughter's hand, "I'm so glad you got away from that Russian!"

"A letter from Maria," Edith announced with great joy. "Did Otto get back from Russia? Will we hear wedding bells?" Edgar closed his book in anticipation.

"No wedding bells. Otto did not return," Edith murmured. "Maria is taking it hard. She'd like to come and be with us."

"She didn't say so in her letter?!" Edgar sat up with a start. "The Russians will ship her to Siberia, if they read that."

"She didn't. Her letter is very circumspect. She says, she is hoping to visit her little chess partner and is counting the days to see him."

Relieved, Edgar, leaned back and pondered the news. "Poor Maria. All the young men are dead, nothing but cripples and grandfathers left. I'd rather see our Maria married to a 'sunny boy' from America than a stone-faced Slav from Siberia."

"She can share our room. I'll sleep on the floor," Paul offered.

"Most generous of you. Are you sure you want to do that?"

"Absolutely."

"Good. Then let's figure out some details. She'll need an income."

"We'll pick up a paper and check the help-wanted ads."

"You can teach her English, Mami. Maybe she can find a job in an Allied canteen."

"They'd love her good bread."

They discussed Maria's future until late into the night. Then it was Edith's turn to convert the family's invitation into skillful words that Maria would understand, but would be meaningless to the Russian mail spies. It was a clever game, this camouflage of meaning in the correspondence between East and West Germans and developed into quite an art form.

The Russians soon grew wise to it, and it took longer and longer for mail to pass inspection and reach its destination. For extra speed and safety, Peter took the letter for Maria to East Germany and mailed it there. On Edgar's insistence, Maria had to meet one condition—if she were to come to the West, she had to have a visitor's visa and cross the border legitimately, ergo safely. For the first time, a year after the war, a few persons were able to cross the border with a visa.

Weeks went by. And then the big day arrived—Maria, with her visitor's visa in hand boarded the 10:28 train. By mid-afternoon, she arrived at the border station. In the children's room an extra bed was waiting for her, and near the American border crossing, Rosi and Paul eagerly waved and shouted, but only for a moment. The sight of Maria made them throw caution to the wind; they ran the sixty feet to the Russian border rail and hugged Maria right across the beam.

Slowly, two Russian guards approached; they were talking to each other. In a friendly fashion, they motioned to the children. "Come on in," one of them said, taking a good look at Rosi, "cookies for you inside house."

The skating pond in the woods! The Russian chasing her! It hit Rosi like lightning. She grabbed her brother's hand and raced back to the American guardhouse.

"What are you doing?" Paul shouted furiously, shaking off her hand.

"We are not going over there, Paul. We are waiting here."

She meant business. Paul could tell from the tone of her voice. And they stationed themselves near the American guardhouse, waving to Maria, urging her to hurry.

Yet the Russians were not in a hurry. They took Maria inside the building, while the children anxiously waited. Waited and waited. Yet no sign of Maria. They beseeched the Russian guards, but the Russians ignored them. They begged the American guards to inquire, but they were reluctant to interfere. Edith came to plead with the Russians and the Americans, but in vain. Finally, one of the Russians explained:

"Papers no good. We sent her back."

Did they?

Maria was young and pretty. For many months, Edith and the children worried and prayed for her. Edith wrote more letters, but Maria's bed in the children's room remained empty. They did not hear from Maria again.

Life in the Russian-occupied zone was unpredictable. There were no rules, no laws, no safety. The victorious Russian soldiers enjoyed absolute power and did as they pleased. It was different in the American Sector where law and order prevailed.

During the war, several dozen Russian prisoners worked for Edgar. They were brought to the company every morning, and taken back to their barracks at night. Edgar provided them with a stove and a pot, so they could cook peas or make bean soup for their lunch. Occasionally, the Russians sang while they worked, and to Edith's delight, from time to time Edgar brought one of them home.

Ivan, the young Russian, had a magnificent voice. Edith played songs from her Russian collection that Ivan knew. Or he sang the melancholic songs of his far-away village. For some of the songs, like *Stenka Rasin* or *Heh Huchla,* the family joined him. Ivan's visits were an uplifting event for all, starting with lunch during which Ivan eagerly memorized German phrases the family taught him; he had a fine ear for languages, too.

Toward the end of the war, Edgar expected the Russian prisoners to rejoice—soon they'd be liberated. Not so. They begged Edgar to let them escape to the West; they did not want to return to Russia. And quietly, one by one, they disappeared.

Twelve months had passed. Still no permit of residency. Their letters and applications were either ignored or answered with an unwavering, "No permit. Go back where you came from." Yet going back was not an option. Communism called for systematic elimination of all educated or moneyed persons and especially those who had fled, a policy rigorously enforced in all Communist-occupied countries.

Fortunately, West Germany was not able to deport the ever-increasing number of refugees. Thousands had fled, and daily more were coming. Deportation of refugees would have caused violent riots, since deportation meant certain death. Meanwhile, Edgar journeyed to other parts of the American Sector, looking for ways to start his business again. Without a permit, though, the family could not follow. Nor could he stay anywhere and work.

That Wednesday, while Edgar was away, a particularly nasty letter denying their request arrived, and Edith decided to take matters into her hands. Early the following morning, she set out for the office of the American District Governor, located in the neighboring town.

She brought a big book, prepared to wait all day and come again the following day until she got a chance to plead her case. She had barely read two pages, when she heard her name being called, her chance for an audience.

John Taylor, the Governor, a young man from Chicago, received her most cordially and listened attentively to her story. Then he took a piece of paper and a pen and wrote:

"Dr. Leuthold and his family are to be issued a Permit of Residency as of immediately." He signed the paper and stamped it. The family could no longer be deported!

Head Held High

After a gray November follows a merry May —German folksong

On wings of joy Edith hastened back to the station. She could barely wait to bring Edgar the good news. The station was packed with people—most of them refugees and displaced persons; all with their tale of woe. She was both—displaced from her beloved ski cabin in Czechoslovakia, and a refugee from East Germany's Communism. Not much difference, she thought. It meant being uprooted, far from home, and without worldly possessions. Her hand slipped into her purse and lovingly fingered her permit—the permit that gave them a chance to start anew.

The next train would leave in four hours, time for a stroll, she decided, when her ears caught a familiar voice.

"Gunilla."

Edith stopped, intrigued. Gunilla was an unusual name. She had heard it before, in Graz at the ball of her college friend, the Countess von H., long before the war.

There it was again. "Gunilla."

The voice sounded concerned but gentle and well modulated, a lovely voice. Edith remembered that voice and the beautiful lady it belonged to, Erne von Bühlhausen. That evening as a guest at the castle Erne had worn an emerald green gown, exquisitely embroidered with lavender roses. From her tiny waist the full skirt gracefully unfolded like the petals of a rose. Edith could still see her waltzing with her handsome husband across the festive Renaissance ballroom.

Over dinner the two couples talked about horses, travels and the books they read. Both had a one-year old daughter christened on the very same day. "Gunilla is our daughter's name," Erne had told her—Gunilla, the name she just heard.

In 1939, she and Edgar visited the young couple. The von Bühlhausens had recently returned to the family estate, their beloved Korschwitz. It had been in Polish hands since the Versailles Treaty, when large chunks of German territories had been torn off and given to neighboring countries. Hitler had recaptured these areas in 1939.

Edith recalled vividly Erne's joy of being home again on the family estate with its rolling hills of lawn and forest surrounded the castle. It had belonged to the Bühlhausens for centuries. She remembered rowing on the lake and feeding a family of swans amidst the mauve water lilies.

Irresistibly drawn by that voice of the past, Edith pressed in its direction. The train station was small and stuffy, bursting with people pushing in every direction. It was not possible to see anyone. But suddenly she stood in front of that voice—a frail lady, much older than the lady she remembered.

We have aged beyond our years, Edith realized. Seven years of hardship and anxiety, deprivation and lack of food do leave their mark. The lady she faced wore an unsightly, ill-fitting garb, yet she had the regal bearing of the Erne von Bühlhausen she remembered. A young, slender girl pressed into her presence. She was clad in crude, brownish sackcloth, her feet bare, her head covered with a scarf in farmer's fashion.

Not a farmer's daughter that girl, Edith thought, scrutinizing her vivacious, intelligent features.

"Here I am, Mama," the young girl whispered, "I got hold of a ..." She stopped short and shot a glance of ill-concealed hostility at Edith, a glance full of passionate pride.

Also refugees, Edith thought, smiling compassionately at the young girl while saying softly, "You must be Gunilla."

Neither mother nor daughter responded, and Edith with some trepidation turned to the mother, "Forgive me for intruding into your privacy, but your voice and face remind me of a lovely lady I met long before the war, at a ball in the castle of Graz. I am Edith Leuthold." She turned to the daughter and added, "And that lady told me about their beautiful, one-year old baby girl they had just christened Gunilla."

The young girl's face brightened. Strangers rarely had a kind word for her since she had become a refugee. Local people despised refugees and made life miserable for them.

Yet her mother did not share her daughter's sentiment. Her mind churned in bitter turmoil. She, too, remembered the ball, the elegance, and the warm glow of joy waltzing in the arms of her beloved husband, the man of her life. Now she was destitute, a displaced person in a hostile world with five small children she could barely feed. She looked down at her clothes, despicable, hand-me-down rags. She blushed with embarrassment and shame. An angry tear rolled down her cheek. But not for long did she succumb to her feelings. She was a lady, composed at all times. She mandated her calm to return, and with a small, melodic voice murmured:

"Edith?"

Edith nodded, and sensing her friend's uneasiness about her plight, she replied, "We, too, are refugees, Erne, my dear. We, too, had to flee."

Yet for Erne it was no consolation to share this unhappy fate. She descended from a long line of valiant warriors dating back to the tenth century. They had conquered lands and garnered fame. Now, the tables had turned. She was among the conquered, deprived of all worldly possessions. Gone were her carefree days of elegance and laughter, gone her happy, well-ordered life in a world at peace. Nothing was left but her memories. And a world in chaos.

"Your feet must be cold and sore, Gunilla," Edith murmured to the barefoot girl. "Mine are sore from these shoes, and sometimes I feel like walking barefoot, too."

Gunilla's face brightened for a moment. She scrutinized Edith's shoes that had been worn day in and day out for a long, long time. Her eyes returned to her own bare feet, and her expressive face left no doubt about her feelings of dismay.

"Her shoes were ruined in the delousing camp," her mother explained, and turned to her daughter, "Gunilla, you can tell the story better than I can."

Intense anguish clouded the child's lovely face and she sobbed the words more than she spoke them: "Mama was not with us then. We thought ..." She stopped, visibly overwhelmed by the memory, but her mother placed a reassuring hand on her shoulder and Gunilla continued.

"Before the war ended, Father sent Mama off in a medical transport. Mama was very ill." She turned to her mother, "We were told you'd never come back."

"Then Father left us to fight the Russians. He simply left us, the five of us—the baby, my sister, and my little brothers! A relative came to stay with us, the Baroness von Leipe." Gunilla pursed her lips with loathing when she pronounced the name.

"And then the Russians came." She heaved a deep breath as if it were her last.

246

The child's pain loomed like a black cloud ready to burst. "The shoes, Gunilla, tell Edith about the shoes," her mother whispered.

But the girl's pain had welled up from deep within her, too intense to be stopped. She would get to the shoes in due time.

Erne, sensing her daughter's state of mind, murmured to Edith, "Our train won't leave for three hours. Let us talk outside, if you have time."

Edith nodded and Erne took her daughter's arm, and gently guided her toward the door. The three ladies walked in silence for nearly a block. The sky was gray, casting gloom over the war-ravaged town. A northwesterly wind twirled clouds of dust, giving the street the semblance of a dirt-baked road in the country. Neither a blade of grass nor a bench were anywhere in sight, so the ladies settled themselves on the concrete slabs of a bombed-out pharmacy.

Gunilla's memories still held her hostage. One in particular was haunting her, one she had never shared with anyone. It was the intense disapproval she felt for the Baroness, her aunt. The Baroness was young and beautiful, and passionately in love with her father. Gunilla knew. When her mother had left with the medical transport not expected to live, the aunt had moved in with them in hopes of marrying her father. The aunt herself had told her so.

Gunilla did not want another mother; she had one whom she loved with all her heart. Dimly, with a woman's intuition, she sensed that it was the aunt's open and shameless flirtation with her father that had caused her mother's long illness.

The aunt was still living with them, which was a source of daily anguish for Gunilla, who was expected to be grateful to her. After all, the aunt had saved her life and the lives of her siblings, and had suffered plenty on their behalf.

Slowly she resumed her story.

"We were waiting for Father to return. Instead, one gloomy day the neighbors came running to the castle screaming:

"'The Russians are coming! The Russians are coming!'

"We ran to the cellar —some twenty of us—and had barely locked ourselves in, when Russian tanks rolled up. Later, we heard them stomping about in the house. That's when the baby began to cry. Luckily, the aunt had sugar cubes and kept stuffing them into his mouth to keep him quiet.

"Two days later the Russians found us."

Vacantly, the girl stared into space, but like a robot she kept talking. "They kicked in the door and waved their guns in our faces. The children screamed. Herr and Frau von Dizelski and their two daughters hid under their bedding. When the soldiers found them, they kicked them and hit them with their gun barrels.

"Other soldiers kept shouting, 'Uri, uri.' They wanted watches. Many of them had already three or four on their arms.

"They searched everyone and everything. Then they fell upon the women."

A slight shiver seized Gunilla. Her face dropped into her hands.

"Poor Katrina," she murmured absently. "She kept screaming 'No! No!' and kicked and struggled with the soldier as hard as she could. But he was stronger, the beast. He beat her and strangled her to death." Gunilla wrapped her arms around her knees.

"They kept us locked up," she whispered. "We couldn't bury her for days.

"Every day they dragged out the two von Dizelski girls. Pretty girls, with blond hair and blue eyes, just like their mother. The first day, their father tried to protect them. He

248

planted himself in front of his girls and kept pushing the soldiers away. 'Don't you dare touch them,' he shouted, 'or I'll kill you!' They got into a fistfight. But it didn't do much good. Those brutes, they killed him, too.

"Several times a day the soldiers came to the cellar to get women. Later, they brought them back and locked us up."

Intense anger and compassion flushed Edith's face—anger at the egomaniac who had caused the war, and compassion for the young girl who had to live with these nightmares for the rest of her life.

Instinctively, Edith reached for Gunilla's hand. She felt a deep love for this girl who was on the brink of becoming a teenager just as her own daughter. Would she be able to cope with what she had seen and suffered? And trust in life again? And ever confide in a man?

Edith's chin sank into the palms of her hands. She recalled an article in a British journal—a most disturbing eye-opener about Hitler's clandestine operations. It still haunted her. On a beautiful, sunny day Edgar had brought home that British magazine, a gift from one of his clients.

She was thrilled to see a foreign magazine again, the first in many years, until she came across that devastating article. The Russians, it appeared, were not the only ones who committed unspeakable acts of cruelty. Hitler's henchmen had done worse. Her own countrymen! She had not yet come to terms with the shocking revelation, especially, the secretiveness that Hitler had employed. Now, a year after war's end, the horrible deeds were slowly coming to light.

The article described Hitler's *Barbarossa Plan,* a codename Hitler gave to the invasion of Russia. He issued express orders to his officers that the enemy on the eastern front must be dealt with "unrelenting, merciless harshness."

It mentioned the Einsatzkommando, a special unit designed to "lead the struggle against the enemies of the Reich." Its commander was a man born in Triest, Odilo Lotario Globocnik, who became a Party member in 1931. Armed robbery and financial trickery had landed him four times in Austrian jails. In spite of it, he rose quickly in the Nazi Party and ruthlessly facilitated Hitler's Anschluss of Austria and was named Governor of Vienna.

Göring did not like Globocnik and fired him. So Himmler took him into the SS, giving him vast authority under the codename, Aktion Reinhard. He was to "*cleanse* Poland without anyone getting wind of it." Globocnik transported countless Polish Jews east. No one suspected they would never return.

Edith winced. Hitler was preaching high ideals and service-to-the-fatherland to his subjects at home, while he secretly ordered his henchmen to commit ruthless atrocities!

Enraged, she turned to Edgar. She could barely find words. "Edgar, this can't be true! Have you read this article?"

"I've read it, and I know no more than you do," Edgar replied, sick to his stomach about the disgrace Hitler had brought upon the German people and the honor of the Officers Corps.

"But I assure you," he continued, "neither my general in France, nor my general in Russia would have stooped to such demands. Both were men of principle, men who upheld the Hague Convention and the dignity of men. They did not follow those directives. The Prussian Officers Corps has long been known for its men of honor and integrity."

"How about this Globocnik?"

"He's a common thief and scoundrel. What do you expect? Give a jailbird unlimited authority, and he'll turn into a big-time criminal. Hitler certainly had a knack for choosing the vilest of men."

"Were SS men generally evil?"

Edgar loathed the SS. Right off hand he couldn't think of a nice one among them. They certainly had caused him plenty of trouble. But he was fair. "We can't condemn eight million men; most of them were drafted without recourse. There are all kinds among them," he said. "First of all, there are two distinct branches—one is the Waffen SS[47], the other is the political SS. Some of our bravest men in the service belonged to the Waffen SS. They were chosen for their bravery, their ancestry and their height. The political SS was less exclusive. It included men like Arno. Many of the political SS men were given extraordinary authority, causing extraordinary abuse."

"Do you remember Franz telling us about the iron discipline and harsh punishment within their ranks? He certainly was a good man and a brave one."

Edgar drummed the table with his fingers. The mere thought of the SS made him edgy. "They did have strict discipline. If you were caught stealing from another SS man, you were shot in front of the regiment. If you were under 18, they put you on probation and sent you to a detention camp. Later, when we needed them at the front, they were sent on the most dangerous missions."

"A cruel regime."

"Cruel and secretive, and with absolute power. No wonder it has caused absolute calamity."

Edith nodded and sank into a chair to continue the shocking report. The British journal reprinted the full text of Hitler's incredible directive that he sent to his generals on the eastern front:

---

[47] Waffen SS is the military SS (Schutz Staffel), in contrast to the political SS.

"The war against Russia cannot be fought in knightly fashion. The struggle is one of ideologies and racial differences and must be waged with unprecedented, unmerciful, and unrelenting hardness. All officers must get rid of their old fashioned ideas. I realize that the necessity for conducting such warfare is beyond the comprehension of you generals, but I must insist that my orders be followed without complaint. The (Russian) commissars hold views directly opposite to those of National Socialism. Hence these commissars must be eliminated. Any German soldier who breaks international law will be pardoned. Russia did not take part in the Hague Convention and, therefore, has no rights under it. Hitler"

Was it surprising that the Russians retaliated?

Evil begets evil.

What has become of our civilized world," Edith sighed, recalling the article and the enormity of Hitler's crimes. The cold concrete she and her two friends were sitting on and the rubble all around them were no comfort either. Her hand slid into her purse. Was it still there, that ray of hope, that long awaited Permit of Residency that John Tailor, the American Governor, had handed her barely two hours earlier?

"What happened to your shoes?" Edith murmured to Gunilla, at a loss for words.

"My shoes?" Gunilla repeated absentmindedly. "Oh, my shoes. They were burned, because we had lice. The women got the lice from the soldiers. In our cramped quarters, they spread from head to head. Months later, when we got to West Germany, we had to be deloused. They put us in a big chamber—gray concrete walls, gray concrete ceiling, and a cold concrete floor. We had to take off everything we wore, and they threw it all, including our shoes, into a hot oven to kill the lice.

"They deloused us, too, by pouring acid over us." Involuntarily, she clasped her shoulders as if to protect herself. "Did we scream! All of us. We had open sores and wounds and the acid burned like ..." She stopped and looked at her Mother, searching for a word that would not offend her. But there was no polite word that could describe the pain. "It burned like ... nechistnaya sila yob twoyu mats svolotch sukin sin," she burst out with fury, using the expletives she had heard her Russian captors use a thousand times. A deep breath of relief escaped her lungs.

Erne's backbone stiffened and her eyes glared disapproval, but before she found words, Edith exclaimed, "A perfect description, Gunilla."

Gunilla stared at Edith in shock, "You understand Russian?"

"Only a little." Edith replied calmly. Then, in halting Russian and with a sly little smile she added, "Actually, I don't know any of the words you used. I learned Russian from a textbook. But I am sure they expressed well what you must have felt."

Against her will, Gunilla's face turned crimson. She was certain they were ugly words. Yet they brought great relief.

"I don't know either what they mean," she admitted in surprisingly good Russian. All children in East Germany had to learn their victor's tongue.

"I don't think we want to know," Edith added with a wry smile. Then she continued in English, "What happened to your shoes, Gunilla?"

Reluctantly, Gunilla returned to her account. "We just stood there, stark naked, and in agony. For an eternity." Her eyes wandered aimlessly over the rubble that surrounded them. Suddenly, her face brightened.

"Look," she murmured. "Over there. A red flower amidst the ruins!" She jumped up, eager to forget the past. In spite of her mother's protestations, she skipped over the boulders with the agility of a young fawn, eager to investigate this joyful sign of life amidst the sad devastation of war—a tiny red bud peaking through the rubble of a collapsed building.

"It's a geranium," she called. "It must have been in a window box."

When she returned, her pain had visibly eased and she settled herself again on the hard stone.

"To top it all off," she continued, her frown returning, "they shaved our heads. That was the worst of all. Hair takes forever to grow back," she moaned plaintively. "All of us—bald like Tibetan monks."

"How about your clothes?" Edith asked, unnerved by imagining the scene.

"We got them back. Everything shrunk in the ovens. Nothing fit us anymore. The shoes were as hard as rock and as brittle as eggshells. We were barefoot and mostly naked. Eventually, they gave us blankets to cover ourselves, so they could send us away, back into the street." Gunilla covered her face and quietly sobbed.

Edith gently stroked her arm, "One day," she murmured, "you will have beautiful long curls again, and lovely shoes and clothes as you did when you grew up in Korschwitz. We will all have well-fitting shoes again," Edith looked at her aching feet, but her mind did not dwell on shoes.

She thought of the moments when she had escaped a similar fate: first at the cabin, when a dozen Czech soldiers had broken down their door and confronted them—two young women alone with a daughter and a small son. But miraculously, they had not harmed them, not even touched them. And later, when they hid under the bridge while a group of soldiers passed overhead and did not discover them. Chills went down her spine when she thought of her son's coughing spell at that crucial moment. Or the day in Hainichen, when they nearly knocked on her mother-in-law's door, unaware that Soviet soldiers occupied the house.

A heavy silence enveloped the three women, perching on cold slabs of asphalt—like slender willows weaving in the wind, each alone with her thoughts, each rooted in her past, each prey to the storms of global events. Like willows, they were swaying to the chords within them—Gunilla, coping with a cruel reality; Erne, clinging to the memories of her privileged past; and Edith, always searching for a kernel of goodness in the world around her.

The silence weighed heavily, and Edith reached into her pocket to find relief. She pulled out a small bag of seeds she had roasted and passed it around.

"Tell me what you think of this," she announced half humbly, half proudly to be able to offer something to eat. "It's a mixture of flax seed and oat flakes." Flax was animal feed, but dire need taught Edith to experiment.

"Flax seed?" Erne looked puzzled. "Didn't we feed flax to the horses?"

"We did. I've heard Edgar say that it gives horses their shiny coat of hair, and who knows, it may make it grow faster, too." Edith smiled and handed the bag to Gunilla, who with interest took a handful. "If you like it, Gunilla, take the bag home with you."

"I'd like that," Gunilla replied. "Taste is not everything."

"It used to amaze me," Edith continued her train of thought, "that the Soviet prisoners, who worked for my husband, always carried seeds in their pockets and chewed on them all day long. Usually hard kernels of peas or corn. They had strikingly strong and good-looking white teeth."

Gunilla cocked her head quizzically. Enemy soldiers with a redeeming feature? The thought had never occurred to her. "They do?" she queried.

The mere mention of a Slavic soldier still caused her instant dread. She remembered the winter after the war, when she and her nine-year old brother had to go to school again. It was a long and scary walk. They didn't mind crossing the open fields, but they had to pass through a stretch of forest. Russians used to hang out there, looking for rabbits and deer. It was a cold winter in 1945/46, with lots of snow, and the soldiers always carried a bottle of Vodka with them to keep warm. Whenever Gunilla and her brother heard or saw Russians, they would run and dive into a snow bank behind a tree.

"White teeth?" Gunilla shook her head, "I never looked at them."

"You were wise not to look," Edith commented, looking at the girl's deep blue eyes. "Tell me, how were you able to escape from the Russians? I mean, how did you get across the border?"

"Mother sent a friend to take us across."

"How were you able to find your children, Erne, and contact them?"

"It is a painful story, Edith, but it ended well." She squeezed her daughter's hand. "Before the war ended, the German medical transport left me at a hospital in West Germany. I was not expected to live, but I did. Six months later, in the winter of 1945, I was able to get out of bed. Every day I walked to the highway. Hundreds of refugees passed by there, some on foot, some in wagons; all moving at a snail's pace. I looked at every person and asked them all the same question,

'Have you seen my five children, my little boy who is two years old, my little girl who is four, my big daughter twelve, and my sons nine and fifteen, accompanied by a young aunt?' Every day I went to search for them on that highway. Every day."

Her eyes filled with tears, but she managed to suppress their flow. "I was lucky. After eleven months of searching, the Red Cross located them for me. They were at Lochow castle, I was told. Its owner, Count Bredow, the aunt's cousin, had fled to the West."

"We weren't staying at the castle, Mama," Gunilla exploded. "We were thrown in its cellar with the rats and the mice, and had to work in the fields like common laborers! You should have seen the Russians soldiers scorn us when we arrived. 'Look at them,' they jeered, 'this is what Hitler has done to his people. Look at these half-dead, lice-ridden remains of Hitler's Thousand Year Reich!'"

"I know, Gunilla," her mother murmured soothingly, but Gunilla's flow of angry words could not be stopped.

"They took us to an empty garden-shed crawling with bugs and fleas. But the aunt refused to set foot in it. She insisted that we be put in the castle's cellar. She knew it had a cooking stove and a door. The aunt did not want every Russian in the neighborhood to visit us in that open shed.

"The soldiers finally consented. I think she struck a deal with them, because the very next day they ordered my brothers and me to work in the fields. We had to work every day, all day long, without food and pay. One day I collapsed in the field from hunger and fatigue. And the Russian guard came and hit me!" She stopped, her face red with rage, her fists firmly clenched. "He kept shouting at me, 'Dawei! Dawei rabotta! Shevelis, suka!!' Work! 'Dawei rabotta!'

257

"The fields were full of thistles that stung our legs and arms and hands. At night, we had to eat those thistles. The aunt made thistle soup, thistle spinach, thistles stew, nothing but thistles, morning, noon and night." Intense pain darkened the young girl's features. Edith tried to distract her mind from the humiliation she had suffered.

"What does it taste like, this thistle soup?" she asked. "Isn't it prickly to the tongue?"

"Not really. I guess the aunt cooked it a long time. When you are hungry, you aren't choosy. After working all day, we would have eaten anything. We cut down trees, too, and sawed them into logs and chopped them for firewood. Once in a while we got milk from a farmer. The aunt cooked gruel for us then. It was good."

"A kind farmer," Edith gently tapped a lump of plaster.

"He was. I think he took pity on my baby brother," Gunilla explained. "Farmer Ed lost four sons in that wretched war. He was a kind man, and smart, too. He was the only farmer in the village who still owned a cow. Before we arrived at Lochow, the Russians rounded up all the cows in the area and had them herded to Russia. When the soldiers came to Farmer Ed's place," Gunilla's eyes danced with mischievous delight, "he hid one of his pregnant cows in his bathroom. His wife kept feeding and patting her so she wouldn't moo."

Edith looked puzzled. Not much surprised her anymore, but she found it hard to imagine that Russians would herd cows to Russia, half way across Germany and Poland.

Erne, divining Edith's thoughts, explained: "Thousands of our cows and sheep have been herded deep into Russia. They use German children and women to do the herding and Russian soldiers to guard them."

"Lochow Castle, what nightmares we suffered there!" Gunilla looked as grim as a gravestone. "The Russian soldiers kept coming at night when we wanted to sleep. They shone flashlights into our faces and waved their guns. They frightened us half to death. They always wanted something. We learned a lot of Russian from them," she glanced sideways at her Mother and quickly added, "and Russian songs."

"You did? Russian songs?" Edith looked pleased; she recalled Ivan's fine voice.

"We could hear them singing in the forest, especially in the evenings. Sometimes, they sang upstairs."

"Their songs are melancholic, aren't they? But beautiful."

"It was us who were melancholic." Gunilla retorted, her eyes shooting dangerous sparks. "We were scared, hungry, and miserable. I did not like their songs. Russian songs meant Russian soldiers were nearby. They were always too close for my comfort."

Edith prudently changed the subject.

"Tell me, how did your Mother contact you?"

Slowly, the girl's face relaxed. It even brightened a little. "A letter arrived."

"A letter? You mean a letter by postal service? I still haven't received a letter from my mother in Leipzig! I've written her several times," Edith interrupted. "I thought postal service is at a standstill in East Germany."

"I sent it through the Red Cross," Erne explained. "After many weeks, somehow the letter did reach them."

"We got a notice from the Red Cross that they had a letter for us," Gunilla eagerly added. "I ran all the way to get it. A letter from Mama! Mama still alive! We were in ecstasy." She turned to her mother, "It would have been the happiest day of my life, the day that your letter arrived."

But her face did not reflect happiness. In a barely audible whisper she continued, "What a shock it was, that letter, telling us that Father had been killed. Father, whom we expected to see again."

The color had drained from Gunilla's face. Vacantly, she searched the sky for her father's face. "I still can't believe it," she moaned.

"I did not say good-bye to him when he left to join his regiment," she whispered, and Edith slid closer to hear her fading voice. "My brother and I hid in the stables. We were most upset. We did not want Father to leave us; we were all alone. We were sure he would stay if we weren't there to say good-bye. But he left all the same."

She hugged her knees and broke down in bitter tears. She had venerated her father like a god. Yet she had denied him her last farewell.

The two ladies sat silently, commiserating. The cold stone became unbearable, and they got up and walked.

"You were fortunate to have found your children," Edith murmured to her friend. "I've heard that newspapers and radio stations will be running search ads for missing persons for at least a dozen years into the future."

A strong gust of wind took hold of Gunilla's headscarf and carried it away. She pursued it with agile steps. Her hair was barely a quarter of an inch long.

"Is your daughter attending school again?" Edith asked her mother with concern.

"Yes, the poor girl, she is. It is a nightmare for her, attending school without shoes and proper clothing and without her long, beautiful braids she used to have. A few days ago, her teacher made her take off her scarf, and her classmates laughed at her. They thought it was funny to see her shaven head."

"How thoughtless of that teacher!" Edith frowned.

"I wish she could wear my shoes, but they don't fit her anymore," Erne sighed, but stopped, aware of her litany of grievances. She groped for a more positive note.

"The pastor promised a pair of wooden shoes for her."

"Wooden shoes from Holland?"

"Donated by a Dutch church. Winter is approaching; I'm praying for any kind of shoes." A weak smile brightened her care-worn face.

"Your daughter is a remarkable young lady, Erne. You can be proud of her. It takes great courage to cope with all she has seen and suffered."

Both women sank into silence again—both wondering how to survive this post-war misery, both wondering whether it would ever end.

An hour later from the window of her train Gunilla waved good-bye until Edith and the station disappeared. For a long time Edith stood there, gazing after the train, into the distant past, and toward an unknown future. How quickly our fate can change! Yesterday comfort and plenty, today abject poverty, suffering and pain. What will tomorrow bring?

Perhaps it is good we do not know.

She had come to the station on wings of joy, but Gunilla's story had shaken her faith. Why this cruelty of men against men? The war had ended a year ago; yet the worst of the tragedies had remained hidden and were just then beginning to surface—the horrors of the concentration camps, the atrocities, the fate of the Jews. Its staggering enormity was beyond all understanding.

Voltaire had put it brilliantly, she thought, "Murderers are punished, unless they kill in large numbers and to the sound of trumpets." But it brought her no comfort.

Edith felt as exhausted as if she had lived through Gunilla's nightmares. She was glad to find Edgar at home and willing to lend her a patient ear.

Edgar was a pacifist at heart, but he was also a realist. "It will take millennia to change human nature," he said. "Lust for power and aggression are deeply engrained in the human race."

"Why can't we share Planet Earth in peace?" Edith retorted. "What good can come of war?"

"A good question. Do you know how General Lee justified the horrors of war? He said, 'It is fortunate that war is so terrible; otherwise men would love it too much.'" Edgar was in the best of spirits, now that he had a permit to stay in the West.

"We are too deeply involved to render sound judgment," he added more seriously. "Nonetheless, war destroys the old and makes room for the new. Cities can be rebuilt with better design, better materials, and better know-how. New factories will be more efficient and productive."

"At a high price."

"A high price indeed, but perhaps to the benefit of future generations. War is lunacy, no question about it. But, like death, it may be part of life—death on a grand scale."

Edith looked doubtful. In her opinion, war had no laudable aspects.

"Nothing forges the unity of a nation more firmly than the existence of an outside enemy," Edgar explained.

"*Enemy*—the word should be abolished! We're one species."

"Still, wars have stimulated trade, knowledge and a multitude of inventions. World War II created radar, the jet plane, the long-range missile, the transistor, the Volkswagen and the atomic/nuclear age." Edgar smiled sheepishly. "Am I speaking in defense of war?" He asked sheepishly. The permit of residency had put him in a most happy frame of mind.

Edith did not respond; her mind was trying to cope with Gunilla's heartrending odyssey.

"Don't you agree that struggle adds spice to life?" he resumed. "We have battled a whole year to get this permit. And it paid off; we finally got it."

Edith nodded wearily, and Edgar wrapped his arms around her, whispering tenderly, "You did it!"

After supper, Edith got out her accordion. She remembered an old, popular folksong that she wanted to play, a special song for Gunilla:

> Im Leben geht alles vorueber
> Im Leben geht alles vorbei.
> Nach jedem trueben November
> Folgt wieder ein froehlicher Mai."

> (In life ev'rything passes.
> Life will bring a new day.
> After each dark November
> Will follow a merry May.)

The Faith of Youth
Nothing is Permanent but Change —Heraclitus

Edgar's oldest son, Peter, was still in East Germany working on the Singer farm. The ancestral love of land and farming, however, had clearly passed him by; he yearned for city pavement, modern conveniences, and a fine bath. To his dismay, his usually immaculate fingernails were an embarrassment, and his shoes were caked with mud.

There were compensations. A farm was the only place where a hungry, undernourished teenager could get something to eat. It also was the safest place during the post-war chaos. In urban areas, Soviet soldiers snapped up young men and women wherever they found them, and few of them were ever seen again. Soldiers rarely came to isolated farms.

Peter's job entailed hard, physical labor. There was no gasoline for the farm equipment; even the plowing had to be done by hand. It was not to Peter's liking. After three months of backbreaking labor, Peter was entrusted with a pair of oxen to do the hard work for him. It was a glorious step forward.

But his joy was short-lived. Disquieting news from his father arrived. Peter did not know that the family had fled to the West; he had not heard from them in many months. Without mail and telephone service, news had to be carried by people, and they were hard to find.

That morning, an old gentleman had brought him father's letter. It suggested that Peter join the family in the West and, if possible, bring a few items they desperately needed. Would he venture to go back to their city home—that is, if strangers weren't occupying the house yet?

Big questions, yet no one to discuss them with.

A glance at his fingernails sufficed to make his decision. He chuckled at the irony of fate—the family had fled to the West to escape political persecution and certain death. Now they faced another grim enemy, the lack of the most basic necessities. Liberty alone was not enough for survival. He knew it all too well. They needed clothing and bedding, pots to cook in, and dishes to eat from. They had none of these. And nothing could be bought—neither in the West Zone of Germany, nor in the East. They could not stay in hotels much longer.

Peter took his knapsack and said goodbye. He was ready for a change. He did not worry about the dangers that lay ahead. He was heading home. The front of the house was severely damaged. But the key was still in its hiding place. And miracle of miracles, no one had moved in! He discovered some food in the pantry and spent the night. Next morning, he gathered the items his father had listed and locked up again.

His father had also sent him his rail pass, a vital permit that enabled Peter to board one of the scarce trains that ran again. The pass had no photo, making it safer to use. It was in Russian, and Peter wondered what it said. Did it give father's doctor title? What if someone questioned him about it? At fifteen, he was a bit young to have an M.D. or Ph.D. What if they detained him to look after their sick comrades?

By evening, Peter found the border guide his father had suggested. And Peter was in luck: the guide agreed to take him across. He even offered Peter a couch for the night.

At the inn, Am Falkenstein, Rosi and Paul had no inkling of their brother's daring adventure until early one morning he knocked at their door. And there he was!

Peter left soon on his second trip. He was gone one morning, barely saying goodbye. His siblings were used to secretiveness and the futility of asking questions; during the Hitler years, secrecy had been imperative for survival. An innocent remark of theirs could endanger everyone in the family. Government oppression had not changed; it was the same under Stalin's Communism as it had been under Hitler's Nationalsozialismus. West Germany, too, was swarming with Communist spies.

When Peter arrived at the border with his next load, his regular guide was unavailable. Since border situations fluctuated, patrol patterns changed and walls topped with barbed wire were being added, his father insisted that Peter take a guide. It increased his chances of survival. So Peter found an enterprising Russian soldier who took him across in exchange for cigarettes and schnapps. Russian soldiers did not receive generous military rations as did American soldiers. They supplemented their income and supplies whenever they could.

On his third trip, Peter decided to bring the sewing machine, an invaluable asset. Curtains had to be turned into dresses, napkins into pillowcases, torn and worn-out sheets mended, and outgrown clothing had to be lengthened and widened.

Peter found a saw, cut off the legs of the sewing table, and stowed everything in a wheelbarrow. Then he took his knapsack and headed for his father's company, which was run by the government then. He managed to enter unseen and hid inside, impatiently waiting for the employees to go home. In the cellar of the warehouse, interred under the brick floor, was the family silver. It had been buried there since the early years of the war. Peter felt like Robinson Crusoe as he tested and poked to find the right spot. By the light of a match and with infinite perseverance he loosened the bricks. Underneath in a large box was the family silver.

His father had wrapped the box in roofing paper to keep it dry. But two years earlier, a bomb had broken the water pipe and flooded the cellar. The box was still waterlogged when Peter opened it. A most hideous smell issued from the muddy mess. Nonetheless, Peter stuffed as much as he could into his bags. Then he settled down to wait until morning—a general curfew reigned in the city.

Back at the house he loaded his booty into the wheelbarrow and set off for the West. He was glad his silver didn't glitter, and its evil smell kept fellow travelers at a distance. His destination was the official border station near the Falkenstein.

The Russian control came first. Peter had brought a carton of black-market cigarettes for the guard, who was delighted and gladly looked through Peter's stuff. Russians were always on the lookout for something appealing, but the contents of Peter's wheelbarrow were revolting. The silver had turned black, the knives were ragged from corrosion, and the smell was repulsive. Bewildered, the Russian examined the five-arm chandeliers. Why would anyone want to bring something so hideous across the border? He broke off one arm after another—but every one proved to be empty. In disgust he motioned for Peter to pass, and turned to his cigarettes for a smoke.

The U.S. border guard was next. The young American couldn't care less about the wheelbarrow. He wanted valid papers and permits, and Peter had none. Yet Peter stood his ground. He kept pointing to the window where his family lived; he was not going anywhere until he had delivered his goods. Eventually, the guard gave in and summoned Edith to the post. And soon it was arranged: Peter was allowed to pass and would return to East Germany within a few days.

Edgar and Edith viewed their silver with melancholic amusement. Nothing was permanent. One day they would restore the silver to its old luster. The knives would be fitted with stainless steel blades, and the broken arms of the silver chandelier reattached. "Don't you think we should leave off one of the arms," Edith smiled wryly, "to remind us that life is full of surprises?"

On his next trip, Peter visited Mina. She was delighted to see her oldest grandson, but chagrined that he looked hungry and thin. He needed fresh milk and eggs. In her basement they found an old bicycle, and Peter set out to visit her farmer friend.

Whistling cheerfully, Peter biked through the fields. He had not owned a bicycle since he was little. The manufacture of children's bicycles had ceased during the war, and adult bikes were issued exclusively to the work force. When Peter entered the village, a Russian soldier blocked his path, calling for him to stop.

"You give me bicycle," he ordered.

Peter glanced at the fellow's rifle and handed over the bike.

Of course, the art of riding a bicycle was a different matter. Peter felt a certain glee when he observed Russian soldiers furiously kicking their new acquisitions. One afternoon, he heard a soldier swearing profusely as he kept falling off his bike. When a young German bicycled by, the Russian stopped him to swap bikes. Did he manage to ride the new one? Peter looked on in joyful anticipation, but wisdom prevailed. He quickly walked away. Why become a target for the Russian's likely fury.

No exchange of bicycles that morning. Peter trudged home on foot, mulling over the old adage: *Might is Right*.

On his next trip back to East Germany, Peter was captured. The four Russian soldiers, who confronted him, were young men of perhaps eighteen. Quite matter-of-factly, they took Peter to a small house, ordered him down the stairs, and locked him into the cellar jam-packed with other men.

The night was not one he likes to remember. Some men stood, some sat on the cold, concrete floor amidst the foulest air. The cellar had no windows, no ventilation, no light, and worst of all no toilet. The little air they had could have been sold as poison gas. They had nothing to eat and nothing to drink.

Many hours later, the door opened and they were herded to the grounds of a local school. Hundreds of boxes and crates awaited them there, apparently dismantled factories and equipment, ready to be shipped to Russia.

"Load them on the trucks, Dawei rabotta! Work!" the Russians ordered Peter and his co-prisoners. "The trucks are parked in front."

Peter was not prepared to haul boxes. He had escape on his mind. How about driving off in one of the trucks? He walked to the front of one of the vehicles, but a guard eyed him keenly, and Peter thought it wiser to abandon the plan. He called to the soldier his need for a toilet. The Russian pointed with his gun and Peter proceeded down a long corridor.

The bathroom was at the far end of the building and had a small window toward the back. And there, in front of Peter, rose a hill. Six hundred yards up the hill trees promised safety. Could he squeeze through the tiny window? He had to!

He took off his shoe and gave the glass a gentle whack. The glass cracked. Carefully he loosened a piece, but it fell to the ground. He held his breath. Luckily, the piece was small and no one came running. He pulled out the next piece and used it to loosen the caulking. He listened. No one. Feverishly he yanked at the glass; his patience was running low. His hands were getting bloody. He smashed out the rest. Then he squeezed head first through the hole. He rolled a few feet, and raced up the slope to reach the trees. Only then did he stop to look back. No pursuers, no pointed guns. He took a deep breath and realized how hungry, thirsty and bloody he was. But he was free.

Three hours later, he saw the trucks with his comrades-of-the-night passing on the road below. Were they being shipped to Russia too? Peter was not anxious to find out.

Eventually, Peter got back to the border town, not far from where he had been captured many hours earlier. He took the train back to the city and assembled another load.

Two weeks later, he was captured again. After a long night locked up in a damp and musty cellar with other strangers, they were marched off to an unknown destination. After an hour or two, a farmer with a horse and wagon came rambling along from the opposite direction. The Russians stopped the farmer, made him turn about and ordered the men to climb aboard and did the same. Slowly the horse and wagon rattled off.

Peter managed to hold on to a spot near the back rail. His mind was feverishly at work to get his freedom. When the wagon neared a bend in the road, he saw his chance. Quietly, he dropped below the rail and off the cart. He lay there like a corpse and did not budge. He lay in full view. Had they noticed him? Would they shoot him? He had to take that chance. The wagon moved on slowly. Every inch seemed to take an eternity, yet Peter did not stir; he barely breathed. If the Russians saw him, they didn't seem to care. They needed able-bodied men, not passed-out corpses. Eventually, the wagon passed out of sight and with it the guns of the guards. Peter was free again.

On Peter's last trip he found the house partially collapsed due to earlier damage from bombs. He had made ten trips across the border, bringing many essentials, also some Meissen China, family albums, Edith's accordion and a few paintings that he cut out of their frames. He never mentioned these feats to anyone, not even to his siblings. Like many refugees and heroes of the war, he felt that these events were part of a past—a past that was best forgotten.

"Weren't you scared at times?" his sister asked him.

"Not really," he replied, "at that age you don't think about danger. You feel indestructible. Danger exists only in theory or for others." A pity we lose this faith when we grow older.

Perseverance

Perseverance is a great Element of Success —Longfellow

As the proud holder of an official permit, the Leuthold family moved to a small Bavarian town where Edgar had secured two sunny rooms at a local inn.

Edgar searched in earnest now. With a permit he could earn a living again and get a permanent residence. In the meantime, Edith and the children combed the woods and meadows for anything edible—berries, mushrooms and leaves—to quell their ever-present hunger.

It was summertime, and they spent many hours gathering blueberries that were to be canned for the winter. Canning fruit in a hotel bedroom was far from ideal. Thanks to Peter they owned a pot and a camp burner. In the woods they found a few discarded beer bottles and corks that had to serve in place of canning jars. But they lacked sugar to preserve the fruit, and one hot afternoon a bottle of overly fermented blueberries exploded.

The effect was devastating. Blueberries covered every inch of the hotel room.

"Draw the curtains," Edith whispered. "Rosi, stand guard outside the door and keep away the maid. Tell her I am sleeping and don't want to be disturbed."

Paul looked puzzled, "are you going to sleep now?"

"No," Edith had to smile in spite of her dismay. "But if the owner hears about this, he'll send us packing. Look at his white walls! And we can't get paint or sandpaper these days."

Edith sacrificed a pair of socks to clean the walls, but the devilish purple stains did not budge.

By evening, the walls showed hardly any improvement. "We have to keep at it," Edith announced firmly.

And they kept at it, washing and rubbing. Edgar returned home that evening. When he entered the door, Edith flew to his side before he had a chance to explode, too. She gently took his arm, motioned silence, and guided him out the door.

"Keep watch," she murmured to Rosi. "We'll be back," and disappeared into the children's room.

When they returned, Edgar sternly examined the speckled walls. Toothpaste might help, he thought, but refugees couldn't get any.

"We'll have to save our breakfast slice of bread," Edgar concluded. "When thoroughly dry, they may serve as a sandpaper substitute."

To the children's dismay, no bread for breakfast. Edith placed the slices on a sunny windowsill, out of the reach of birds. After a day or two they were ready. And miracle of miracles, they worked. All they needed was more bread. Slowly and surely the stains became lighter and finally just about disappeared.

Amazed, Paul gazed at the walls, "They're cleaner than before!"

Edith nodded, "Elbow grease and resolve can accomplish a great deal."

"That's what you keep telling us," he admitted. "Get started, keep at it, and nothing is impossible!"

Compassion, Where have you Gone?
Seek and Ye shall Find —Luke 11:9

Not long after the blueberry incident, Edgar found what he had been looking for, a place to start his business again. It came in the shape of an abandoned military complex. If he could lease it and convert it into warehouses and offices, he figured, he'd be in business. Above the offices he envisioned a home for his family. The large concrete courtyard could serve as a tennis court—all that was needed was a bit of white paint to draw the lines and some chicken wire to make a net. The slight slope and the rough spots—well, they would constitute an extra challenge.

It would take much persuasion to get the necessary loans since he had no security to offer. But he was hopeful.

He moved Edith and the children to nearby Ingolstadt, a small town on the blue Danube, six miles from the barracks. Fifty miles from Munich.

As everywhere in Germany, living space was scarce and allocated by government agencies. The family was assigned to move in with a retired, childless couple. The hapless couple were allowed to retain their living room and had to move their bed into the breakfast nook, while the five refugees moved into their two upstairs bedrooms. All seven shared the tiny bathroom, and the small kitchen.

The owners had survived the war unscathed. Now, by government decree, their peace was to be cruelly disrupted. Five refugees, three of them children! They were determined to get rid of them!

Every sound or step in the tiny house could be heard everywhere. This did not disturb the children. They were eager to live and starved to hear new music. If the radio played a good dance tune before breakfast, they joyfully dropped their toothbrushes and practiced the step, on tiptoe of course. Still, it set the chandelier below in motion, and provoked an angry tirade. Edith was always ready to apologize and soothe her ruffled feathers, but it only doubled the poor woman's ire. From her point of view, those refugees were savages. From the children's point of view, the landlady was a sad and sorry nuisance.

The Shakespeare play, *A Midsummer Night's Dream*, was coming to town. The children had never seen a play and were thrilled. Edith secured tickets for the family and a book of the play, so they would be prepared. But when the great day arrived, Rosi came down with scarlet fever. Instead of the trip to the theater, she was moved into the attic, where she spent many months in isolation, with leisure to read all of Shakespeare's plays.

It was a dreary, unfinished attic without electricity. No one but Edith was allowed to see her. Food rations were meager, and lacking a vegetable garden or farm connection, her recovery took forever. On a walk one day, she collapsed, and Edith hurried off to get a bite of food from a nearby farmer, while her daughter drifted off to sleep by the wayside. When she awakened, her mother was sitting by her side, triumphantly holding a slice of bread and half an onion that a kind farmer had given her. It was like a gift from heaven.

In grateful silence they shared their meal, both shedding secret tears—tears of a child's frustration and of a mother's pain at being unable to feed her child.

The American Marshall Plan came as a Godsend. It provided school luncheons for German children—a thick noodle soup made with horsemeat. Lunch became the children's happiest moment of the day. In effect, the Marshall Plan became Europe's savior; without it, Europe could not have risen from its ashes. Germany, for certain, would have plunged into a deep depression, and possibly another war. As it was, America offered millions of dollars to victors and vanquished alike. And Europe eagerly rebuilt. Not so the Soviet bloc. Stalin ordered all Communist countries to refuse the Marshall Plan aid.

When she was fifteen, Rosi got her first government voucher to buy a dress—a big event, her first new dress since 1942, four and a half years ago. The dress was to be mailed from a government warehouse after receipt of payment and documents. The application did not specify size, color or style. Nor did it give a description of the garment. When the eagerly awaited package arrived, everyone watched in suspense as Rosi tore away the wrapping.

At last the mystery dress emerged. It was big and shapeless, made of rough, brownish sackcloth and had white polka dots. Even the boys were struck speechless. Rosi dropped it to the floor and fled to her room. After a week, Edith suggested that she wear it just once. On a pretty girl, she figured, even an ugly dress might look better than expected. But Rosi did not look pretty. Peter summed it up ably: "You look like a corpse dug up from a grave." Her skin broke out in a rash, and Edith quietly left the dress at a school occupied by refugees.

A few days later, Edgar signed the lease for the barracks. Now he needed permits, loans and contractors. In time, he would have a business again, and the family a home.

To celebrate, Edgar and Edith went to see a film with the great French comedian, Fernandel, their first movie in many years. Arm in arm they returned to the house, happy after so pleasant an evening. To their surprise, two police officers stood by the front door and blocked their way. They did not handcuff them, but they insisted on taking them to the police station— without a warrant or an explanation.

Flanked by officers of the law, they were marched through town to the station. Not much has changed, Edgar thought sadly, being reminded of the Olympic Games ten years earlier, wondering about the officers' past.

At the station, they were questioned about their where-abouts that evening, which they could easily explain; the movie stubs were still in Edgar's pockets. Besides, they had plenty of witnesses. Edith had complimented the cashier on her lovely broche made of Bohemian quartz. They sat not far from the mother of Anna, whom Edith had helped with her French paper. And when they left the theater they ran into Fred whom Edgar frequently gave a ride.

But why did the officers want to know? And what was their alleged crime? She pondered about possible enemies. But she could think only of Arno and the landlord. They had not heard from Arno in ages. As to the landlady, Edith recalled how adamantly she had urged them to see the film. Could it be that she had done so with a motive? She mentioned the fact to the police officers, and Edgar made sure they wrote it down. On a hunch, he requested that their landlords be brought to the station, or they be released to go home.

"They are on their way," the officer replied leisurely. He was not in a hurry; he had to spend all night at the station.

When their landlords arrived, they vigorously denied having mentioned the movie.

"They didn't see a film; they set fire to our house," they maintained. "We got home just in time to extinguish the blaze."

Edith wasn't sure whether to laugh or cry. "Why would we burn down the house? Our children are asleep upstairs. All our earthly possessions would have burned."

"They should be expelled from our house," the landlady insisted, "and their permit of residency revoked."

For a split second Edgar had to smile. So that was what they were after. The situation was serious. Like most locals, the police officers resented refugees, too. Refugees caused overcrowding. They were *Sau-Preussen*, Prussian pigs from the north. And the Leutholds were refugees.

The following day, Edgar engaged a lawyer. "Check the landlord's fire insurance," Edgar suggested. The result was illuminating. Three weeks earlier, the landlord had tripled his fire coverage. As to the landlords' alibi—they claimed to have gone for a walk. Yet no one had seen them.

The damage from the blaze? Half a burned newspaper and a partially burned, old wicker chair on the back patio.

Eventually, all charges were dropped. The family was neither evicted nor deported, and reluctantly remained the tenants of a landlord who had openly declared war. They had no alternative. Thousands of refugees were in desperate need of housing. Families able to pay were moved in with local homeowners in exchange for rent. Others not so fortunate were placed in schools—an average of forty people per classroom with barely enough space to stretch out at night. They cooked on a makeshift stove and lacked shower and laundry facilities. They had nothing but the school's sinks and toilets. It was not an attractive alternative.

The odds of the Leuthold's ending up in one of those schoolrooms had alarmingly increased, also the likelihood of vengeance from their landlords whose scheme of getting rid of them had failed. Their animosity toward the children was palpable. And they lacked other distraction.

To keep the children out of harm's way, Edgar decided to send them to a boarding school until their own home would be ready.

Edith found a reputable boys' boarding school near the Starnberger Lake, an area hardly touched by the war. Rosi was boarded with a kind couple nearby who had a large garden of roses. On sunny days, the owner, an enterprising septuagenarian, lovingly tended trays full of rose-petals. Cigarettes were unavailable then, so he experimented with various combinations to create a tobacco substitute, though none really proved satisfactory. Occasionally, the aroma of roasted wheat and rye kernels wafted through the house when he was making *Ersatz-Kaffee* for his wife.

Rosi attended the local school for girls. She had lunch with her brothers at the boarding school. Lunch was served on tables of eight, decked with white tablecloths and white cloth napkins, and circled by grim-looking instructors. An awesome silence reigned, not as if sixty boys were enjoying their noon-time meal. They didn't! Instructors with eagle eyes and eager ears observed every move and every word they said.

"Max, would you pass the potatoes, please?"

"Thank you, Tom."

The British concept of Manners Maketh the Man was pitilessly hammered in. The smallest trespass—reaching for something, not sitting straight, elbow on the table, or talking with a full mouth—resulted in an immediate slap in the face. And mercy, if anyone soiled the tablecloth! Rosi was glad to have only lunch there.

Weeks turned into months. The children rejoiced in this atmosphere of peace. They made friends, studied, played and laughed again. It seemed like a different world. Nonetheless, they were jubilant when they were summoned home.

The workmen at the military barracks were still at work. The offices downstairs were already in use. Upstairs, their new living quarters were near completion, a bedroom for each child, a kitchen for which they pumped water from below, and everywhere a peaceful view of the wetlands of the Danube. To the children's delight, beyond the living room lay a stretch of unused barrack space, ideal for games and a ping pong table.

Visions of the Great

The Future Belongs to the Brave —Ronald Reagan

The devastation of World War II gave birth to the glorious idea of European Unity. Europe's history is a litany of alliances, counter-alliances and wars. Virtually every European nation has been allied with and fought against every other nation on the continent. It was time to change.

On November 19th 1946, Churchill in one of his memorable speeches advocated a "sovereign remedy" against the peril of another war, "the creation of a European family." Schuman, the French Foreign Minister, heartily embraced the idea. In Germany, the Reverend Niemöller wrote the country's "Declaration of Guilt," an essential first step toward Germany's admission to a common European future.

The driving force behind a United Europe was France's Jean Monnet. Like the creators of the American Declaration of Independence, Monnet envisioned a European parliament, a European court, a bill of rights, a tariff-free market, a European anti-trust agency, the removal of borders, and a common European currency.

Unattainable castles in the air, of course, but they ignited the hearts of the brave. They were tired of war. Nonetheless, after six years of ruthless war, 55 million dead, and unspeakable destruction, Europeans also harbored strong feelings of hostility toward each other.

At this crucial moment in history, America with its extraordinary Marshall Plan came to their rescue. It put Europeans back on their feet by financing the revival of their industry. Yet when Adenauer sought the Allies' approval to restart the German steel works, Germany's neighbors were gravely alarmed.

On the other hand, they were tempted. Steel production in Germany would mean an upswing of the economy in its neighboring countries—the sale of French coal to German steel works, and much needed shipping orders for the quiet ports of Holland and Belgium.

This was the moment Monnet had been waiting for, an opportunity to turn potential profit into an instrument of peace—the creation of a French-German industrial syndicate that guaranteed peacetime production of steel, and profits for all concerned.

The idea of European Unity also swept up Edith and Rosi. They attended EU conferences and read everything on the subject. Rosi mobilized her high school peers and formed a local chapter of Youth for a United Europe. Before long, some forty members attended the weekly meetings, intelligent and eager young students rejoicing in the idea of One Europe and Peace on the continent.

Yet Communism was also on the rise. Communist spies were everywhere, keeping a keen eye on all political movements, just as Hitler had done during his first post-World War One army assignment. Stalin distrusted people and like Hitler was a firm believer in exerting absolute control over everyone and obtaining total information. Germany provided the perfect infrastructure for Stalin's network of spies—Hitler had trained thousands of people to spy on their fellowmen; and as is to be expected, spies are not picky whom they spy for, as long as they get paid.

Stein, the chief of the local Communist Party got wind of the gatherings of Youth for a United Europe and attended them all. He was stocky and broad-shouldered, eloquent and sarcastic. He was older than the high school youngsters, a smooth politician, crafty and clever—an awesome enemy. They were no match for him.

Rosi was working and studying at the University of Erlangen then, but she came home regularly to meet with her European Youth group. Meetings had turned into a fierce ideological battle with the Communist chief, who savagely ridiculed their idealism, and was determined to win them for Communism. Yet the youngsters were just as resolved as he was. So Stein resorted to other means. During each meeting, Stein had his men vandalize Rosi's, or rather her father's, car in which she drove to the meetings. No matter how far away she parked the VW, Stein's men found it and left their eloquent warning—stop this European nonsense!

One night, two tires were slashed and the windshield broken. Rosi walked home six miles on a dark, perilous country road, and her parents realized that their daughter was in harm's way. They found an *au pair* program in England and signed her up. Two weeks later Rosi arrived on British soil.

Full Circle
The Wheels of Justice keep Turning —Anonymous

The sound of swift steps echoed up the stairs. It was Edgar, taking two at a time.

"Mail for you," Edgar announced with a broad grin. "A letter from Viola, a letter for Rosi, and one for us."

Edith reached out eagerly. She had not heard from her sister in nearly two years. Much had happened since then—five months of heavy Allied bombing, Russian tanks and troops fighting in the streets of the city, and since 1945 the Russian occupation.

When Edgar and Edith fled from East Germany, they lost touch with their friends and relatives. What had become of them? Had they also fled? Were they still among the living? Would they ever be able to reconnect?

"Mother must have sent our address to Viola."

Edith studied the envelope. "Viola's letter was mailed in Frankfurt five days ago! Mother's letter from East Germany took eighty-seven days for the same distance. A lame donkey could have walked it in less time."

"Because your donkey wouldn't have to read each piece of mail. Not even Hitler invaded the sanctity of mail!"

Edith did not hear his last remark; she was stunned by Viola's news. She turned to Edgar, "Arno is missing."

"Probably still ruling Latvia."

"Edgar!" Her tone was only slightly reproachful; a similar thought had struck her, too—Arno, the self-proclaimed Tsar of Latvia.

"Viola writes that he got back to Leipzig a day or two before the Russians arrived. He brought with him a truckload of merchandise and had Viola drive it to Frankfurt. She's living there now. Can you imagine Viola driving a truck? Arno was going to follow with the company furs and their furnishings as soon as he had loaded them. She never heard from him."

"That's Arno. Always full of surprises," Edgar responded, unmoved.

"Viola sounds heart-broken; she still loves that man. What could have happened?"

"Maybe he drove elsewhere or found another girl," Edgar suggested. He had no intention of expressing sympathy for the man who more than once had tried to get him killed. But he was a practical man. "How will Viola manage? Someone will have to support her?"

"The truck Viola drove to Frankfurt was loaded with black-market items—cigarettes, alcohol, stockings, coffee, all the things that fetch high prices."

"Not surprising."

"She says they are better currency than German marks. With five cigarettes she can buy five eggs or a quart of milk. She bought a beautiful china cabinet for five packs of cigarettes."

"How about her living expenses? Rent, clothes, school books?"

"She pays for everything with goods. Can you imagine, Viola bartering like a fishmonger?" Edith shook her head.

"Adversity can be a stern taskmaster," Edgar replied. "Your father would have been amazed."

"But how long will it last?" Edith knew her sister's expensive taste. It was unlikely Viola had changed.

"Viola the spendthrift and Arno the want-it-all," Edgar replied, but then grew pensive. "Instead of letting Arno have the company, we may have to support his family."

Edith wrapped her arms around his waist, "I do appreciate your attitude," she said. "I am glad Father has been spared to see this day. His business gone, the world in shambles." Tenderly, she eyed her father's picture on the wall that Peter had brought across the border.

"I doubt we will have to worry about Viola," she added. "Mother won't let her starve. Besides, I am sure Arno has stashed away plenty of assets."

"If she can get her hands on them. Who knows who else may lay claim to them?"

Edith was about to comment, but thought better of it.

"Did you say you have a letter for Rosi?"

"Here it is."

After her year as an Au Pére in England, Rosi had returned to Ingolstadt, but only briefly. Jean René invited her for an extended visit in France. René was married now and a doctor, and his wife Susanne was expecting a baby.

Edgar and Edith were receiving enthusiastic letters from their daughter in the *Provence*. Susanne had taken her to the sites where Van Gogh had painted his vibrant, golden sunflowers and twirling, sun-baked fields, his gray-green, twisted olive trees and the reddish, iron-rich soil.

"It looks like official mail," Edith remarked, studying the envelope. "It wouldn't be another Communist threat? Do you think we should open it?"

"I think you should. If we forward the letter, it may not reach her for a month or two."

Gingerly, Edith opened the envelope. She did not like to violate someone's privacy, and that included her husband's and her children's.

The letter started with congratulations, and Edith's smile widened.

"Edgar," she murmured. Tears of joy were misting her eyes. She tried to speak, but her voice did not cooperate. She handed him the letter instead.

"I say! A Fulbright scholarship for our Rosi—to study in the United States of America. The Land of the Free! Edith, think of it! One day we will join her there."

After a joyous discussion they sent a telegram to France, and turned their attention to the third letter.

"This one is for both of us," Edgar smiled broadly as he handed Edith a mysterious envelope.

"From Sigurd and Sylvia!" Edith rejoiced. "How did they obtain our address?"

"From your Mother, Sigurd told me. He is teaching psychology at the University of Berlin and wrote to her."

"What a small world," Edith murmured, eager to read their news of several pages.

"A smaller world than we realize," Edgar replied. "Would you believe that Sigurd ran across Hitler in a cheap men's dormitory some thirty years ago?"

"Not possible!"

"Sigurd has kept it secret for all these years. It happened after his tiff with Sylvia, when he took off from the university and roamed the countryside. He spent a night at a dorm where Hitler happened to be staying. This was back in 1914. No one knew Hitler then."

"Why did Sigurd never mention it? He must have figured out who the man was."

"He did. Eighteen years later, in 1932, when he saw Hitler on the front pages of the newspapers as the new Chancellor of Germany."

"But that was over a dozen years ago!"

"True, but remember, Sigurd is a psychologist, and a shrewd and intelligent one. He recalled the young Hitler as a ruthless fanatic, likely to eliminate anyone who knew about his shady past."

"What in the world was Hitler doing in a cheap dorm?"

"He was a hapless, penniless vagabond then, living off charity."

"Hitler a hobo? How come no one knew about it?" Edith exclaimed.

"It is hard to believe! But then, Hitler always cloaked himself in mystery and secrecy; not only himself, his relatives, too."

"His own family?"

"Hitler wanted no one to know about his past. He forced his half-sister Angelika to change her name; he wanted no other Hitlers beside him. He wiped the village of his forebears from the face of the earth![48] That is why Sigurd decided not to mention their encounter. Even today hardly anyone knows that for nearly six years Hitler was a penniless tramp. I did not know."

Edgar paced the floor. "Sigurd was wise to keep quiet. He would not be alive had he talked. Read for yourself."

Edith read the letter about Hitler's past and Hanisch's murder. "Truth is stranger than fiction," she murmured.

"Sigurd did some amazing research to get the facts."

"How calculating Hitler was, and how vain! To have his photographer take two and a half million photos of him."[49]

"Even more amazing is the account of Sigurd's daughter. She recently saw her old friend Traudl[50] again, Hitler's last secretary." He handed her the letter, but changed his mind. "Let me read it to you. It is so different from what we were told."

"... I had lunch with Traudl Junge yesterday. She stayed in the Berlin bunker as Hitler's secretary until the very end. It is a miracle she survived. Here are some of the stories she told me:

'By April of 1945, Hitler had aged a thousand years. Restlessly, he shuffled back and forth in his underground bunker—from bedroom to office to bedroom. We felt sorry for him, and for ourselves. We simply could not conceive of life without him. We were dependent on him.

---

[48] Hitler turned it into an artillery practicing ground.

[49] Heinrich Hoffman, the Nazi-sanctioned photographer, took 2.5 million photos of Hitler. *"Hitler, Eine Biographie"* by Joachim Fest, p. 646

[50] Traudl Junge, Hitler's secretary; author of *Until the Final Hour*.

Hitler had not left the bunker in many months. He was afraid of people; but then, he never trusted anyone.

On April 29, Hitler's aide Günsche reported that Himmler had been located in England, trying to negotiate a peace treaty. Hitler flew into a violent rage—we were used to his tirades.

But then he turned pale; he remembered that Himmler had procured him the poison for his final exit. Had Himmler betrayed him with the poison, too? He ordered Günsche to fetch the doctor, and the three men went to find Blondi and her puppies. Hitler selected a pill from his pocket and had the doctor feed it to the dog. Almost instantly the poor thing collapsed.[51] It was dreadful. He loved his dog.

'Is she dead?' Hitler asked.

The doctor nodded.

At four o'clock, I took Hitler's dictation of his Scorched-Earth Directive. "Everything is to be burned to the ground," I wrote. "If the war is lost, this nation must perish." Outside, we could hear the sound of Russian artillery, while the radio on his desk gave a vivid description of Hitler's valiant defense of the city.

At 4:15, Hitler dictated his personal will.[52] His associates have amassed vast riches, but Hitler's possessions are few, mostly his sketches.

Later, Eva Braun came to my room. She brought me her gorgeous fur coat. "I won't need it anymore," she sobbed. "I want you to have it." A pity I had to leave it behind when we fled from the bunker.

---

[51] Ibid. p. 181
[52] Ibid. pp. 183-185

Toward midnight, everyone gathered for tea. Another painfully long night. Outside, the enemy was closing in. Gunfire was only a few blocks away. No one slept.

The next morning, Hitler ordered a festive table to be set. Champagne for eight, but simple vegetarian food for him. One of his aides was sent to find a registrar—he was going to marry Eva Braun, his long-time, secret mistress.

After a brief ceremony, Hitler shook hands with everyone. He stooped low, his eyes were glazed, and his mind far away. He repeated his instructions that his body and Eva's were to be thoroughly burned. Then the heavy steel door of his room closed behind them.

I was dazed and mortally afraid of what would happen when Hitler was gone. And so was everyone else. To distract myself I looked in on the six little Göbbels children. They had been forgotten during the wedding ceremony and were hungry. I got them some bread and jam.

Suddenly, a gunshot echoed through the bunker. It seemed to herald the end of the world. Günsche told me later that they found Hitler and Eva on the sofa, both dead. The two containers of poison lay empty on the floor. Günsche, Linge, Borman, and two SS men carried the bodies outside and put them into the ready, shallow grave near the entrance. They poured large cans of petrol over the bodies and burned them. The burial party did not linger long. Shells of Russian artillery were exploding all around them. They covered the still burning remains with dirt and hurried back into the bunker.'

Susanne"

"Do you think Hitler felt remorse during his last hour?" Edith wondered aloud.

"No, not Hitler. I am sure he felt nothing but loathing for the Wehrmacht that did not win the war for him, and for the German people, who did not multiply fast enough to conquer the world. No insight, no common sense, and certainly no remorse. His last directive to Admiral Dönitz, his successor he appointed, says it all: 'Above everything, I demand scrupulous obedience and continuation of my race laws...[53]'"

Edith could barely believe her ears. "Doc was right," she said. "'Hitler was a madman, a dangerous madman.'"

"What became of his charred remains?" she added.

"Germans claim the Soviets took them to Moscow. Stalin asserts they were never found. Some people insist that Hitler escaped to Brazil. Only one fact is certain, Hitler opted for the most cowardly way out."

Both were silent; both dwelled on the same thought— will we ever have the wisdom to elect politicians on the basis of their past performance, and not on their promises for the future?

Edgar slowly folded the letter. Wrapped in thought, Edith got up to open the window. Birds were chirping. A solitary leaf floated leisurely toward the ground. Spring was in the air, the rebirth of Earth.

***

---

[53] Hitler's political testament, dictated on April 29, 1945, ended with these words: "Vor allem verpflichte ich die Führung der Nation und die Gefolgschaft zur peinlichen Einhaltung der Rassengesetze ..." N.B. 3569-PS

Index

About the Author

The author grew up in Germany as daughter of an upper class family. Her father, a royalist, refused to join Hitler's party and paid for it heavily. During WW II, he was drafted into the cavalry. In 1943, his wife and children escaped to a remote mountain cabin in the Sudetenland. When Germany collapsed, the Czechs dispossessed them. They returned to the city, but three months later, they fled from the Communists and became refugees.

After a year as an *au pair* in England and France, she won a Fulbright scholarship and graduated from Smith College and the Harvard/ Radcliffe Program in Business Administration. She and her husband settled briefly on a Caribbean sugar plantation and later spent months at sea with their infant daughter, Mimi.

McIntosh has since made her home in the San Francisco Bay area where she edited the German newspaper, obtained further degrees and taught at Golden Gate University. As management consultant, she was editor of *Practical Risk Management*. In spare moments she learned to hang-glide and windsurf, and skied with the National Ski Patrol.

The author's autobiography, *Live, Laugh & Learn,* was published in 2004.

Printed in the United States
102313LV00002B/280-285/A